HAUNTINGS AND HOARFROST

HAUNTINGS
AND
HOARFROST

EDITED BY

RHONDA PARRISH

TYCHE BOOKS LTD.

Published by Tyche Books Ltd.
Calgary, Alberta, Canada
www.TycheBooks.com

Cover Design by JV Arts
Interior Layout by M.L.D. Curelas
Interior Artwork by Niken Anindita
Frontspiece by Dean Spencer
ID 73752346 © Mashakotcur| Dreamstime.com

Tyche Books Ltd Edition 2025
Print ISBN: 978-1-989407-84-4
Ebook ISBN: 978-1-989407-85-1

Dedicated to Jo

With special thanks to Tonya Redpath, Tina Foo, and Barbara Tomporowski, whose support over the years has meant more than I can put to words.

Thank you so much!

Table of Contents

INTRODUCTION

RHONDA PARRISH

I miss the winters of my childhood.

No doubt this is due in part to the soft filter of nostalgia, and I expect some of it has to do with the dread and fear with which I greet climate change. Regardless, missing those winters is one of the reasons I really wanted to put this anthology together.

Winter was different then. It was a playground with teeth and claws.

Winter was drifts as tall as houses, that rose up from the ditches at the side of the road so that it felt like driving through a snow tunnel. It was a December blizzard burying the fence and spending the rest of the season walking over the crusted snow because it was easier than trying to dig out the gate. It was digging forts out of piles of snow, and being allowed to stay inside during recess. It was frost on the inside of windows, thawing frozen fingers out under cold water and running awkwardly up hills so you could slide back down them on Crazy Carpets.

Of course it was a lot of less bucolic things too. It was being snowed in for a week and figuring out how to stay warm when the power went out. It was stories with only one degree of separation about people getting lost in a blizzard and freezing to death fifteen feet from their barn. It was an empty desk because the car a classmate was riding in, slid into a snow plow, and near misses when someone misjudged the thickness of the lake's ice.

The stories in this collection are not like my tranquil memories of winter; they all land on the dangerous side of the spectrum. They are not softly packed snowballs that explode delightfully when they strike something; there are stones hidden away in their centres. Do not make the mistake of thinking that the stories which feel like fluffy white flakes drifting gently from the sky are less dangerous than the ones with the flavour of a blizzard because you don't know what the beautiful, peaceful flakes are concealing.

Most of these stories do not hide the presence of their teeth, though they may make you wait until the end to see their exact shape, and a few will likely leave you with unanswered questions even after multiple reads. I make no apology for them. If they leave you vaguely unsettled after reading, I think they have done their job. But don't worry, I've made sure to include several stories that will offer you answers and closure as well.

Think of it like looking out over an unfamiliar landscape after a heavy snowfall. Everything is covered in a sparkling, shimmering white blanket, but it is not flat; you can still make out shapes beneath the snow. Some of them are immediately recognizable—there is a picnic table, and there a swing set—but some require more effort to decipher. If you stare really hard at that shape over to the left, it will slowly resolve into something that is probably a barbeque but might be some sort of planter. On the other hand, the drift to the right? No matter how long you look at it, you'll never quite be able to figure it out. Oh, you may be able to make out that it has a handle of some sort (or is that a horn?), and at least one wheel (did it just shift?), but the only way to know if it is a garden cart or a wheelbarrow (or something different altogether) is to wait until the snow melts in spring.

But what if spring never comes?

Rhonda Parrish
Edmonton, Alberta
4/4/2024

FOR THE SEER, WHO SEES IN THE SNOW: THE WINTER HOUSE AT THE ROAD'S END

SARAH VAN GOETHEM

The snow always stirs something inside of Tessa, something that reaches back into her childhood. Perhaps that's why she remembers the strange Winter House at the end of the road on the afternoon of her mama's funeral. She stands on the stone steps of the funeral home, silent and alone, surprised by a world that has changed into a snow globe while they've been inside.

Am I an orphan now? she wonders. She feels like a child again, even if she is twenty-five. She turns her face to the leaden sky and lets the thick flakes fall on her cheeks, her nose, her chin. She lets the cold spots remind her she is still alive, that her heart hasn't stopped beating like her mama's. But there is something odd about that, something that makes it a little harder to breathe now.

Tessa sucks in the crisp air, waiting for her brother, who's gone to warm his van, and her sister, who is directing the funeral assistant in the dispersal of the floral arrangements, and she thinks, for the first time in years, about the day they stopped at the Winter House.

It is the snowy afternoon, of course, that is making her think of it; it is so similar to that day. *How old was I?* she wonders now. *Four? Five?* She drudges up a faint memory of how it all started,

3

of the shopping trip to Riverford, of a new green velvet dress, of a grilled-cheese lunch in a diner on a red swivel stool, and a hot-chocolate layered in whipped cream. Mama had drunk coffee, black.

In her mind's eye, Tessa can see the waitress, in her frilly white apron, pouring her mama a refill. *Storm's moving in,* the waitress said, gesturing at the big front window, pot of coffee sloshing. Sure enough, snow had started to swirl while they were eating. *Hmm,* Mama murmured, a frown furrowing her brow. It had only been Tessa and her mama that day, she realizes. Ben and Brooke must have been at school.

A hand on her arm startles Tessa out of her reverie. "Done," Brooke says, all business. "The rest of the flowers will be delivered to Mom's house." Tessa is the only one to call their mother *Mama,* anymore. It's a habit she can't break, just like Brooke, who is the oldest, is always taking charge. Tessa knows it's easier for Brooke to be in control than to feel the hurt, but it has the effect of putting a wall between them. Between a grief they could share. Brooke rubs her palms together. "God, it's cold now. There's Ben, let's go."

The girls pile into Ben's minivan, Brooke up front in the passenger seat, and Tessa in the captain's chair of the middle row, an empty car seat strapped in beside her. Ben is five years older than Tessa, Brooke seven. The two of them have always been close, and Tessa envies them their relationship among other things. Not that they ever exclude her, but being closer in age has allowed them a very different family experience than her. For instance, they both remember their father, while Tessa does not. Still, the three of them together, alone right now, feels right. It's a rare event, now that both Brooke and Ben are married, and especially now that Ben has a baby.

"I'm so glad there isn't a stupid luncheon," Brooke says.

Ben turns on the wipers to clear away the snow. "I don't know. I could go for some triangle sandwiches and—"

"Stop," Brooke interrupts. "Mom would have hated that."

She isn't wrong. It was Tessa's idea to have a celebration of life in the spring and everyone had gone along with it. But that meant right now was wide open, with nothing more to be done except go back to Mama's house where Brooke would want to start packing up what they no longer needed and Ben would insist they needed to keep all the things. Tessa would be the swing vote, as usual.

"You know," Brooke says, "she would've preferred if we'd dressed her in a long dress and a flower-crown and pushed her on a raft out into a body of water and lit it on fire."

Ben clears his throat. "I don't think that's legal."

Brooke turns on him. "Okay, but don't you remember her saying she'd like that?"

"I do," Tessa chimes in. Mama was eccentric at times. A dreamer. A romantic.

Brooke looks back at Tessa, thoughtful. "We should drink wine at the house, just the three of us."

She's probably come up with the idea to make sure Tessa's not alone tonight, but Tessa isn't about to say no.

Ben doesn't either. "It's a plan," he says, but his voice cracks. Tessa's six-foot tall brother was always a mama's boy.

For once, Brooke doesn't make a joke about him being "the golden child," or the "favourite." Instead, to Tessa's surprise, Brooke turns her face to the window and brushes the back of her hand across her cheek.

Everyone is crying, except Tessa. She is all cried out. She is strangely numb inside, as frozen as the world outside. She looks out the window at the snow and then she's slipping, slipping, slipping, into the memory of the Winter House once more.

The snow is nearly blinding, thick and heavy. The car smells of leftovers; a greasy bag of fries sits on the back seat beside Tessa, her lunch, hurriedly packed to go. Mama has turned the radio off and the only sound is the frantic swiping of the wiper blades. Tessa knows better than to talk or make any noise. In the rearview mirror, she can see Mama's pinched face, the way her jaw clenches. Usually, she eyes Tessa in the mirror, or makes kissy-faces, but not today. Now, she only has eyes for the road ahead.

At some point, she turns off the highway. There is a new sound—the crunch of stones under tires. A gravel road. Tessa has no idea where they are, but she hopes it's close to home. She presses her thighs together; her bladder is full.

But then they reach the end of the road and Tessa realizes it's a dead-end. They pull into a driveway dotted with towering pines.

The snow falls softer as they slow, and she can see more clearly. A house materializes in front of them: a simple stone house with a peak in the front, laced in gingerbread trim. There are blue shutters on either side of the two front windows, and a holly bush with bright red berries beside the front step. With the roof crusted in snow and icicles dangling from the side porch, Tessa cannot imagine this house existing in any other season.

Tessa always gives made-up names to objects and people. This one comes unbidden. "The Winter House," she whispers, but Mama is no longer in the car to hear her.

Ben's voice brings Tessa back to the moment. "You've been really quiet, kid." Ben still likes to call Tessa "kid." Maybe he will forever. "You okay?" He winces. "Never mind, don't answer that."

They're on Oak Street now, only two blocks until they reach Mama's house. The thought of returning home without Mama makes Tessa sick. "I was remembering the day Mama took me shopping."

Brooke sniffs. "Man, I loved those back-to-school shopping trips she took us on."

"Oh, um, actually I meant the one where she only took me." Tessa shrugs. "It's probably just the snow making me think of it, but do either of you remember that day at all?" To jar their memories, she adds, "She bought me a green velvet dress?"

"Oh yes, the Christmas dress," Brooke says slowly. "How can I forget? *I* didn't get a dress that day." She gives Ben a playful punch on the arm. "There's no way you forget. The buses took us home early on account of the snowfall, and Mom and Tessa weren't there, so we made huge ice cream sundaes and ate potato chips."

Ben nods. "Oh, right." Of course, he would remember the food. "Ruined our dinner. We thought it was great until they got home and we realized they'd gone shopping without us. And had fries." He shakes his head. "*I* didn't get fries."

"And *I* didn't get a dress," Brooke repeats. They are teasing Tessa in fun, but sometimes Tessa thinks they are just adults who become children the moment they are with each other. "The kid peed her pants that day," Brooke adds. She laughs, but it sounds weak and wrong.

Tessa bristles. "I did *not*—"

"Okay, you *almost* did." Brooke looks over her shoulder at Tessa. "You bolted to the bathroom faster than I've ever seen you move before or since."

Tessa's cheeks redden. "Whatever. Can I get to the point? I have a question about that day." The one person she'd like to ask is no longer here, so she'll have to settle for any information her siblings may have.

Ben slows, flicking on the blinker to turn into the driveway. Tessa doesn't miss the side-eye he gives Brooke, like they're communicating without words.

A prickly feeling crosses Tessa's collarbone and she almost doesn't want to ask; sometimes she still feels like the little sister who everyone is making fun of. Like everyone knows something important, except her. But this—she has to know. "Is there any chance Mama mentioned whose house we stopped at on the way home that day?"

A pause. And then a length of silence that stretches out while they all sit and stare at their childhood home.

It's the Winter House that Tessa is seeing, though.

Mama climbs the steps to the Winter House. Someone must answer the door, though Tessa can't quite see through the swirling snow. Mama goes inside.

Tessa squirms in her seat, uncomfortable. The car is silent. Mama has turned off the engine and taken the key. It already feels cold. Tessa stares at the house, willing her mama to come back out. As she watches, the lacey curtains in one of the windows part, and a tiny face with a head of dark curls appears. A child.

A friend, Tessa thinks. She doesn't have any friends yet. Maybe when she goes to school like her big brother and sister, she will make friends. She waves at the little girl. But the little girl does not wave back. She only cocks her head to the side, her mouth turned down, her eyes dull and empty. She reminds Tessa of a china doll: pretty, pale, sad. Sad because china dolls are not played with, of course.

Tessa's seatbelt clicks as she unfastens it. Maybe she will go to the door and see how long Mama will be. Maybe she will find the dark-haired girl and ask her why she is so sad.

But when Tessa goes to open her door, a man lumbers from around the back corner of the house. He seems to be made of hard lines and jagged angles, his skin the colour of the grey stones that form the house. Tiny icicles coat his beard and moustache. Even his eyes are steely grey, like the sky. He glares at the Winter House, at the little girl, and Tessa pinches her eyes shut and wills her mama to run from the house. Now.

Tessa doesn't remember her mama coming out of the house. She doesn't remember her climbing back into the car, or the drive home.

"The house?" she tries again. The atmosphere in the car has shifted perceptibly.

Finally, Brooke sucks in a deep breath. "Okay, so when you were done in the bathroom that day and you came out, Mom said to you 'if you had to pee that bad, why didn't you come out of the car and go when I did?' You said you were going to, but then you got scared. Then you kept talking about the China Doll Girl and the Frozen Man . . ."

Tessa is surprised to hear she told them all of this back then, when she'd forgotten it for years until today. "Right. So, who were they? Why did she stop there?"

Brooke licks her lips. She casts another look at Ben, and he gives her a small nod. "Mom only stopped there to pee, Tess. She said she wasn't going to make it home after the slow drive and all the coffee. Mom told us there were no people there."

"But I saw them," Tessa insists. "We stopped at a house."

Ben turns toward Tessa now, too. He's wearing a strange look, one filled with sympathy and something that looks a bit like awe. "There was *no* house. It was just some leftover ruins."

Tessa sits there, staring at her brother and sister. No one gets out of the van. Nothing makes any sense, because Tessa can *see* the Winter House in her mind, can *see* the China Doll Girl and the Frozen Man. "Why would Mama have lied?" she asks finally.

Brooke is still twisted in her seat, looking back at Tessa. Her hazel eyes widen. "She didn't lie."

"Neither am I," Tessa says, hearing the defensiveness in her tone.

"She's not saying you are," Ben cuts in. "But you've always been able to . . . see."

Brooke purses her lips, and Tessa knows her older sister doesn't necessarily agree with their brother. Brooke is the skeptic and has always thought Tessa never outgrew her childhood imagination.

Tessa knows what Ben means, though. She's heard the story multiple times over her life, how at only one year old she saw their father after he died. The story makes her feel funny, like it was a comfort to Mama and Ben, but she can't even remember it. And if she's being honest, she wants to know why she can't see her Mama now. Why she didn't see her today. Why she isn't giving them a sign, something to say that she's okay, that Tessa *will be okay.*

Suddenly, Ben backs out of the driveway.

"Where are we going?" Tessa asks.

"To show you," Brooke says with a sigh, like she can read Ben's mind.

It occurs to Tessa that they've known where this place was the entire time. That everyone, it seems, really does know more.

The towering pines still line the driveway, heavy once again with snow. Ben parks the car near the road. "We'll have to walk. It's not like anyone is coming to plough out this lane."

Tessa pulls her hat over her ears, glad she had the sense to put boots on this morning. She steps out of the van hesitantly, half-afraid the Frozen Man will still be here, waiting for her after all this time. She wedges herself between her older siblings as they walk up the long laneway, their footsteps sifting through the powdery snow. White silence hangs over them, over this place, as quiet as a tomb. The sky is bleak, yet blinding, stretching on into nothingness, choking out the rest of the world. There is something about it, about the grey and white deadness of it all, that claws at Tessa's insides. It's lovely, in its own way.

Almost like her own sadness is offering clarity. Beauty even when the sun has gone.

Tessa is both surprised, and yet not surprised, to see a pile of stone rubble up ahead. There is no house any longer. Only a big bank barn still stands in the distance, boards weathered, windows broken. She never noticed it before, not with the house standing in the way. And behind the barn, a forest. The Winter House feels like it exists at the end of the world, not just the road.

Ben's arm snakes over Tessa's shoulders, and he gives her a squeeze.

"When," Tessa asks, slowly, "did the house come down?" There is still the possibility that it only happened in the last twenty years, and that Tessa did, indeed, see a real house.

"Mom researched it," Brooke says. "She was quite interested after everything you said. The house burnt down sometime in the nineteen-seventies."

The possibility is snuffed out like a candle.

Brooke crosses her arms, self-assured, like she is doing Tessa a favour by showing her what is real and what is not.

And yet, even as Tessa stares at the old foundation and the craggy stone walls, it's as if she can see the imprint of the Winter House in its glory, laid over top of the ruins, like a hologram. And there, in the window where the China Doll Girl was, a spot of fog clouds the glass, as if someone has let out a breath, as if someone was *just there*.

Tessa narrows her vision, squinting into the crisp air. She's always done this, in winter especially, when the air itself seems visible, made of tiny crystals. It dawns on her she's always been trying to see more, something hidden, something that once was.

Because how can something exist and then just be gone? How could *someone* exist and then not?

"You ready to go now?" Brooke asks, shivering. She adds, "Now that you've seen it."

But Tessa isn't ready to go. She hasn't seen what she was meant to see. It's a feeling deep inside her, of something unfinished. A pull she can feel deep down into her bones. "I need a minute," she says. "You can wait in the van." She doesn't mean it to sound like a dismissal, but she knows it does.

Brooke doesn't fight her; they are all tired, their nerves frayed. This trip down memory lane is an indulgence. Brooke would rather be drinking wine and cleaning out the house. Moving forward. "Whatever." She looks to Ben, to see if he's coming, but he only hands her the keys.

When Brooke is gone, Ben stares straight ahead, same as Tessa is doing. "You can still see it," he says. It isn't a question.

"It is—was—a pretty house," Tessa tells him. "But it is sad." She only realizes, as she says it, how true it really is. Everything in this place, including the ghostly Winter House, is shrouded in a despondency, a sadness heavier than the one they've brought with them. "Something happened here."

"I feel it, too," Ben admits. "Have you ever heard the theory that ghosts or hauntings are like tape recordings?" Ben is a big fan of theories, of research, of thinking outside the box. "It's like place memory, the idea that buildings are capable of storing memories of past events, which can later be played by gifted individuals."

Tessa considers this. "So, *I* can see these memories somehow?"

Ben blows warm air into his hands. "You've always been sensitive, tuned in." There is something comforting in the way he says it, as if Tessa is indeed "gifted" and not just strange. Or possibly delusional, as she is sure her sister thinks. "There is also the concept that environmental elements are capable of storing traces of human thoughts and emotions."

The snow, Tessa thinks. Even as a child she thought the Winter House could never exist in any other season.

Because it doesn't.

It only exists for *her* in the cold, ice-laden world.

Ben waves a hand in front of him. "Perhaps *you* are capable of seeing into . . . the psychic ether."

As if he's given her permission, Tessa suddenly sees it all. Her vision is flooded. The Winter House comes alive in front of her, the lacey curtains swinging as if someone has just left the window. The air smells of wood smoke, too, a curl of grey spiralling from the chimney. The imprint, the recording as Ben calls it, speeds up. Suddenly the solid side door whips open, and the China Doll Girl leaps down the steps. She is wearing a red hat that ties under her chin and matching mittens. In her hands, dangle a pair of ice skates.

Tessa inhales sharply; it is all so real. And yet she knows she is the only one seeing it, seeing the girl. Ben is not looking at the Winter House rubble at all, he is only studying Tessa, as if she is the one who is the mystery and not what is happening here.

The China Doll Girl takes off then, a flash of red in a bone-white world.

Before she can think better of it, Tessa darts after her.

She makes it past the barn, before Ben catches up to her. She never expected to outrun him, not when he goes to the gym religiously.

He catches her under the arm. "Where are you going?"

He's barely winded, whereas Tessa's weak lungs are burning with the frigid air. "The China Doll Girl," Tessa says, drawing breath. "She's headed to the forest." But she blinks and the girl is gone, swallowed by the trees.

Tessa sags in defeat, shaking Ben's hand from her arm. She whirls on him, ready to tell him she's going to the forest anyway, she *has* to—but she is stopped by the look on Ben's face. His mouth is open slightly, his brow furrowed. He is staring at the clean napkin of snow in front of them, untouched save for tiny footprints.

The sky grows darker as they follow the footprints into the forest. The forest itself is frozen in time, sleeping, yet biting. Tessa can feel the hunger, the ominous crawling up the back of her neck. The woodland is a hundred different greys, a charcoal sketch, bitter, bare, and beautiful. White drifts rise over mossy stumps and curving hills, icing the barren branches like frosting on a cake.

Their own footsteps are rapid, full of tension.

Tessa knows she is following the China Doll Girl. She cannot be sure what Ben thinks, but he is here with her, and that is what matters.

The footsteps stop in a wide clearing. There is a pond, freshly scraped clean of snow, the ice a clear sheath.

Ben cocks his head to the side. "Do you hear that?"

And Tessa does. She can hear the sounds—the faint laughter, the slice of skates—before the scene materializes.

Then, like at the Winter House, the image unfolds. It is the red hat and mittens Tessa spots first. The China Doll Girl is attempting to skate, holding the hand of a woman who has the same pale skin and dark hair. *Her mama,* Tessa thinks. The woman's cheeks are pink with the cold, her ears covered in fuzzy earmuffs. Her coat is a striking blue wool, the shade of cobalt. Tessa cannot tear her eyes from the two of them, from their happiness. A warmth spreads through her own chest, nostalgic and bittersweet. Tessa has the uncanny sensation of her own hand in her Mama's. She half-imagines she is the China Doll Girl, and the woman is her mama, and they are skating on a forest pond on a wintery day.

Tessa can practically feel the lightness of it, the freedom, the swell of joy in the China Doll Girl's chest. Wait. Isn't that why she is here in the first place? It dawns on her, with alarming clarity, that it is not only the snow, but the sad look she saw on the China Doll Girl's face in the window that day, that has drawn her here. A sadness that now sweeps over her once again, straight to her core. And as she watches the pretty scene in front of her, another hint of warning pitter-patters through her brain. There is misery in the breath of wind now, misery where laughter once was.

The threat of pain where love lives.

The sound of a phone jolts Tessa back to the here and now. The scene begins to fade at the edges, but Tessa notices the Frozen Man beside her in the trees, leaning forward, arms folded over a snow shovel. He is smiling a wide smile as he watches the woman and the girl.

He isn't frozen now, Tessa thinks vaguely, her mind spinning. And then, *no, he isn't frozen yet.*

Yet.

That is the keyword. If this is a recording, has Tessa seen the end before the beginning?

The scene is gone.

It is no longer the Frozen Man and his shovel, but Ben with his phone. Did it ring? He has put Brooke on speaker. Her voice is an assault in the silent world. "*Where* are you two? I walked back up to the house and you're not here."

Ben glances at Tessa. "Sorry, we're just . . . uh, in the forest."

"Tell me you did not say that." Brooke's breathing becomes heavier; she's on the move. "I found your footprints, I'm coming. I don't know what's going on with Tessa and this place, but I did some googling in the car and you will not believe—"

Brooke cuts out, replaced by crackly static. Tessa is no longer listening. She has noticed a star in the ice, a fractal-like pattern. Darker, clearer tendrils that seem to stretch out from somewhere in the middle.

Tessa barely registers Ben still trying to salvage the conversation. "Brooke, you there? Brooke?"

Tessa steps out onto the ice. With slow, shuffling footsteps, she slides her way over the eerie shapes under the ice. They are like the roots of a tree, like arms gathering her in.

"Stop." Ben has noticed her now. "The water may not be completely frozen."

Tessa turns toward him slowly. He is still gripping his phone. His nose is red.

Tessa points at the ice. "Do you see the shapes?" He saw the footprints and heard the laughter. Will he see this, too?

Ben nods. "There was probably a breach in the ice and this happened when it refroze." A simple explanation for something so mysterious. Tessa wonders if Ben will spend his life trying to explain everything. Has he wondered why the ice here is cleared when no one lives here any longer? Does he not see that he, too, can glimpse into the past, if only a bit? "Now come back."

But Tessa cannot come back. She is only a few feet away from the dark centre where the tendrils come from. *The breach.*

Eyes still trained on Ben, she backs up slowly, toward the breach, a single, imperceptible step at a time.

"Tessa," Ben warns. He has always looked after her since the day she was born. An older brother perpetually trying to fill the void of an absent father. He takes a step forward but stops. There is a sharp cracking noise; Ben weighs much more than little Tessa. He cannot go to her or the ice will crack. "Shit," he says.

The irony is not lost on Tessa. They are so close in this place, in this grey world, and yet so far apart.

Brooke crashes into the clearing while the two of them are still locked, eye to eye. Immediately, Brooke shakes her head. "No, no, *no!* Get off the ice." There is an urgency in Brooke's tone that sets Tessa's nerves on edge. Brooke rarely sounds anxious, but now she is flailing and rambling. "Before the house burnt down, it sat empty for twenty years, after the death of Helen Winter."

Tessa stiffens. "Winter?" *The Winter House?*

"I know," Brooke says. "I *know.* I don't know how you know things and see things, but you do, Tess. I get it. I'm sorry. But right now, *I* know things, and you *have* to get off that ice."

"What is it?" Ben's teeth grind together. "What did you find out?"

Brooke holds out a hand to Tessa like maybe she can stretch her arm far enough to yank her back. "The woman fell in the pond ice-skating. Helen Winter drowned."

Drowned. The breach.

There is a change in the air again, a shift. Tessa feels like she's vibrating.

She looks down. In the black ice beneath her feet is a familiar face. Brown eyes dart about frantically, a palm pushes against the unyielding ice. *Help,* the woman mouths, and bubbles obscure her face.

Mama.

No, no, no.

Someone is screaming, but Tessa's heart is thundering in her ears, too. She drops to her knees, pummelling her fists against the solid surface. *Bang, bang, bang.* On the third try, Tessa slows, staring at her red mittens.

Red mittens.

Tessa holds her hands out in front of her, incredulous, and filled with horror. When she finally looks down at the ice again, it is not her Mama there. Instead, it is a woman's bloated face. Her skin is alabaster under a powder of snow, wrinkled with time, her eyes vacant and unseeing, her mouth, with frosted blue lips, open in a never-ending wail. Her dark hair twists in thick strands around her neck, strangling her, over and over.

Helen Winter, Tessa's foggy mind tells her. *She drowned.*

She is drowning.

She will drown.

Time is curling in on itself here, here in this loop, in this never-ending recording. It is a collage, pasted together images. Tessa is at the centre.

"Get away from the hole!" a deep voice yells. It doesn't sound like Ben. *Papa,* her mind registers. The Frozen Man.

Sure enough, there is a hole in the ice now. A *breach.*

A dainty, gloved hand is hanging onto the shelf, her head barely above the water. "Get back," the woman screams. It is Helen, the woman she saw under the ice only a moment ago, but she is still alive in this scene. Not dead yet. Not bloated with icy water.

Somehow, it is Mama, too.

Tessa has broken the recording, mixed it all up.

Tessa's limbs are frozen, from cold, from shock. She wants, more than anything, to dive into that hole, to save her mama. Or perhaps die with her. One or the other, rather than the separation between life and death. She inches forward. The ice groans.

Her mama screams again, "Get back, Peggy!"

Peggy.

The name rings wrong. Tessa is not Peggy. Tessa is not the China Doll Girl, and she isn't wearing red mittens and it isn't her mama who fell through the ice.

"Get off the ice!" This time it *is* Ben. His voice cuts through the past, calling to Tessa from the here and now. Calling her back from wherever she's gone.

Ben, she thinks. She still has Ben and Brooke.

She crawls away, far enough away, toward the voices of her siblings. Oddly, she can't see them, Brooke and Ben, but she can feel them, their warmth, their safety. Her bare hands are freezing on the ice; she is no longer wearing the red mittens. She is not Peggy. She has shed the ghost of the China Doll Girl.

Tessa glances over her shoulder. The scene is still playing out. The Frozen Man is on his belly now, his face, his beard, his arms, submerged in the frigid water. He thrashes about, searching, searching, searching.

Tessa collapses on solid ground. A whimper makes her roll to her side. Beside her, the China Doll Girl covers her eyes with her red mittens, but she is peeking through them to watch the last moments. She doesn't know it yet, but her mama will die. Or maybe she does know it.

Maybe, even in her child's mind, she knows this moment will mark her forever.

Tessa pulls herself up and watches with the China Doll Girl, the two of them united in their shared grief, connected through time.

When the Frozen Man finally stops searching, when he lays his cheek on the ice and sobs, Tessa reaches out to comfort her. Tessa's hand slips through empty air. "She's gone," she whispers. Like a recording on a loop, she says it over and over. "She's gone, she's gone, she's gone."

Maybe if she says it enough times, it will all make sense.

Or maybe it never will.

Maybe the China Doll Girl will sit here on a loop, replaying the scene over and over, an imprint ghost that can't—won't—stop.

No.

It's too cruel, too unfair. Tessa can still picture the little girl's face she saw in the window that snowy day when their worlds collided. Tessa can see how it all played out. The China Doll Girl had likely run back to the house, with some faint hope that her mama would be there, that it'd all been a bad dream. The Frozen Man had come up later and stared at the house, at his little girl in the window, unable to fix any of it. That is the moment Tessa had witnessed that day, the two of them drowning in their own grief, with only the house between them, only the stone house and the snow to absorb it all. And only Tessa to see it.

Beside Tessa, the China Doll Girl rises. Before she can run off, Tessa says, "Peggy, it is over now." She only hopes it really will be, that the act of her seeing it all, of witnessing it, can make it stop.

Accepting it? Well, only the China Doll Girl can do that.

As if the little girl can sense something has changed, she looks around at the forest. Rather than running back to the house, rather than starting the loop again, she walks slowly across the ice, following the dark tendrils to the breach. But there is no longer a hole, and no longer her mama. The China Doll Girl stares at the ice for a long time, and then, rather than down, she looks to the trees behind her, where the Frozen Man once, minutes ago, years ago, leaned against his shovel.

To Tessa's surprise, he's there again. He drops his shovel and walks across the ice to the China Doll Girl. He takes her red-mittened hand in his and the two of them keep walking.

It's then that Tessa sees where they are going.

There are two women standing on the other side of the pond. One is Helen Winter in her cobalt blue coat. The other is Tessa's mama, wearing a long, flowing dress and a flower crown. They smile at Tessa with golden smiles. The China Doll Girl and the Frozen Man are enveloped into their light.

The scene shimmers and fades.

They are all gone.

"She's gone." Tessa says it again, but this time with awe, and for all of them. A bittersweet warmth flows through her chest. There is a shift again, a discernible quietness that settles over the clearing. The image, the past, fades away. The light has changed, the sky a softer dove grey.

Brooke is on one side of Tessa, shivering.

Ben is on the other side, his tears frozen lace on his cheeks.

They did not see what Tessa did, but she can tell them later. For now, she reaches for their hands and holds them tight.

It is the three of them in this snowy world.
It is only the three of them.

It takes Tessa a month to track down Peggy Winter. Tessa had half-expected her to be dead, like she always imagined ghosts to be, but the woman, it turns out, is still alive. She married in her twenties and changed her last name to Delrue. Luckily, she was easy to find; she became something of a famous local artist, painting wintery landscapes that feel distinctly gothic.

Tessa takes the three-hour drive to visit her on a bitter-cold Saturday in January. She's concocted an entire story about being an art student and wanting to interview the now seventy-one-year-old artist, but the moment Peggy opens the door, Tessa forgets all her well-rehearsed lines.

Peggy's face pales and she raises a hand to her chest as if she's forgotten how to breathe.

Tessa isn't sure what to make of it, but she, herself, does no better. Despite all the years she's aged, Peggy's eyes are still the same—a striking blue.

It is Peggy who speaks first. "Come in," she says. She waves a shaking hand at the arrangement she's set out: a pot of tea and china cups, a plate of sugar cookies—her preparation for the stranger who was coming to interview her about art.

But the ruse has been forgotten. Tessa settles into an overstuffed arm chair, her legs like jelly, and Peggy lowers herself slowly onto the couch. That is when Tessa notices the painting on the wall behind the couch. It is *the* wintery woodland. It is barren branches and snow-dusted ground and . . . the pond. There is a hint of golden light permeating through the greys.

Tessa is startled to discover that even this she had seen. The day she had raced into the woodland after the China Doll Girl, she'd thought how it had looked like a sketch, like something that deserved to be caught in time and live forever.

Peggy had done that.

"It's so beautiful," Tessa says, a tear snaking down her cheek. Tessa has studied all of Peggy's paintings she could find online, and although all of them evoked a sad beauty, this one is by far the best. It still holds the darkness, but catches the light.

Peggy tries to talk, but her voice catches and she clears her throat. Then, she says, "I only painted it last month."

Tessa drags her eyes from the painting and back to Peggy. "A month ago?"

Peggy nods. "I had the strangest dream, like a memory. I've painted my whole life, since my mother died, as I'm sure you read in other interviews. It was a way to work through my grief, you could say." She sniffs. "Or maybe I was simply haunted all these years."

Tessa clasps her hands together in her lap. *Haunted.* She can see how events can haunt people or places, stay with them forever, like a recording you can't stop seeing. Haunted is different from what Tessa thought it was.

Peggy goes on. "But then, a month ago, I awoke from an afternoon nap with the strangest memory. I remembered something I'd forgotten from that day."

Tessa leans forward, her elbows on her knees. "What did you remember?"

Peggy's lip quivers and she takes a moment to answer. Finally, she says, "I remembered a girl with brown hair and brown eyes. I remembered *you.*"

A chill climbs Tessa's spine and makes her scalp tingle. "Me?" she whispers.

Tessa is the seer. But is it possible the China Doll Girl saw her back?

"I didn't think you were real until fifteen minutes ago when I opened my door." Peggy is crying now, too. "I only saw you for a split second, but I remember what you said. You said '*It is over now.*'"

Tessa lets out a tiny sob.

"When I woke up, I felt . . . lighter. Like I could finally paint this scene, the moment I skirted around all these years."

Tessa turns her attention to the painting again, to the golden light. She squints. There are light-filled shadows on the other side of the pond. Tessa rises and goes closer. The shadows form into two figures. *Mama.* Tessa knows no one else will see them unless they are looking for something more. The figures are hidden, a secret in the painting, a secret in the snow.

On the drive home, it begins to snow and Tessa takes the back roads. She is still reeling from the turn of events, replaying the afternoon in her mind. That is why she almost misses seeing the stately house on the hill. Tessa slams on the brakes and backs up. She jumps out of the car, shielding her eyes from the softly falling snow.

She blinks.

There is no house.

Sarah Van Goethem is a Canadian author of short stories and novels. She lives in a century farmhouse where she hibernates in the winter, only venturing out to take a walk in her snowy pine forest.

Her first middle grade gothic novel, *The Witch of the Dark Wood*, will be published by Kids Can Press in the fall of 2026.

Three of her short stories have been nominated for a Pushcart Prize, and one of was a finalist for the CBC Nonfiction Prize. All can be found on her website at SarahVanGoethem.com

WHITE ONES

ALEX T. SINGER

The fur trappers are stuck when the blizzard sets in. It will take days before the bat can reach them. It is not the first time this has happened, so at first, they laugh. They are not too bothered. They built a cabin out in the white years ago. They are well fortified. They have a lot of food, a strong generator, and a healthy supply of alcohol. Jean-Pierre wins at poker. Tomas sings along to the old CDs he keeps in the bathroom. Augustin drinks heavily. Julian sits nervously by the window but even he smiles at times.

On the second day in their cabin Julian says, "I think I see the rescue team."

Jean-Pierre tells him this is silly. The veil of snow is too thick to see anything.

Tomas says that Julian is full of shit, there is no way that anyone could see out that far.

Augustin is sleeping on the couch and misses the entire conversation.

All they see are whorls of snow in the horizon, any one of which could be a person or a mirage and the radio is too staticky to answer their argument one way or the other. The men mock Julian heartily—he has always been too cautious on these trips.

"Screw you all," says Julian, who decides to ski out to meet with them. He packs his gear and leaves.

Augustin wakes up some time after he leaves. "Where's Julian?"

"Jumping at shadows," says Jean-Pierre. "He'll be back before night."

Julian never comes back.

"Should we have let him go?" asks Tomas, after a bit.

"He's gone to the harbour to sulk," says Jean-Pierre.

The next day Tomas wants to go out to find Julian, but Jean-Pierre does not let him go. The blizzard is too thick, and there was a cave in the harbour they often used, surely Julian is there. "Julian needs to toughen up," says Jean-Pierre.

Augustin sighs and puts his sleeping bag over his head to ignore the argument.

Jean-Pierre decides they should play cards again, by the window if Tomas is so worried. They do this for half a day, until Tomas sees something.

"Julian?" he asks.

"Not you too," says Jean-Pierre.

But they both see something this time, through the blowing blizzard: a line of shadows. Tomas and Jean-Pierre put on their coats and step out. They see very little. They hear the scream of the wind and, on occasion, a crunch that could be feet in the snow.

"Julian, you ass," cries Tomas.

There is no answer.

"Back inside," says Jean-Pierre. "If it's the team they'll be here by night."

"Have fun out there?" asks Augustin, when they come back.

The team is not there by night, but by morning the blizzard has died down some. They can now tell the white of the clouds from the white of the snow, and there is indeed a line of people on the horizon. Distant, thin figures, colourless in the still falling snow, but trudging dutifully, swaying side to side as they walk.

"They are taking their time," says Augustin.

"Is Julian with them, you think?"

"Forget Julian," grumbles Jean-Pierre. "They must have stopped for the night. Pack up, everyone."

But by mid-day the trudging men are no closer to them, nor are they any clearer on the horizon. They must have run into trouble, the trappers think. They must have had to divert around an ice flow. Jean-Pierre radios, but he gets nothing but static. They are left to speculate. Tomas paces. Jean-Pierre glares at his boots. Augustin decides to check the generator. They argue on and off about what might have happened. Finally, Tomas has had enough. He grabs his skis and his bright yellow coat, and says he will go out to meet them.

"Fine, if it will shut you up," says Jean-Pierre.

"If it will stop you from sitting on your ass," says Tomas. He goes. Jean-Pierre is too angry to watch him leave.

"You let him go?" asks Augustin, when he returns.

"He went himself," says Jean-Pierre, and that is the end of all discussion.

By evening, the figures on the horizon are only a little closer. They cannot spot Tomas' yellow coat among them. Augustin tries to call Tomas and Julian. He gets nothing.

The blizzard gets stronger in the night, but has ebbed enough the morning after that they can see the line of men have managed to get closer. Now they can make out the colour of their gear: grey and white.

"How stupid," says Jean-Pierre. "Who wears white in a blizzard?"

"And you are the expert now?" asks Augustin.

"Say that when you are not in the bottle," says Jean-Pierre.

Augustin shrugs. It is fair enough. Jean-Pierre supposes they have given Tomas and Julian some of their gear. He supposes Tomas and Julian are with them. He supposes they will reach the cabin soon. He can see now that they do not seem to have much gear, and they must be wearing snow shoes, for how they shuffle back and forth on the snow, without sinking in.

"Keep your things by the door," says Jean-Pierre, "they'll be here soon."

Evening falls and they have not come. Is it possible, the men wonder, that the team does not know the location of the cabin? Augustin goes out to fire a flare gun. He comes back wide-eyed.

"They are still moving out there," he says. "I don't think they've stopped."

"You're letting things get to you," says Jean-Pierre. "If they were still moving, they'd have reached us by now."

In the night, they think they hear footsteps in the snow. But of course, that could not be the case—the winds are high and would make that impossible. It is snow falling from the cabin roof, nothing more.

By morning the line of men has gotten closer. They can see now that they are wrapped from head to toe. This makes sense, in a storm like this.

"They are marching like soldiers," says Augustin. "Their arms at their sides."

"Are you still drunk?" asks Jean-Pierre.

"No, but I am beginning to wish I was," says Augustin.

"You are useless," says Jean-Pierre.

So, Augustin goes to check the radio. No answer. Augustin and Jean-Pierre both sit uselessly by the window, trying to make out individuals among the silhouettes. It is quite impossible, their bindings are identical, and their body language is exactly the same.

"Have you ever heard," says Augustin, as the sun sets, "of the white ones? The ones who walk and walk and never stop?"

"No, and you are an idiot for trying to spook me," says Jean-Pierre. Augustin shrugs and goes to bed.

Jean-Pierre stays up that night with one of Augustin's bottles. He steps out to light more flares. He sees, in the dark, the men swaying in the distance. He shouts and waves his arms, but there is no response. Jean-Pierre lowers his arms.

He thinks, for a moment, that this is Julian and Tomas' revenge.

He thinks also, for a blurry moment, that they should have known better.

He takes his flare gun and aims it at the horizon. He fires. The light dies in the snow, for a moment illuminating the line of men—their long arms, and the glare of light off of their huge shining goggles. They do not even stumble as the fire falls in front of them. They do not even flinch.

"Sons of bitches," shouts Jean-Pierre. "We're over here."

There is no response. Jean-Pierre goes back inside for one of the rifles, but Augustin is awake by then and Jean-Pierre changes his mind.

"Jean-Pierre," asks Augustin, distantly. "Have you ever killed anyone? I mean the seals, they are easy, but men, that is much harder. They're bigger. And it's very hard to make yourself aim at them. Oh, the sounds they make as they die. Have you ever done it?"

"You're drunk," says Jean-Pierre, sitting unsteadily across from him.

"And you are not answering me," slurs Augustin, who drifts off after that.

Augustin sleeps. Jean-Pierre does not.

By dawn the blizzard has mostly cleared. He can see the men are wearing fur gear. White, battered fur with yellowed edges, like the pelts of young seals from much farther north, and Jean-Pierre is all at once warmed by hate. So, these men are thieves! So, they are here to take their bounty!

"Oh, you bastards," he says. The men are still walking, strolling really, in the snow. They are close enough he knows they can hear him shout, but still, they don't speed up. Their arms lie stiff at their sides. Their heads are stiff and set straight ahead.

"You won't get them," shouts Jean-Pierre. "I won't let you."

He gets the rifle. Augustin is cocooned in his sleeping bag. He belches but does not stir. Jean-Pierre steps out, takes aim, and fires. At first, he fires into the snow in front of them.

"Leave off," cries Jean-Pierre, "leave the hell off."

But the men ignore this. They just keep walking. Jean-Pierre fires again, this time aiming for the white space between them.

"Leave off," cries Jean-Pierre. "We don't *want* you here."

The men do not even turn to look between them. This has been warning enough. Jean-Pierre shoulders the rifle, and this time, he aims for their legs.

He fires again. And again. And again. But the snow has affected his aim, because the men do not stop. They walk forward, slowly, swaying. They walk forward, long arms stiff at their sides. Jean-Pierre aims for their chests. Their heads. Somehow, he always misses. Somehow, they keep walking. Jean-Pierre has enough. He takes out his club.

"Fine," he says, "fine."

He runs out and his ugly shout is cut off by the great hush of snow.

In the cabin, staring up at the ceiling, Augustin sighs softly and shuts his eyes. He goes to check the radio. There is static again, but then he gets something:

"—ustin? Tomas?" says a rickety voice. "We have broken through. We are here in the harbour. Where are you? Where *are* you?"

Augustin turns the radio off. He goes and puts on his gear. He laces up his boots, and his red coat. He reaches for his goggles, but decides against it. He leaves his hooks and clubs.

He opens the door.

The figures on the horizon are almost here: the white ones, with white furs and long arms, at first stiff at their sides but now, as they draw close, now, as they draw near, their arms are raised high. Raised, in greeting, in an embrace . . .

"Ah," says Augustin, who does not run. What would be the point, after all? They will come either way. "I suppose it is about that time."

Augustin steps out to meet them. It is what one does, when meeting old friends.

Alex T. Singer lives in coastal New England, which is cold, but not quite as cold as the remote part of Newfoundland where her poor protagonists wound up stuck. She is the author of novels *Minotaur* and *Song of the Bullrider*. Her short stories have appeared in *Crossed Genre Magazines, Empyreome Magazine, Apparition Literature*, and *Pseudopod*. Samples of her work can be found on her website: http://littlefoolery.com/. She has been known to enjoy an occasional walk in the snow.

WHAT THE OLD-TIMERS SAY

BETH CATO

they say that when
the leaves turn colour
and drift earthward,
the squirrels scurry, and the fog
rises thick from the river at dawn
the season is beginning to shift
and everyone ought to be prepared
for normal storms and
the other sort

they say there's little warning—
when one of the peculiar storms comes
the sky can be cloudless,
the sun even warm
if a person's not in the shade

they say between one second and the next
the wind rises with the very might
of God's breath, that the air becomes so cold
nearby birds plummet like stones
an instant before the world
turns a brilliant, terrible white

they say things live, hunt
amid the blinding torrent
a snared person has time
to start to scream
then there's nothing
but wind

afterward
however many minutes or hours
the storm has smothered the prairie
feet of snow can't cover
the red and pink that dye
fields where wheat rustled
months before
that blood, and maybe scraps of cloth
perhaps a hat
are all that's ever found
no bodies, no parts

they say that people who are fast
with a gun or hustle for indoors
can survive
that even schoolchildren caught out at recess
can live if they keep cool heads and mind
their teacher, but every family
in this county
has someone they mourn, every family
leaves flowers at empty graves

they say a person's a fool
to live here if they can afford to get away
but even so
they
the old-timers
remain
they say they love this place

I think they do, but that
they're also
stupidly stubborn

they can't let winter win
that one way or another—
through their rows of wheat and corn,
by their blood atop the soil
or their bodies beneath
—they'll mark this land
as theirs

Nebula Award-nominated Beth Cato is the author of *A Thousand Recipes for Revenge* and *A Feast for Starving Stone* from 47North plus two fantasy series from Harper Voyager. She's a Hanford, California native now moored in the Driftless Area. Her new Minnesota home and its fabled winters provided the inspiration for her poem in this anthology. Follow her at BethCato.com, Twitter/X at @BethCato, and Instagram at @catocatsandcheese.

EVERYTHING IN ITS PLACE

NICOLE M. WOLVERTON

On the mid-September day that Mother moved to Brightview, the crows perched on the telephone wires outside my childhood home were watchful. Mother insisted that I *not* accompany her to her new living arrangements, so I stood on the well-tended doorstep, flowers perfect red on either side, as the taxi trailed after the van with her things. I waved half-heartedly at the small, departing caravan.

It was with no little trepidation that I pushed open the front door and returned to the cheerless foyer where I had hugged Mother, stiff-armed, before seeing her off. Like the exterior, the interior of the house was as pristine and as proper as a museum. Not a speck of dust. Not a decoration out of position. Everything in its place. If I had not grown up in this meticulous house, I would think a cleaning crew had rendered it so sterile—but Mother has always been particular and exacting. I could easily imagine her slowly scrubbing the corners of the parlour, polishing the crystal that stood watch in the dining room cabinet.

I had not willingly entered the house for nearly four decades, it being largely unnecessary after I moved out on my own. Mother was happy to come to me for the occasional brunch. She never pushed me about coming to visit until a few weeks ago. "Won't you please stay after I'm gone and look after the place, at least for a few days? It would mean a great deal to me."

Her voice over the phone had pleaded as innocently as a child, but Mother is as intentional about her person as she is about the house—and she has card-catalogue knowledge of every item in the place. She knows each item's provenance and its rightful location, whether atop the gleaming rolltop desk in the office or in the built-in cabinet with the handsome, hand-tooled scrollwork in the dining room.

I know that when I walk into the broad and shining kitchen the café table will be set neatly for one, a pointed reminder to me of my absence. And when I stick my head into my childhood bedroom, everything will be as I left it. There could easily be a tiny placard below the light switch that reads, "Living space of artist Lola Litchfield, 1970. *In situ* in the home of eccentric dowager Izzy Litchfield."

I choose not to remember much of my childhood, but the quiet, painstaking showpiece of this house is burned into my retinas—into my very bones—as is Mother's penchant for manipulation.

And so I was both surprised and not surprised that in the living room Mother had left an artificial nine-foot spruce, decorated for Christmas. I would have thought she'd insist on packing away her pair of beloved Victorian children with the bisque heads, suspended on braided swings (1901, once owned by German royalty) or the rare silver filigree dove (1855, Japan)— but there they were on the tree, twinkling amid stark white strings of light.

She'd mentioned in passing that the realtor—an old friend, she'd said—had asked her to stage the house for the winter holidays. Create a cozy, family atmosphere (as much as one could amid all this perfection). This scene, though, smacked of more than a simple warm tableau. I would have expected a raft of shiny red and green presents nestled beneath the tree and stockings hung from the cold marble mantle. Instead, there was only one: a large square box wrapped in blue foil and festooned with an oversized silver bow.

Shivering with the sudden cold—perhaps I was getting into the spirit of the holiday display after all—I bent down to read the white tag tucked in with the bow. There was my name, hand printed, Mother-perfect, in precise block letters: LOLA LITCHFIELD. On the back of the tag, she'd printed:

I FOUND SOME THINGS IN A CRAWLSPACE IN THE UPSTAIRS CORRIDOR WHILE PACKING. I DON'T KNOW WHAT THEY ARE—YOURS, PERHAPS?

The frigid silence of the house rose to a scream. As if it were possible that something that existed in this perfect, arranged exhibition space that had eluded Mother's attention for four decades. As though I would have left anything of importance behind. It could only be one final attempt by Mother to make a pointed commentary about her eternal disapproval over the life I had chosen. I tucked the box under my arm and left the house, days before I had promised. For once, mother would not have eyes on this house and would never know.

Back in my apartment I sat the silver-bowed box just inside the door and circumnavigated it for weeks. The thought of throwing it away without opening it was ever-present, yet something tugged at the corners of my mind, refusing to allow it. Whatever message Mother was trying to convey with the box—and there was *always* a subliminal message—it would have to wait until I ran out of excuses not to open it. The box transformed into a drab, makeshift table pushed against the wall, piled with unwanted mail. Eventually my apartment subsumed the box until it was an invisible component of the décor. I just . . . forgot about it entirely, and Mother never asked. It was as though the box no longer existed, for either of us.

Except I *did* know it was there. I simply continued to refuse to acknowledge it.

Mother died the day before Christmas. She was alone in her senior living apartment when it happened, nothing suspicious about it: she was seventy-two and, despite her perfection, had a bad heart. I blamed her constant vigilance to ensure that everything, including me, was in its place.

"Yes, yes, of course I'll come," I said to the retirement village attendant over the phone. The air in my apartment was cool enough that I wore fingerless mitts, my nails drumming on the scratched kitchen table as I considered that I was now an orphan. "I'll be there . . . perhaps in a few days. I wouldn't want to interrupt any activities on Christmas Day. Will that be okay? Do I need to empty her room?"

I hadn't been to visit her in Brightview, but I could imagine a spare, blindingly white apartment, neatly organized. Perhaps she'd kept a few of her holiday decorations. The hand-painted creche scene, circa 1840 from Madrid . . . or the delicate replica Fabergé Winter Egg (c. 1924, Russia). Something to satisfy her need for precision placement that would unsubtly remind people of her station.

"I'm so sorry for your loss," the attendant said. It must take training to sound that sorry yet so completely uninterested. "Yes, we'd certainly appreciate it if you could see to her possessions before the beginning of the new year. Izzy was well liked here. Our Friday morning canasta tourneys will never be the same."

I hung up and sat in my living room for five minutes—I counted, thinking about how much Mother would appreciate the exactitude of knowing the precise duration of time spent considering her death. I thought of that house, all decorated for the holidays, still completely pristine. It had sold shortly after she'd moved out. I'd never heard anything more about it.

My apartment—by contrast to my childhood home—was undecorated and cluttered, with only the lights from the decorations on the building across the street to mark the holiday. I was determined to be Mother's opposite—there was something about her house that had repelled me though I could never quite name exactly what it was.

And Mother. She repelled me, too.

Getting a handle on how to feel about her death was . . . difficult. It was hard to think of Mother as anything other than just a relative. We'd always gotten on as properly and coldly as the state of our old home, especially after Daddy went away. He'd at least brought *some* warmth to the situation. He went missing when I was little, though.

The mystery box that still lay under a blanket of the old and unwanted mail suddenly felt like a glowing beacon—almost as loud and bright as the Christmas star from all those stories. This remnant of my old life, this reminder of my orphanhood. Now it was just me and the box and the dust that layered over everything in my apartment and the snow outside, falling just hard enough to make a soft sound against my dirty windows.

Perhaps the box was important in some way I hadn't considered. Perhaps it contained information about my father—I'd long suspected Mother knew more than she'd said. There could be *anything* nestled inside. Maybe a rusted knife with blood still caked along the edge. I heard more than once that people thought Mother had cracked under the weight of her perfection and stabbed him to death, hidden his body in the basement.

Mother would never have allowed his body to remain in the house, though, I was sure of that. Everything in its place, and that museum of house was no place for a corpse unless Daddy's body was preserved, labelled, and carefully displayed in some way.

"Murdered body of engineer Earnest Litchfield, 1976. *In situ* in the home of eccentric dowager Izzy Litchfield."

My knees were stiff as rusted hinges when I finally moved from the chair to the box. I pushed the mail and unopened Christmas cards off into an untidy heap on the cold floor and ripped up the cardboard around Mother's perfect tape job, around her precise block capitals on the address label. Bits of newspaper spilled out, and bubble wrap the colour of ruined roses. Finally, a hard, brown corner poked through the packing. I tore at the cardboard until a wooden box lay on the cluttered floor.

The box was . . . I'd never seen it before. Not the latticework carved into the top, nor the brass latch holding the lid fast. If it had been stowed away in the crawl space of my childhood bedroom all these years, shouldn't it have sparked *some* recollection?

I shivered and blew warmth into my frozen fingers.

Beneath the tissue paper inside, a stack of documents—again, nothing familiar-looking. I lifted out the documents, and that's when I found it. The air in my apartment thickened to ice until I could barely breathe. The bridge of my nose prickled. I clapped my hand over my mouth.

A framed needlepoint, gleaming and unblemished, wedged into the bottom of the box, as though the box were built around it.

I lunged to click on the lamp, then climbed to my feet and sprinted around the room, turning on every single light. The black corners of my apartment felt occupied, as though someone watched. It felt impossible to stay in the same room with the frame for more than thirty minutes—yet I couldn't bring myself to leave even if the snow hadn't rendered the streets slippery and dangerous. I could only pace like an agitated cat and let the memories return.

Fourteen is such a strange year for girls. Every moment is at once crucial and not crucial enough. Entirely too dramatic, yet not dramatic enough to make life interesting. Even begging Mother to tell me about Daddy was disappointing—her recollections were unsatisfying and vague. Mother's eyes were unfocused when she spoke of him. It was the one subject that, for her, was indistinct. The most frequent story she told was that he'd headed out one night for cigarettes but never returned. No more detail than that . . . in any of her stories.

The cigarette story was laughable. My father never smoked. The very idea of him leaving a cloud of smoke anywhere in our home was unlikely. Mother would have followed behind him, erasing any evidence of the stench and the ashes . . . just as she erased any evidence of his existence after he was gone. She could not permit any deviation from the perfection she created.

I made up my own stories about my father, imagining him a bold explorer or a daring bank robber, some scenario that required him to go into hiding to protect us from his action-packed and perhaps dangerous life. I inserted him into the books I checked out from the library.

The morning I saw that needlepoint for the first time I'd bicycled to the library, glad to be away from the funereal pall of my house. I slid my pile of books across the desk to a librarian—a gaunt, grey woman in wire-rimmed glasses I had never seen before. She looked over those glasses at me and frowned.

"*'Salem's Lot*?" Her voice was raspy as nails against metal. "*Frankenstein*? Too old for you."

My reflection, frizz-plain and brown-haired, frowned back at me from the librarian's glasses and jutted its pointy chin up, daring the woman to refuse me. That day I wanted to imagine my father as a hero fighting monsters . . . or perhaps a man made into a monster against his will. Perhaps *that* was the secret Mother kept.

"I can read what I want," I said.

The librarian's thin, pale lips tightened. "A girl like you could get in trouble, knowing more than you should."

"There's nothing in these books I don't already know." Except the whereabouts of Daddy, but that was family business according to Mother. *Everything in its place,* she'd say—*and the place to discuss your father is here in this house.* Nowhere else.

"Is that so?" Every molecule of air in the library seemed to freeze with the librarian's voice. "The Tree of Knowledge is not that of Life. Byron said that. Satan with this black hand, he tempted Eve—"

"Eve was framed."

"I knew your father." It was an accusation.

I said nothing but shivered and rubbed my arms.

"He was tempted, too, and now, he with Eve, and Eve with her Adam, and both of them damned. You are damned as well." She packed the books into a bag. "You should pay reverence, girl. Repent before you know darkness, too. It will do you no good, of course—the curse still reaches for you. Your mother should take you out of that house."

The temptation to ask was almost too much. I *felt* cursed so much of the time in that house, under Mother's scrutiny and amid the whispers I'd heard around town.

I snatched the bag and glared. "You don't know anything."

The feel of her gaze was heavy on my back as I raced from the library into the sunshine.

By the time I arrived back home to my perfectly ordered, perfectly organized house, the sting of the woman's words had dulled.

In the confines of my pink bedroom—still pink despite my mother insisting we repaint white the interior walls of the house each year—I unpacked the library books, one by one, feeling dangerous. Standing up to adults was not something I did. It filled me with power, even though it felt as if I had also defended Mother, as well. It's the last thing I intended. Is this what it felt like to be an adult? Off-kilter and excited at the possibilities, yet still conflicted? I shoved the library bag off the bed.

It clunked on the floor. I dug through the bag and pulled out a small, black-edged frame. It held a stark white needlepoint, stitched neatly with three dark crosses.

The librarian's words came back to me. I am *damned*. Maybe

she had cursed me, not Mother, and certainly not the house. Who knows what that woman was trying to say. She was only trying to scare me into respect.

Instantly, the shadows in my pink-cheery room lengthened, and for all that it was a sunny day, the air in my room turned raw and bitter. Frost crawled across the windows, and the frame slipped from my numb fingers to land on the chenille bedspread and stare up at me, the glass shattered jagged.

It was just a needlepoint.

A high-pitched creak-ping snapped. I whipped my head toward the sound—toward the mirror. It fractured slowly at first, then screeched out to the corners. A cold breath blew down my spine, and I stumbled backward. The shadows stretched toward me, one agonizing centimetre at a time—with long, dark fingers. They whispered my name.

Looooola.

The voice pealed in my head, expanding, expanding, filling it until the sound licked the inside of my skull. It wanted me. It hated me. And suddenly, this house, the curse—whatever it was— I knew it had something to do with what happened to my father. I could feel it wriggling under my skin, waiting for me to admit it aloud. To think it through. A second after that, something touched my throat, a single ragged caress that felt as final as death.

My scream was a train whistle. The doorknob was ice under my hand. I backed out of the room, wailing, and slammed the door behind me before racing down the hall, with the bleak and biting darkness at my heels.

I hid in the bathroom with the shower curtain wrapped around me, every light shining bright, until Mother discovered me and lectured about destroying her décor and the sanctity of the house.

Everything in its place, she'd said. *And now you've destroyed our peace by stepping out of line. Why can't you just obey my rules? Rules ensure order. Rules keep us safe.*

From whom? Rules certainly never saved my father. I told Mother about the librarian after babbling out the story—the mirror, the hand. Her eyes narrowed, but she said nothing.

If I was cursed, the librarian had cursed me with *knowing.* And Mother cursed me with what she had done.

After forcing me to help rehang the shower curtain and tidy the bathroom, Mother marched me down the hall to my bedroom.

The needlepoint was gone.

The shadows were gone.

She eyed me dubiously when I replayed what had happened again and again, then insisted on deep cleaning the room—both of us on our hands and knees, scrubbing the corners, dusting out the cobwebs. We *did* paint the walls stark-white that day. I didn't even argue this time. The day after that, she installed lighting so bright I had to squint against the glare. The curse faded until I remembered nothing at all. After all, everything in its place.

Just like my childhood bedroom, my apartment now was lit like the surface of the sun and the curse returned as brightly. The shadows in the corners hung heavy and dark, as they had the day the needlepoint fell out of my library bag. My heart hammered like I'd just run a mile, as though someone had chased me. I seized the needlepoint, the wooden box, and packing paper—all of it—and sprinted to my bathroom.

The sound when that frame landed in the bottom of my bathtub was louder than the silence gripping my apartment, louder than my memories. I doused that cursed thing with paint thinner and struck a match, tossed it into the tub. It burned until the tub held nothing more than chunks and ash and jagged glass bits and burnt embroidery floss.

My chest loosened. My fingers uncurled.

I turned off the lights as I made my way back through the apartment. With each dimmed light, the shadows grew longer, and still I felt pursued. Pursued by the darkness—by the curse. I forced myself to walk slowly, to move with slow purpose. To ignore the suspicions echoing in my head. The feeling of it running soft over bone. It was only a nightmare. Some strange flashback orchestrated by Mother, made worse by the loneliness of the holidays and the isolation of the snow.

Still, the compulsion to paint the walls stark white, to deep clean my apartment took hold of me strongly.

My mother's voice rang in my head. *Everything in its place.*

My living room was still lit bright, the corners edged in a growing black. The reflection of the Christmas lights from across the street pulsed through my window. There in the middle of the coffee table—the needlepoint. Unburned. Pristine. A small, black-edged frame. A stark white needlepoint, stitched neatly with three dark crosses.

My skin was abruptly entirely too tight.

The mirror on the opposite wall cracked, slowly at first, then screeching out to the corners. My reflection's mouth opened in a scream, and I could hear a curse in the sound,—along with Mother's voice whispering my name.

Looooola.

The smell of the musty books from that long ago library filled the room as Mother's face appeared in the mirror behind mine, behind the lies and the death and the cleanliness and the order.

Behind what she had wrought.

A black hand snaked out of the darkness. I closed my eyes and felt its touch at my throat. The fingers tightened. *Everything in its place.*

Nicole M. Wolverton is the author of the young adult horror/suspense novel *A Misfortune of Lake Monsters* (2024) and the adult psychological thriller *The Trajectory of Dreams* (2013). She is a Pushcart Prize-nominated writer; her short fiction, essays, and creative nonfiction have been published in over forty anthologies, magazines, and podcasts. She served as editor of *Bodies Full of Burning* (2021), an anthology of short fiction that centres horror through the lens of menopause. Wolverton lives in the Philadelphia, PA area, where she earned a Masters of Liberal Arts in Horror and Storytelling from the University of Pennsylvania.

AND WE ALL COME TO THE
END, AROUND, AROUND

BETH GODER

1906

The cabin in Vermont is covered in snow, ice spiderwebbed across windows like winter's first breath, so fragile that Tonya Redpath almost turns back before opening the door. Despite being thirty-two, she has never lived on her own, but the cabin is hers for six months. The owners plan to sell it next summer, when the heavy snow melts, disappearing as if it were never there.

She makes herself tea with the rusty kettle. The wood pile is small. She'll have to go out with the axe later.

The cabin is sparsely furnished, two rickety chairs shoved against a faded green table, a musty bed in the back room, and an oak wardrobe that creaks. Cold creeps in through the stacked log walls.

Before lunch, Tonya goes for a walk. There is something unsettling about the cabin, and she has the desire to be out under the open sky. She thrusts her old coat over her dress, the skirts billowing out. Her button-up boots stick in the snow.

Fallen trees remind her of the terrible earthquake in San Francisco, reported by telegram before she left New York. *We are such tiny bodies on the surface of the world*, she thinks.

All her life, Tonya has dealt with winter's snow, but it has been light city snow, a nuisance, nothing more. The snow of the wilderness has a different heft, like a heart underground beating,

41

like frozen giant's tears.

She does not see the hidden ravine until her feet are slipping, until she is falling, the snow like aching fingers, pulling her down, down, down.

Her leg will not work, and the snow keeps falling. She is cold, so cold, until suddenly she is warmer than she has ever been. Tonya forgets to pray. She forgets everything but the white that stretches on forever.

1907

Tonya's brother finds her body in the summer.

He does not know that she watches him.

Her essence is in the trees, in the earth, in the dark dirt where seeds wait, ready to grow.

She dreams until it is winter again, when she stretches herself to the cabin. She becomes the ice that clings to windows. She becomes the cold that seeps in.

The owners have abandoned it, unable to sell after Tonya's death.

No one lives in the cabin for decades.

1944

It is summer, so Tonya cannot see the man well. She cannot find his eyes, his mouth, only the shape of his body, his broad shoulders, his long legs.

In summer, he fixes up the cabin, taking out rotten logs, throwing away the rusty kettle. No matter what he does, he cannot change the nature of the cabin, the ungodly shadow that falls over it.

It is not his cabin, but that doesn't seem to bother him. No one owns it, anymore.

In winter, Tonya stretches out. She whispers in the night with the song of owls. She sings in the patter of snowfall, through the footprints of hares, and the soft chirps of winter wrens.

The man never hears her.

Tonya spies on his letters, pushing into envelopes, reading his signature in his cramped scrawl, Thomas Herrings. He writes of a terrible war in Europe, and his hopes for the summer, for a garden and a wife. He has saved two hundred dollars from his work at the general store.

Each year, she guards the hidden ravine, making sure no one falls.

1949

Thomas still has no wife in the winter of 1949. He takes his axe to chop wood, going down a new path where the trees are plentiful.

Tonya calls to him through the shudder of trees, the gasp of snow on snow.

He does not see the patch of ice, the slick, glassy sheen hidden under dead leaves. When he falls, she tries to lift him, but he slips through.

The axe digs deep into his arm. He lies in the cold, gasping, shivering, staining the snow a gentle red. If he had been in town, with someone to bandage his wound, he might have lived, but not here. In the wilderness, there is no one but Tonya, who cannot touch him.

When he dies, Tonya catches him.

1953

Tonya and Thomas are the trees, the sky, the dark undersides of mushrooms. They dream in spring, floating in the twitch of hares' legs and the green sweetness of leaves.

In summer, they cradle each other. They cannot speak as they once did, in words, but they speak in the hushed bloom of flowers and the clouds that paint the sky.

In winter, they stretch to the cabin, always the cabin, which pulls them back like a shadow devouring the light, where they wait for the next occupants.

1963

James dies in the woods after only five days in the cabin. He walks down a path that leads deep into the forest. As snow falls, his footprints are erased. The trees look too similar, their austere branches reaching for a darkening sky. He curls against the bone-white trunk of a birch, growing colder.

The ghosts call to him through the rustle of branches and the sharp, gentle fall of snow. They know the way back to the cabin, the twists to take through the darkening woods. But he cannot hear them.

Like Tonya and Thomas, when James dies, he reaches himself into the trees. They take him up, enfolding him in icicles and the gentle touch of winter's dark.

The cabin waits, as it always does, infinitely patient.

1969

Martha is quicker in death, though she lasts several years before she succumbs to the grim stillness of the pond.

Martha lugs her fishing gear through the woods—a rod, her lures, a basket, a small axe to pierce the ice. She fishes every winter, enjoying the solitude and the satisfying gleam of fish scales in her basket.

As she approaches the pond, the ghosts shout, rattling the trees, throwing branches in her path, for they are stronger together, strong enough to take the wind of winter and fling it against her.

Headstrong, Martha marches across the pond. Falling snow obscures the ice's dangerous opaqueness, its twig-thin cracks.

When she falls through, desperate coldness pierces her bones, and she cannot move, cannot even cry out.

She joins the ghosts in the trees, in the sky, in the soft brush of snowflakes.

Martha has ideas about life and death, having been a philosophy major at Dartmouth. She believes time is a circle, that death is only the part before everything begins again. She believes we all come to the end, around, around.

1972

The cabin has a reputation for danger. No one lives in it now, and the ghosts rejoice. They dream in summer and come out in the winter, roaming the lands, quick as foxes.

Tonya thinks perhaps the cabin will not call anyone else to it, that even the cabin's strange pull cannot overcome the knowledge of the deaths that have happened there.

But collective memory is a fickle thing, and the cabin continues to sing its unsaintly song, its wordless, irresistible yearning.

1982

Robert moves in during the summer of 1982. He is a striking man, with his thick beard and predilection for finely tailored coats. He hikes everywhere in summer, finding places to paint.

The ghosts dream, but Tonya's hibernation is disturbed. In fragments come snatches of her life in New York, and she cannot push them out. Thomas, sensing something is wrong, cradles Tonya. He sings her a lullaby with the voices of blue jays. Finally, she sleeps.

In winter, the ghosts wake again, stretching into snow-bogged branches, coming home.

Even though it snows fiercely that winter, Robert continues his hikes. He has an interest in mycology, often harvesting mushrooms to fry in butter. On one hike, hunger blooms in his stomach, the small bit of cheese he packed that morning not enough to satiate him. He searches for mushrooms, as he has done so many times before.

The false morel waits for him, masquerading as its edible counterpart.

The ghosts can sense the poison twisted up in the false morel, a secret death hidden in soft folds. They call out, as they always do, and as always, they are not heard.

The false morel is delicious. Robert begins to search for another, until a terrible pain clenches his stomach shut.

When Robert dies, too weakened to reach the cabin, snow falling around him like tears, Tonya and the others reach out to him, taking him up.

The cabin calls to them all, laughing through dark and ice and the wet stench of things left too long under snow.

Tonya stretches out to the cabin, filled with Robert's paintings. There is the little bed, mustier now, and the creaking wardrobe. Matches sit by the stove.

She calls the others to her, in that way of ghosts, without words.

They all settle in the stove among the wood.

The stove is the best place for a ghost to suggest fire. It has known fire before, as the whale knows the sea. As Martha would say, time goes in a circle, and the cold stove is only trapped in the moment before the fire begins again, around and around.

Tonya stretches and pulls until she has a spark. The spark becomes an ember.

Within the stove, the ghosts stretch, breathing the fire into life with their dead breaths.

The cabin pushes back. Wind rushes through the door.

The ghosts push the fire out of the stove. Together, they are strong.

Tonya stretches over the tiny chairs, and they catch flame.

Next the table, the kitchen rug. The paintings are the last to catch fire. Painted trees curl up from the roots, vast skies shrink.

The cabin rages, it sings, it rattles its rooftiles. It calls to the cold snow. But it is not enough.

As she watches the burning, Tonya stretches deep into the earth and up to the sky, full of joy and sorrow and pain all at once.

It is not until the logs catch fire that Tonya stops stretching. The logs are wet, hard to burn, but the ghosts burrow into them, insulating against the cold.

The cabin becomes a sepulchre of fire, then the wick of a candle burned down.

Tonya is suddenly warm. Warmer than she's ever been.

2025

There is a place you can go in the summer where ghosts lie dreaming. They dream of meadows and sunlight and the gleaming scales of fish. They dream of hares' shadows and sky and the sweet taste of honey. They dream of lives long ago, in fragments that brush against them like dragonfly wings.

Mind your step in winter. The land is unforgiving. The snow is deep. No one has been here for many years.

As the ghosts fade, (and they will fade, as everything does, only waiting for the moment they begin again, around, around), they cannot tell you their stories, only sigh through the branches of trees and the bright, shy voices of winter wrens and the ashes of a cabin that is now only a memory, fading as the wind brushes past.

Beth Goder is an archivist and author. Over forty of her short stories have appeared in venues such as *Escape Pod*, *The Magazine of Fantasy and Science Fiction*, *Analog*, *Clarkesworld*, *Nature*, and *Horton's The Year's Best Science Fiction & Fantasy*, among others. She lives in a sunny state where the winters are mild and it never snows. You can find her online at http://www.bethgoder.com.

The Wanderer and the Wight

KEVIN WEIR

For My Love,

 I hope these times have been treating you well. It's hard to believe it will still be four months until I see you again. I know your schooling is important, and I don't want you to think I would've preferred if you had passed on this excellent opportunity, but I do walk by your father's woodworking shop some mornings on my way to the vineyard and wish you were there.

You'll return with such stories, I am sure. Holmburg's own archeologist daughter. I can only imagine the wonders you will find.

I'm sorry to ramble. You must be wondering why I'm not talking about it. Your parents likely told you of the unseasonable frost and the stranger who saved our town. They likely wrote of how I travelled with him, too. I told the town what I could of our journey but didn't tell them everything. I couldn't. I didn't know what to tell them that they could understand when I hardly understood myself. Perhaps, with the considered speed that comes from writing ink on paper, I'll be able to find the words.

Early on church-day morning, Saddie Quill found her well water frozen. The next day, young John Copperhouser said he found snow in the ox fields. It wasn't long before the entire town could feel the chill on the wind, and by the time the first snowflakes fell, the talks began.

Fortunately for us, the government finished running the power lines to the service station two months ago. Father Ruthbaker shipped in heaters using church funds and folks donated the little firewood they had since many had yet to stock up for winter, still three months away. With a fire roaring and heaters abuzz, near half the town crowded the hall.

Vern the baker spoke the loudest. He shouted that it was a freak wind. He read about how cold air can push under warm air, lifting it into the atmosphere and bringing sudden chill. It would blow past in a few days, he said. He always was reassuring.

Rita the washerwoman said she had been having trouble drying her clothes for the past week, and taken to using the heaters. She said she nearly set her husband's overalls on fire. Let me tell you, it took all of my power not to burst out laughing from the image of Mr. Horace in flaming denim. No one laughed. But when she said it was a punishment from God, I saw a few of our friends nod sagely.

But it was that old farmer, Hector—the one who barely spoke other than to run you and me out of his corn field—who truly brought the fear to our town. He stood slowly, drawing all attention to him like a howl in the night, and told us about the Cold Woman.

Hector moves like a glacier at the best of times, but that day in the town hall he took long breaks in his speech and some moments his eyes drifted up to stare into a dark place none of us could follow. He hasn't changed in the past year, you should know. Despite his age, Hector is still a mean sight with calloused hands from decades working the field, but he seemed softer that day. Even his wrinkles, like cracks in granite, were worn down like someone had taken sandpaper to round the edges. It was fear. Hector was afraid.

But I was enraptured.

He explained that he'd been examining the edge of his land, looking for signs of wolves—they always liked to come down from the mountain in early winter, looking to turn his sheep into food. Though winter was a long ways off, the sudden cold had already confused the birds and the predators weren't likely far after.

As he circled the eastern side of his farm, he spotted a woman walking up the mountain path. Fearing for her safety with hungry wolves about, he opened his mouth to shout. But the words never left his lips.

The hem of her dress drifted like fog, obscuring her feet and curling into hazy snakes before scattering into the wind. Her skin glowed pale ivory, like bones picked clean and dark hair flowed and drifted in the air like seaweed in the waves. Her dress was an extravagant piece fitted for a noble lady of times long past— fHector wasn't a tailor or follower of fashion, but even he could recognize fine work when he saw it.

He covered his mouth to stifle his breathing. The action came before the thought, but some ancient urge within him said that if he brought on this dark spirit's attention, she would steal his breath and leave him cold. So he knelt in the dirt, one hand over his mouth and the other gripping the shotgun he couldn't bring himself to fire and watched as the Cold Woman drifted through the trees toward the mountain. Her face never turned from the peak.

I didn't know what to make of the story but, as you know, Hector is as honest as they come. Whispers filled the room and turned to a panicked roar as horrible recognition appeared on the faces of the older townsfolk.

Rita had seen her out her back window from the corner of her eye. Vern had seen her passing from the post office to the pub. And little Frankie had seen her upon the Callow Hill as he played with his brother. None, however, had seen her face.

It was Father Ruthbaker who spoke last, his attention directed toward the confused youths. I don't know if I ever told you, but I always found Father Ruthbaker's sermons quite dry. He knew the Book well; I simply was bored near tears by every one. However, in that town hall, where the heaters buzzed and the fire crackled, I couldn't turn away.

He told us a story of his grandmother, who told him a story from even longer past. Centuries removed—back before the mines shut down and the town shrunk to a village, when Holmburg thrummed with energy. She told him of a beautiful, yet vain, duchess who lived in the mountains. The legends say she murdered her father, the kind duke of these lands, and then abducted young women from the town, using their blood and flesh to extend her youth.

The townsfolk heroically stormed her manor to return their lost daughters and sisters, and finding them already sacrificed to the duchess's vanity, they burned the manor to the ground. Alas, not before the duchess laid her curse upon those who slew her. A curse that would place a chill as cold as her heart upon the people of Holmburg.

When Father Ruthbaker's grandmother was a child, she too saw the Cold Woman wandering the streets, bringing an unseasonal frost with her. The livestock grew ill. Many crops froze before the harvest, leaving the farmers with less to sell and the town with less to eat. One day a stranger arrived—an angel some would say—and journeyed to the mountains to return the valley's warmth.

"The Whore of Frost walks again," Father Ruthbaker said, clutching his hands around the cross on his chest. "To see her horrid face is to have your soul turned to ice. And only an angel can deliver us from this demon before she turns our home into a frozen wasteland. We must pray for deliverance."

It was hard to pray that night. I had nightmares of a woman with no face descending from the mountains, backed by a wave of icy air. My skin turned blue, then black. The marrow in my bones turned to ice. All the while, I lifted my face to the stars and watched them freeze in the heavens. I woke with no rest.

Early the next morning, the oddest sight met our town. A simple cart tethered to a massive horse sat in the middle of the square. Simple now, but the golden filigree paint flecking off the side spoke of elegance long past. I spotted a carving on the back with a long crack through the centre. It looked to be a family crest—one with twin ivy mantling and three parallel keys. I'd normally think nothing of it, but you told me once of the old Holmburg families and I recognized the design. Though, I can't remember the family it belonged to.

A man in fur-lined leathers and a winter cap with the ear flaps down stood upon the bench, reins in one hand and his other stretched out to welcome the town to his presence. He knew of the Cold Woman and had come to rid us of her terrible visitation.

The town was overjoyed. I think the only other time I've seen them cheer so loud was at the harvest festival when Mrs. Blanche won the largest pumpkin.

"You must be our angel!" Father Ruthbaker proclaimed as he stepped forth wearing his morning robe atop his vestments. "Here to drive out the Whore of Frost!"

The man twitched, then gave a tight smile. When Father Ruthbaker asked his name, he took a long moment then said it was Wanderer. No one believed that was his real name, but if he could truly slay a wight, some may have called him God.

Wanderer had a strange way about him. He was undeniably odd, and yet perfectly plain. Not an angel, or not like any I had read about in the good book. His gentle face hid behind an unkempt beard and shaggy dark hair. A scar running up from his lip cut a pale valley through his moustache. I found my attention taken by his black scarf wrapped up to his chin. It was the only thing he owned that wasn't leather or fur, but instead a fine silk. Undeniably old, fraying at the seams in places where someone, likely him, had roughly stitched it back together. Still, it was an elegant piece among untamed wilderness.

No one batted an eye when he laid out his price. His cart was to be filled with various foods and supplies. He would then head into the mountains and return a week later, at which point the cart was to be filled again. A fair payment, people whispered, as without him our valley would freeze and our food and supplies would be worthless.

As he produced his list of requests, I spied a revolver with a dark oak grip on his belt. A similar rifle rested on a rack at the back of his cart, above a weathered trunk bound with heavy leather straps. I was reminded of the day you left, with your gear laden over in the carriage. You and he both travelled with substantial paraphernalia, but while yours was to discover stories from the past, his was presumably to slay them.

Fruits, vegetables, dried meats; Wanderer's list was simple save for two items—cheese and a single bottle of our signature Holmburg Wine. It was quite a luxury to haul out, and I'd expect him to request them on his return, not his trip up the mountain. A dark thought made me wonder if he never intended to face the wight at all, and instead take our goods and leave us to our frozen fate.

Bringing him a vintage was my job. My mother gave me an old bottle from long before her time. If our vineyard froze, we'd lose the entire crop, she said. But still, someone could buy a house with that bottle! So far, Wanderer had proven he was capable of nothing but bravado.

I hadn't seen the Cold Woman. Not yet. And if Holmburg were to freeze, how could we leave the duty to save it to some stranger? I did something very foolish, yet I don't regret it at all.

When I brought Wanderer his wine, I said I wished to travel with him to see the Cold Woman. He initially refused, said he knew the way to the mountains and he didn't need someone slowing him down. I explained the path may have changed and he needed me.

Do you remember that avalanche from about a month before you left? It covered most of the southern trail and pushed the wildlife westward. My father brought me out there on one of his hunts and showed me another way around to the hunting grounds. I could, I said, show Wanderer the same.

He gave me a curious look when I told him this and let out a sigh that seemed to well up from somewhere deep in the earth. He turned to leave, and I pointed at the crest on his cart and told him that I recognized it. I said that if it was his family, he was from Holmburg. He was saving his home and I simply wanted to do the same.

Wanderer recoiled in surprise and explained his family indeed used to live here, but left long ago, even before the mines closed. He asked how I recognized it, and I told him about you and about how you'd gone off for schooling almost a year ago. Despite myself my voice trembled and perhaps it was that moment that changed his mind. He looked briefly at the mountain peak, then snatched the wine bottle from my hands.

He would take me, but I had to follow his rules.

One: don't touch what was his.

Two: follow his direction, no matter what.

I agreed without thought. I took my father's hunting rifle with a handful of bullets and rode out with Wanderer. His cart rattled with the supplies the town had given him, and people waved and cheered as we passed by. Despite my growing fear, I couldn't stop smiling from the adoration, and I waved back.

Wanderer kept his eyes on the mountain.

The first day was quiet. Wanderer said very little to me other than asking for directions as I steered him toward the new path. He said he'd be back in Holmburg within a week for the rest of his payment, and even with the detour we were likely to keep to that schedule.

The first night we stopped in a clearing surrounded by massive pine trees. The frost on the ground cracked beneath our feet as we set up our tents. Wanderer lit a fire and stared into the flames while we ate carrots and salted pork. Occasionally he rose and returned to the cart, opening the trunk and checking the contents. He never retrieved anything but would shift things around wordlessly, then return to the fire.

Only when the flames went low did I try for after dinner conversation.

I asked what we were hunting. No answer. I asked why he hunted it. Still, no answer. I prepared for a cold, silent night when he finally spoke.

"Do you miss her?" he asked.

He was talking about you. I told him the truth, the same truth I've shared with you in these letters. Of course I miss her. You. I told him how we met when your mother came to buy wine. How I snapped the leg off a chair for an excuse to go to your father's shop to see you. I shared how I proposed on your birthday and nearly dropped my grandmother's ring because I was so nervous.

His gaze grew distant. He tilted his head back to the stars hanging above the arboreal spires and stroked his beard.

"I also love someone," he said.

He met her when he was young. One day while walking through a market he glimpsed a woman with eyes of the most vibrant green. Though, her right eye held a unique quirk. Split right in the middle like a waning moon, her iris turned from green to a dark blue.

He was hers in an instant. But he didn't know what to say, so when she politely smiled and passed him by, he worried it was to be the last time he would ever see her. It wasn't. He found her again. And again. They seemed drawn to each other, meeting in places when they never planned to be there.

They shared their first kiss beneath a sapling of an oak tree down the hill from her home one hot summer day. They had snuck away during a banquet and, from that moment on, it was them against the world. Just him and Eveline.

He jerked his head toward the cart, where the bags sat open

from our meal. "They say Holmburg Wine is made for lovers. Did you ever share it with your love?"

We did. I snuck a bottle out to celebrate your acceptance into university. My mother was furious, of course, but the look on your face when I popped the cork was worth every scolding.

A wolf howled in the distance, breaking Wanderer from his reverie. He laid his rifle across his lap and told me to sleep. Part of me wanted to pry deeper, to hear more about his past but something told me I'd have to wait. As I laid down, I saw him take the silk scarf off his neck and clutch it against his chest.

Of course. It was Eveline's.

I slept amid fleeting visions of frost, and when I awoke with the first rays of sunlight, Wanderer had already packed his supplies and waited at the cart, stroking his oversized horse's mane.

Once again, he said nothing through the second day. The animals dared not to break the silence. Perhaps they too feared the Cold Woman's gaze.

Our breath slipped from our silent lips, visible in the cold wind as we rattled by a partially frozen lake, and my thoughts drifted to Wanderer's story. Something about it stuck in my mind. He spoke of bustling markets and banquets, and his crest should place him among high society. Yet here he was, a ragged vagabond hunting ghosts. What had happened to Eveline, the young woman with the half-blue eye? Perhaps when the sun set, Wanderer's tongue would loosen again.

We set up camp next to a narrow river flowing down from the mountain. We were close enough that I couldn't see the peak anymore past the cliffside. Wanderer filled his canteen from the crystal-clear creek and we once again ate in silence. Birds flitted among the trees and to my delight, Wanderer spoke again.

Eveline's father never liked him, but he passed away in the second summer of their courtship. Her mother had died in childbirth, and there were no siblings so Eveline only had Wanderer to visit her. He explained that he couldn't stay in one place for long, but when he saw her, it was like he had a home. She lived far from the town. It felt like they had their own little world. He smiled when he said they made their vows to each other next to the Timmons River, even though it was only the two of them.

Do you remember that blind near the Timmons River? We'd spend hours there in spring watching petals drift down the water and float out of view. You held my hand and whispered what your friends had done that week. About Sara flirting with the boys at the pub. About Rebecca trying to braid her own hair like she saw in a magazine and getting her fingers knotted up.

When Wanderer spoke of their house, I thought of that blind. A space no one could touch.

I couldn't hold it back any longer; I asked him where Eveline was. His smile faded.

"She was taken from me," he said, and looked at the mountain.

He told me no more of his story that night.

My mind itched throughout the third day. The cartwheels groaned as the mighty horse pulled us through piling snow, but my thoughts stayed with the Timmons River. It flowed right through Holmburg. And though Wanderer said his family left long ago, he didn't seem that much older than you or me. We would've known him if he lived there. But I'd never seen his face before he arrived a few days earlier.

His story, lovely as it was, didn't make sense. I worried he was taking me on a long con and his story of love was a lie to distract me. Yet, Holmburg was surely freezing. Something else must've been going on.

That night, we camped against the cliffside. The air grew steadily colder the further we climbed, but the cliff and tarp we set up kept the winds away. We ate and I wondered if I would get the continuation of Wanderer's story. Fact or fiction, the only way to learn was to hear more. Instead, he pulled his bedroll up to his neck and shut his eyes.

It seemed the tension I felt during the day wasn't in my mind. Perhaps my question from the night before ruffled his feathers and reminded him I was an intruder on this journey. I stared into the pale landscape beyond the campfire light. His trunk sat on the cart with only the horse to stand guard. I always fell asleep first and woke last, so there had been no time to sate my curiosity. What did the trunk contain? His wight-hunting tools, perhaps? Or something darker. Something that proved him a charlatan, as I suspected?

Once I heard soft snoring from his side of camp, I crept to the cart. The horse eyed me, but for all its size, it was a gentle soul. Wanderer's trunk sat just behind the bench, near the still untouched cheese and Holmburg Wine. I unclasped the belts and eased the top open. I don't know what I expected to be inside, but at first glance it was nothing spectacular. Some women's clothing and old knick-knacks. As I looked deeper, my mind only knotted further.

He had old newspapers. Very old. He left them open on stories about madmen who claimed to see spirits. He had roughly bound copies of writings from great thinkers—I may dare to suspect they were originals. He even had foreign currency printed with dates from over a hundred years ago. But there were no tinctures or silver-forged weaponry, nor anything I could imagine was key to exorcism. Not that I could claim to be an expert.

I prepared to seal it again, disappointed, when there, stitched into the fabric inside the lid, I saw a name. Eveline.

You once told me how archeologists looked at society through the things they had left behind. And that's what was here. History, contained in a box.

I felt a tug on my collar and in the next instant, I was on my back in the cold dirt. Wanderer stood over me. His eyes flared in the moonlight, reflecting off the snow like a demon. A sudden power I never knew I had brought me to my feet, and I demanded he tell me how he intended to drive away a wight with nothing but his old revolver. I demanded the truth.

The fire in his eyes died down. He turned from me and climbed onto the cart. He carefully shut the trunk and bound the leather straps tight. Once again, I demanded he speak to me. I thought of the revolver on his belt, and I dreaded the feeling of a bullet suddenly entering my body. Instead, he faced me with sad eyes.

He said nothing. So we slept.

Wanderer woke first in the morning, as usual. I found him packing a large bag. The trunk laid open and empty next to the cart. Charred newspaper scraps sat among the ashes in the fire.

He told me to take the cart and horse back to town, that he shouldn't have brought me and it had been a moment of weakness. I asked about the trunk, and he said he had everything he needed.

You wouldn't believe the anger I felt in that moment. After three days, he wanted me to simply go home. I refused.

You should've seen the fury I brought upon him. It was our town's fate he toyed with. I didn't understand why he wouldn't tell me his plan for slaying the wight, but he'd distract me with stories about Eveline.

He let out another one of those sighs from the earth and tossed his bag back onto the cart.

"We'll be there by nightfall," he said.

So we rode together, still in silence. Wanderer seemed older than the days before, and there was grey in his beard that I must not have noticed earlier. The sun set on this fourth day, and I expected us to stop to camp, but he pushed on. The moon rose high into the cloudless sky, and our breath glowed in the lantern light. I'd never been that far into the mountains before. I was shocked to find a house—or at least the shell of one.

It must've once been a great manor, but centuries had rendered it to foundation and studs with only the cold preserving it. I thought back to Father Ruthbaker's story. The duchess's home, where she took the young women to extend her vile life and beauty many centuries earlier. My breath quickened and my skin grew even colder than the wind. I reached back to grab my rifle, but Wanderer placed his hand over mine.

I began to protest, to say we needed to protect ourselves, but he started to talk.

"Have you ever held onto anger?" he asked. "Have you braced it in your gut until it made you sick? Have you ever cursed the world for cruel fortune?"

He pulled the cart next to a well and set down the reins.

"My father used to heat up a fire poker and press it against my back. He would say it was to burn evil spirits from my body. It didn't matter what I did; his only answer was to burn me. I know the smell of my own flesh turning black because of him. When I would ask my mother for help, she'd slap me and tell me it was my duty to listen to my father and that he would not have to do this if I would just be a better son. I was to carry on our legacy, and that required purification. So I tried to be better, to make them love me, but the burnings continued."

He spoke steadily, without pause and without a glance in my direction. Like he needed anyone to hear this story, and I was simply the lucky audience.

"One day, my father knocked over the coals he was using to heat up the poker. It had been a dry summer, and the house caught in an instant. I ran as he and my mother tried to save their paintings and furniture, anything that was worth anything. They screamed at me to help, but when the centre column collapsed, I didn't hear them anymore."

He stepped over the bench and sorted through the supplies. A whisper flowed on the wind. Something dark and feminine. I wanted to grab my rifle, but Wanderer's story continued, and I worried if I moved, I might never hear the end.

"Her father—Eveline's father—blamed her for her mother's death. She wore long sleeves even in summer to hide the bruises caused by his drunken rage. His favourite thing to do was to press ice against her skin until it burned. Winter was worse. He would leave her outside, chained to the stable, until her face turned blue and she'd beg to be let inside.

"I found her crying near Timmons River. Ice burns and bruises littered her thighs. I wanted to kill him, but she wouldn't let me. She believed there was goodness somewhere deep inside her father, and she could bring it out."

The way he told that story, flat and emotionless, made my stomach curl. Two people, so abused by those who should care for them.

"Eveline once stopped me from doing what I needed to do, and I think about how much unnecessary pain followed. There are days where I wish I could've smashed her father's head across the stones. I wanted him to feel pain. I wanted someone to experience the pain she had endured. I thought that somehow, that would help us sleep. But I couldn't, and then she was gone."

The wind howled again, and I saw her. The Cold Woman. Just for a moment she drifted between the dilapidated windows of the manor. A duchess who took young women. Eveline had been taken. It all became clear. Wanderer wasn't there for payment, he was there for vengeance. Somehow, he had lived far beyond his years, borne through time by anger. I have to say I understood.

I don't know what I would do if someone hurt you, but keeping death at bay seems like a simple task compared to facing that.

I shouted at Wanderer, asking him what we should do. The winds picked up, spreading snow across the manor walls. I expected him to take his gun or some occult tool to slay the wight. But he set his revolver down and picked up the bag he packed earlier that day. He drew out the cheese, a blanket, and at the bottom, the single bottle of Holmburg Wine.

"Anger makes you sick," he said. "And Eveline didn't want me to become something I couldn't come back from. I only thought of how angry *I* was. I thought I could save her from her pain, without realizing how deep that pain went. We were both people who loved those that hurt us."

I lunged for my rifle. He caught my arm and shoved me back with surprising strength. But there was no anger in his face. He simply grabbed the lantern off the hook and settled back on his knee.

"I still remember the morning I heard the news. Eveline and her father, drowned together in their family well. Some said she must've fallen in and he climbed down after her, but I saw the blood in his hair. She had snuck up behind him as he read the evening paper and smashed him over the head with an iron. So small, but she dragged his body to the well. But he wasn't dead. As he fell, he grabbed the scarf she wore to cover the bruises, dragging her down with him."

He jumped down from the cart and looked to the manor. The Cold Woman waited in the ruins, her back to us so we couldn't see her face. My gaze drifted from her ghostly form to the well, then to the stable, then to the large oak tree down the hill.

"She once told me the world was cold, and she always loved how I could make it so warm."

My mind roiled. I tried to ask Wanderer a question, but I wasn't his concern anymore. He approached the woman, the black silk scarf around his neck whipping in the wind. I cursed under my breath and followed. He stepped across the threshold and the woman's head shot up. She turned, her entire body pivoting like a gear, and I knew I was about to see the Cold Woman's face.

But it was just a face. Pale and slender, but like any woman from the town. She smiled at Wanderer as he set down his lantern and held out the wine. Crouched by the door, I could just make out the colour of her eyes. One green, one half-blue. Her voice came low like a winter breeze.

"Hello again."

Wanderer went off with the woman toward the back of the manor while I sat on the cart, my mind lost in a chilly haze. I didn't see him again until the first glow from the sun appeared in the east and he left the empty wine bottle at the front door.

I had so many questions but no words to ask them. He told me to take the cart and horse, and that I could return the food that remained to the townsfolk. He said the cold would be gone soon, though his voice cracked as he spoke and the grey in his beard was unmistakable in the dawn's light.

People celebrated when I returned and asked me what had happened to Wanderer. The truth felt like a lie, and so I kept it simple: the Cold Woman was gone and Wanderer went his own way. They called him a hero. An angel. Father Ruthbaker proclaimed he sent the spirit of the evil and vain "duchess" to Hell.

It's easier to see evil than pain, I suppose.

And so the town moved on and the warm weather soon returned, but I still think of that moment when I sat outside the ruined manor, watching that stranger walk away. His once flawless beard had been flecked with grey. I wondered how many times over how many years he had made that trek up to visit the Cold Woman.

Someday, I will tell our children to watch for the man with the black silk scarf. When the early chill comes, he will return, and I hope they take him up the mountain to her. The wanderer and the wight; whose broken edges fit together so even death could not find the strength to part them.

I wonder where he goes. I wonder if he knows how long until the cold calls again. But I don't wonder if those few hours are worth the years he wanders. They must be.

I will wait these months until I see you again. Because I know some wait much longer.

Kevin Weir is a multidisciplinary writer of fantasy, science fiction, and just enough horror to keep things interesting. Never content to stick to one lane, he's swerved across the fictional landscape with his novels *Endless Hunger*, *All Gods Fall*, *Ink for Blood*, *Rogue*, and many short stories. After spending the year creating comedy with Full Circle Theatre in Calgary, he's thrilled to bring his take on Gothic chills to readers. When not lost in the world of his creation, Kevin Weir keeps warm by playing overly intricate board games, convincing friends to play TTRPGS, and making crafts. Visit him online at KevinWeirBooks.com.

FREOSAN

KONN LAVERY

I can never be warm, not with this everlasting hunger. There used to be heat inside, which is the same I crave in others. It doesn't matter the abundance I find. It extinguishes faster than I can absorb its embrace. Cold, nothing but cold everywhere.

I recall my appendages being bitten as the frigid blanket of frost covered my skin, turning my blood solid and face numb.

When my body stopped moving, and the final cells in my flesh ceased to move, I became a believer in God, any god, to comfort my dying emotions. Fear and confusion dissolved when the thoughts of losing my wife and son departed. The bleak sting reached its highest point and remained constant in my soul. I asked myself, *am I alive?* I knew the answer to be untrue because I seeped below my open eye sockets, past the brain and bone, and into the snow. No creator would allow something so cruel.

It felt like a dream: the watcher of events. Physical space warped and bended without a solid state as I moved. My vision portrayed colours that differed from the living. I could see the thermal levels of my environment. It told me where the heat was to feed.

The isolation was overwhelming at first but I learned to channel it. What else could I do? Life isn't supposed to continue after the heart's last pump. Yet, here I am, stuck wandering the endless winter up the Canadian Rockies, weaving in and through the bitter wind that others huddle together to resist.

I am the ice that solidifies their fluids, the blizzard covering the once lush forests, the chill that puts the animals to sleep.

For the first year, I had lost my memories, overtaken by a demand to devour heat. At first, I thought spring and summer would release me from the cold. Oh no. That's the paradox: the sun's strength inflicts an unmatched burning in the warmer time.

I was forced to retreat to the mountain's desolate wilderness during the baking seasons to alleviate my endless pain. At the high peaks, subzero remained and no other life lingered at this elevation. It gave me time to reflect on my new existence. I sang to myself to pass the time, trying to recall the niceness of my loved ones. Once fall set in and winter loomed, I returned to the lower slopes, closer to the warmth, and forgot reason.

I was starving, reckless, and rode the breeze with the falling snow. My bite was sharp, causing trees to drop leaves while animals escaped into their burrows, flew south, and swam far, as I converted their habitat into a frosted landscape. Humans, on the other hand, remained.

My first victim was a tourist visiting the town of Banff. I don't know his name, and I wish I had been resilient to the ever-need. The man was middle-aged, a hiker who went too high up the mountain. His hot blood was a beacon, signalling for kilometres around. It was his face, nice and warm. I remained in the air, humming at a high frequency, creating the familiar whistle of the wind: *niiiiice faaaaace*. He heard it, though he never saw me. The heat that projected from his exhales called me in.

I had a moment of rational thinking—this was another human being. At long last, I had someone I could talk to! But I failed to withhold, and my humming morphed into words through the growing cyclone: *nice face . . . nice face . . . such a warm embrace.*

My voice reverberated off the mountainside, and he backed towards the cliff's edge, falling.

I went after him.

His spine met the boulders below with a whipping crack before I could reach him. I wormed into his esophagus and grabbed the escaping heat as it fled his body. The blip was wonderful, kissing my frozen cheeks, returning a memory to me—hazelnut eyes, two sets. My wife, my son.

The heat left, and so did the welcoming gazes of my loved

ones. I slithered out of his remains through the nostrils and the elements once more pricked against my invisible, iced face even while the clouded sky I roamed told me I was not human. I had no face. No flesh. Nothing.

The locals of Banff found the frozen corpse and were shocked by the symmetrical red icicles projecting outward from each orifice like a paused explosion. Its skin wasn't mangled by an animal, rather it was shredded from countless diamonds scraping across the surface.

I was horrified too, but my horror numbed, as one victim after another fed my endless desire.

Not all victims died before my arrival. I became more systematic. The force of my attacks ravaged their skin and pushed out their fluids. Gruesome as it may be, I had to—the memories, of my past returned with each new body I took. My previous life beamed before my eyes, and the heat reminded me of who I was before this.

My son's first word was *dad*. I watched him go to school. His birthdays, year after year. His mother, Elizabeth, myself, and he would head for the cabin in the mountains, the same region where I died and became this hyperborean post-human entity.

Another human slain and I saw Elizabeth with a unique heat inside her eyes. It was fire, but why?

Death after death, I removed souls from this world to nourish my dual hunger: memories and warmth. I had to piece together these scattered recollections. My family, their nice faces, such embraces.

Pockets of remembrance bloomed. We had taken my brother, T-t-tom! Yes. Tom and his wife J-e-e-jenny to the cabin the last year I was alive.

My wife was distant that trip. Tears. I removed myself from her long before. Foolish boredom. I don't think that was my bed. My son, not quite a teenager, cared little about tradition. The family was not warm. Another body would provide answers.

If repetition causes insanity, then that is what I am. Seeping life became my nature. Seasons passed, and time mattered little.

A couple on a winter vacation wandered too far when the cold was prominent at night and I took the warmth from their crystalizing bodies. Their souls gave me the connecting puzzle pieces.

Eight years ago, I was transformed. We went there for Christmas. On the eve of, I went to the outhouse and couldn't get back into the cabin when I returned due to the sudden locked door. Tom and my wife were in the living room sharing a passion that Elizabeth and I lost years ago.

Frozen gusts silenced my shouts and chilled my limbs as I pounded on the window and then I ran.

Hysteria, fear, or maybe I wanted the winter to embrace me. I couldn't live that mirage of a life. I needed to be anywhere but there. I needed to extinguish my hate.

That's when I fell to never get up as a human again.

My brother and wife's actions birthed the wrath of the thing I now am. Dualism of desire, hatred melding with a longing to inflict pain onto those who've wronged me. These emotions merged into the frosted flame I embraced to suppress the hurtful memories that once made me human. I cared little of their disloyal reasoning, for I would expel revenge.

If my former family continued their Christmas ritual of going to the cabin, I didn't need a standard calendar to know when they would arrive. The darkest day is always in December when my power is most prominent. I swirled through the air, raising a snowstorm, watching and waiting. I plummeted into the snow, weaving through the dunes. Eight years gave me the patience to wait and hunt with precision.

The first day, Elizabeth and Jenny used the outhouse under the sun. Elizabeth's narrow jaw was as I recalled—such a nice face I once embraced. The cinnamon irises were not there. It wasn't my heat vision removing the colour, it was the sparkle from our love that extinguished them long ago. Regardless, seeing her didn't bring me warmth. She would pay for her actions.

Daylight was not an opportune time because a death so soon would end their trip. I had to wait for the moon to be full.

That evening, Tom went to use the outhouse with my son Charlie. Almost a decade had changed the boy into a young man. I still knew his unsatisfied drooping frown at performing a task he despised, whether it be chores or acting as an outhouse watcher. The flashlight they used cast little thermal energy compared to their flesh. Tom would suffer.

They must have heard my eager tune as a soft whisper through the wind. *Nice face* ... turning into a sharp howl as sheets of snow flew under the stars. . . . *such a warm embrace for ice face.*

Tom tried to guide Charlie back to the cabin, but due to one strike from my biting air the cheap bulb cracked inside Tom's flashlight, leaving them in darkness. Nevertheless, they tried to follow their footprints back to the cabin, but I dove deep into the snow and wiped them away with one swoop.

"Bill?" Tom called out.

The word made me stop and look back at the man. Charlie stood behind him. Both squinted into my blizzard, white speckles covering their brows.

That name, I knew it. It was something profound inside my psyche that wanted to rip free but I couldn't resist the frozen flame's command and sprung into the air, sending up a cyclone of wind.

Waaaaarm.

The air vacuum lifted the snow and ice off the ground, creating my newfound physical form. I took my first step forward, causing the loose snow to shake from my body. The sharp icicles forming my fingers extended out to them. To Tom and Charlie.

Tom looked back at the void inside my eye sockets. His own widened at the darkness of my mouth, encaged by ice shards. I raised my crystal digits higher with a creaking arm, causing Tom to step back. He wasn't watching his step and slipped on a hill with my son following without a second's hesitation.

I returned to the snow, swimming after the fools. A low rumbling rage bellowed from my core, rippling towards Tom who attempted to stand. He slid on the frozen ground as I reached him. My form sprung high, casting speckles of snow over his raised palm pleading for mercy. The terrified animal could not move. My humanoid form became the wind, funnelling into his open mouth, nose, and ears and slipping under the eye sockets. The former icicle fingers and teeth fell, penetrating the ground around the seizing body.

Vengeance isn't cold. Oh no. I flourished with the heat inside his body, worming through the veins and leeching the delicious hot essence of life. My power sucked out each molecule from head to toe until I left him a frigid carcass.

A flood of the past—my brother, one year apart, had been by my side since childhood. The best man at my wedding, aided in my liquor recovery, there was more . . . slipping.

Our yearly tradition included him and his wife, Jenny. Why the betrayal?

Those sheets weren't mine. Why?

I dug through my human memories. They fell out of my reach with his passing breath, the answer eluding me.

I needed to know.

Winter's cyclone spun around my brother's corpse as I exited through the blood-mixed icicles projecting out of his ears and reformed into the monster I had become. Charlie stood not far, locked in fear. The moonlight cast a soft shadow against my iced face.

"Dad?" Charlie called out. A pang colder than any other struck my chest. The wind stopped and a hot bruising formed where my heart should have been.

Charlie's hazelnut eyes were bright the day he was born, the first time I wrapped him in my arms.

My body washed away with the wind.

His first word was *dad*.

Charlie stared at his uncle's corpse.

I couldn't comprehend this growing emotion. It was . . . it was . . . regret.

I had frozen long before my death, isolating my family from the man they loved.

This knowledge, this anguish petrified my hunger for the season, and I retreated from the cabin to reflect on what I once was: a failed father and husband.

I was missing the complete picture of how my family rotted before I perished. The pockets of what I now know paint an unsettling truth. This conclusion is all I have while resting on the mountain's highest peak.

I wander to no end.

Vengeance did not satisfy my need.

I await the next nice face to feed.

I forget, soaring through the wind and snow, so I can mend.

Konn Lavery is a Canadian author whose award-winning fiction has reached the bestselling charts on Amazon and in his hometown, Edmonton. Don't let his nice face's warm embrace fool you, for Lavery's words freeze the hearts of readers who describe his Dark Fantasy and Horror work as uncanny and immersive. He started writing at a young age while being a homeschooled vegetarian looking at the frosted Albertan winters, letting the snow drift his imagination into the unknown. His short stories, novels, and audiobooks are available at konnlavery.com.

There Was a Tooth in the Coffee

VARIAN ROSS

The small white object at the bottom of my
handmade mug matches the blizzard that hasn't
ended. I cannot bury the bodies.
Requiems should be sung for all this
everlasting storm has taken from me but
wind howls through my parents' bones,
and I cannot tune the piano because Sister
sliced Father's head off with the last piano wire.
After she dropped his head on the mantle, she
turned to poisoning Mother's tea. The resulting laudanum
overdose left her body curled cold by the fire.
Over the weeks Sister has stalked me through this frozen
termite mound of a mansion after hanging herself on the
half rotten remains of Mother's wedding veil, her ghost
invisible yet able to scatter my baby teeth to show how
near she is. I fear the taste upon my lips is not coffee, but
the bitter remains of some poison, a cup that cannot be
handed to another once drunk from. But I have no garden
except for the skeletal remains of roses that surround the
coffin this grand mansion is doomed to become. There is no
omnipotent god to hear my call, or if there is I am being observed
for some cruel amusement. I stopped longing for heaven, I only
fear that from this place, I will only find escape in death. And

even if I take my life by my own hands, who says that is not
exactly what Sister has wanted all along?

Varian Ross is a blind author who lives in the Midwest. When
not hiding from the sun's reflection on lake-effect snow, they
enjoy knitting, baking, and playing guitar. They have been
published by Ghost Orchid Press, Horror Tree, and their poetry
has appeared in the National CFIDS Foundation's newsletter.

A Puppet to His Thoughts

LORINA STEPHENS

3rd July, 1732

We disembarked today at York Factory after five weeks, two days at sea. For the most part the crossing was uneventful, and despite the immediate misery of biting insects upon landing, I am determined to make my position as clerk for the Hudson's Bay Company the first step in my career with them.

The master of York is one Thomas McCliesh, and his second Thomas White—a surfeit of Thomases. I wonder if any of them doubt?—although I only met the latter upon reporting for duty. I was given lodging with three other clerks, all older than me, who seem pleasant chaps albeit reticent, and gone quite native.

The factory itself is much larger than I anticipated, made of stone, and more of a military installation than a factory, complete with gun emplacements which seem insufficient to allow for recoil. Still, it is hard to believe France might venture into this lonely land, and so I suspect the construction of the emplacements was more to satisfy HQ, than any real attempt at military standards.

The outbuildings are primarily of rough-sawn timber, precaution having been taken to ensure good insulation. Already my mates assure me nothing can prepare me for the onslaught of cold come the deep of winter. There are, apparently, but two seasons, and they are marked by cold and snow, and humidity with a plague of biting insects. They have also warned me about the great white bears which roam the pack ice and shores, and have been known to stalk man where none other will.

It is hard to imagine such cold now, what with these swarms of insects bent upon the exsanguination of every living mammal, but I have been told stories of men who have suffocated in the swarms.

Still, I shall endeavour to do my best, build a career with the Company. It is the most for which I can hope given my circumstances.

19th October, 1732

While it was my very best intention to keep a personal daily journal, I have found myself quite exhausted at the end of each day, something I had not expected as a clerk. It would seem there is more to this position with the HBC than I had expected back in London. At all times I do whatever job is required, whether negotiating the trade of furs, hauling bales, or taking inventory. I am still learning the native languages. Food here runs primarily to what we hunt and fish. We maintain a garden, planting a variety of root vegetables, cabbages, mustard, and other such greens, but the latter are now done what with temperatures hovering around freezing.

I am glad for the drop in temperature, as the torment of insects has disappeared. My face and hands sometimes were so swollen with bites I could barely see, and although I tried not to scratch, in my sleep I would flay my skin.

I do find myself in want of society, the men here not given much to discourse, being occupied by work and exhaustion. But for the sounds of the factory's activities, there is a silence here so profound it leaves my ears ringing. Even when the wind picks up on the bay and drives rain and surf, I feel as though I am at the end of the world, that we each of us wander in our own spheres, bumping into each other in our orbits.

25th December, 1732

There is a celebration for Christmas in the mess, a surfeit of roasted meat, fowl, and roots, and the men are deep in their cups, enjoying their country wives and given to sport. I absented myself as soon as I might for the preference of my own company and my own thoughts, although I wonder if I am not becoming too acquainted with solitude. It does seem inevitable that I should choose isolation given my lack of common experience with these rough men.

The cold here is beyond anything in my experience. There is ice so thick on our bedroom walls we take precaution to sleep in our overcoats not only for warmth, but to prevent our arms from freezing to the wall should we stray from our solitary huddle in our bunks. I feel as though I am under threat of entombment by ice, that the winter of my wall seeks to claim me body and soul. There is no escaping the cold of this place.

15th January, 1733

There is aught to see here but ice and snow, a world of white. This endless expanse of white is what death must look like. When the gales kick up, a man may get lost from one building to the next, a handsbreadth from a door, and so we run lifelines, like a ship's, from building to building.

I am sure this land means to kill us all.

Finding wood for fuel is difficult, there being mostly scrub, quickly consumed. We burn a quantity of peat, which is poor substitute, but needs must. I almost feel it might be better to surrender to the cold and isolation, rather than rail against it as my comrades seem to do with drunkenness and diversion. We, all of us, stink.

For myself, I retreat early after we mess, burrowing fully clothed under blankets and furs, and by the light of my one glim, turn my face to the ice of my wall and watch patterns flow and transform before my wandering imagination. Yesterday I thought I saw a face, like melted wax, and now I cannot stop thinking about it.

28th January, 1733

The face in the ice by my bunk grows nightly. First it was but the barest outline of a cheek and mouth, what I thought was a bit of fancy on my part. Then a nose and one eye turned out from the three inches of white, which was astonishing, but still something I could attribute to my unfamiliarity with this world in which I find myself, and my own increasing sense of isolation.

But now the face is fully realized, what looks to me like a young lad, his eyes closed as though frozen in slumber. I find myself drawn to it, to him, in the hours before my light sputters out and my bunkmates tumble in, marooned in a state of drunkenness quite beyond my ken.

I turn away from him, pulling the blankets over my head, to no avail. Still he calls to me.

5th February, 1733

My days are lost, sliding through inactivity and twilight, every moment an exhaustion to try to stay warm, to find some light. I would take the endless rain of February in England in exchange for the implacable menace of this land.

My only comfort is to retire to my bunk and turn my face to the wall where he awaits me, the youth—perhaps some fey spirit?—locked into the ice. I touch the fine, glassine plains of his cheeks, his eyes, his lips. Such a young face. Seemingly lost. I could weep for the beauty there, for the longing I see captured in ice, and I wonder: how? How did this face come to nestle by my pillow? Surely, I imagine this, the way we all can find patterns and shapes in the grain of wood, the formation of clouds, the wind-sculpted rocks of a tor. This is but my own loneliness working upon me, I'm sure.

7th February, 1733

I asked the face last night what it was, and for response there was only what seemed an inscrutable smile. And so I whispered my question again, closer this time to those white lips like marble. My breath was moist there, and my lips moist also. There was a moment I was sure that the mouth moved under mine, all shadows and dimness, only to find myself becoming one with that crystalline spirit. A frisson of horror when I realised my lips had adhered. I tore away in a frenzy of fear, the wool of my mittens rough and stinking when I pressed them to my mouth. And that face watched it all with the eyes of this wild place, bright, implacable.

But for just that briefest of moments, I am sure there had been life.

8th February, 1733

I do not remember when last I messed with the men, nor

attended to my duties as clerk. There is a heaviness upon my chest I cannot shake, breath too ragged and rough with which to labour. My only comfort is this Galatea of ice by my bed, and I, Pygmalion, lost upon his shore. I will close my journal tonight, and turn again to this Arctic gift, and perhaps, finally, find rest.

It is so peaceful in his cold embrace.

For the past forty years, through the wonder of winter or summer, Lorina Stephens has worked on all sides of the publishing desk: journalism, ghost-writer, author, editor, publisher. She has four novels, two collections of short fiction, and three non-fiction books in publication. She co-edited *Tesseracts Twenty-Two: Alchemy and Artifacts* with Susan MacGregor, and is also an editor and reviewer for *OnSpec Magazine*.

Her short fiction has appeared in magazines such as *OnSpec, Pulp Literature, Polar Borealis, Neo-Opsis,* and *Postscripts to Darkness.* She also had short fiction included in the anthologies: *Murder on Her Mind, Volume 1; The Bad Day Book, Deluge, Untold Stories, Strangers Among Us,* and *Sword and Sorceress X.*

She's also an artist, working landscapes primarily in watercolours, although she does venture into abstracts in multi-media.

When the winter winds cease howling, she also gets her hands dirty in the gardens of the 150-year-old historic stone house in the bucolic hills of mid-Western Ontario she and her husband call home.

Too Many Midnights

CHARLOTTE E. ENGLISH

A nimbus of rime traces a bright halo over clouded glass; I press my hand to it, palm-flat, fingers splayed, let the chill seep into my frigid flesh. My face is numb with it, my lips so stiff with cold I could scarce form words, should I dare to try. There's no fire laid in the grate, not today, not ever.

The world beyond the window dazzles my eyes, white as parchment, as bleached bone. A lawn lies sleeping, somewhere under the snow, and a sweeping driveway, but nothing breaks the glittering sea of white save a row of elms, black and bare.

Nurse's quick step shatters the silence; she's already scolding as she enters, her stout figure swathed in starched whites, crisp and rustling, "Come away from the window, Evangeline, you'll catch your death." She goes to the twins, my small sisters turning dolls in listless fingers. I linger at the window, despite the sense of her words, the truth of them. The cold has never hurt me, yet, never laid me, sick and shaking, in white sheets, nor hastened me on my way to my grave. I do not think it is like to.

Nurse bustles out again, driving Bella and Dora before her like livestock, two placid little creatures in silk dresses with ringlets in their hair. Silence descends anew, thick and velvet; then, in the distance, the bells of St. Mary's toll the hour. Eight slow chimes. Nine.

A brisk rapping sounds at the great front door, sharp, staccato.

79

I blink, press my face to the frozen glass, but I cannot see who has ventured to Bellfield House in the dark of the morning. I see only a chill, blank sea of white, unmarred; nothing has disturbed it, there are no marks, yet, of passage. Perhaps my sluggish mind dreamed the knock at the door.

I leave the window at last, and as I cross the nursery in Bella and Dora's wake, I hear the low murmur of voices echoing from below.

"Your cuff is soiled," hisses Nurse, lifting my arm high; the lace at my wrist is smeared like blood on snow, white streaked with red.

"My scissors slipped," I say with practiced ease, "when I was stitching—"

She is not listening. I am already being hustled back to my chamber, stripped of my lace and silk, wrapped and presented in fresh florals tied with ribbons. Father awaits, downstairs in the drawing-room. My sisters are already there, displayed like matching ornaments before the marble mantelpiece; within minutes I am among them, set into my place between Dora and Bella. We wait in silence. Father does not speak, only watches us—watches *me*—with perfect composure. Only once does his cool gaze move to the lace at my wrists, and then away. There is no blood there, now, no betraying crimson smudge. I am immaculate.

Nurse bustles away, her duty performed. We are a credit to her, we three, and she leaves with her head high.

"Girls," says Father. I hear someone else's footsteps approaching, a soft, slow stride across the cold tiles of the hallway. The door swings open; "In here, miss," comes John's voice, the first footman, and he is thanked in low, cultured tones even as Father says, "You are to have a governess. You shall oblige me by obeying her directions in every particular."

She enters, this governess, this stranger. A young woman, as fair as Dora and Bella and I; had she curls in her hair and a silk gown, she might ornament the drawing-room herself. She wears drab grey, her hair arranged as though to subdue its beauty. She is all softness, warmth, her manner, her smile, of the utmost gentleness. I think of Mother, indisposed, laid down upon her solitary bed upstairs, and feel a stab of hatred for this creature.

"This is Miss Deverill," Father informs us. "She is to instruct you in music, drawing, and deportment." He speaks chiefly to me; the twins are too young, yet, for accomplishments, for society. Bella leans towards me, almost imperceptibly. I take her hand, and Dora's. They wobble as they curtsey, but my obeisance is perfect.

"It is a great pleasure to meet you all," declares Miss Deverill warmly. "I am sure we shall get along charmingly together." She radiates delight, her entire person suffused with warmth—love, even—for we three half-motherless girls. I watch her, watch the way she regards Father.

He has not moved, barely even blinked, since Miss Deverill entered. He is a study in opposites, whitest skin, blackest beard and hair; a statue, carved in dramatic planes, swathed in a dark suit. He regards the new governess with keen attention, impassive, unreadable.

She smiles upon all his imposing grandeur, untouched by it. She is either a simpleton or a fraud, I decide, as false as the smile I produce for her when she turns to me.

"Miss Simmons," she says, and for an odd, suspended moment I don't recognise myself in the name. "I shall be delighted to take care of you."

She's focused on me, now, her back to Father, and she seems to harden, solidify; she assesses me, brisk, cool, and I feel she has read something in me, on me, but I cannot see what.

Then she turns back to Father and she's softness again, quietness, meek and biddable. It's a camouflage, like the twins', like my own. Underneath, she's a wolf. She's like him.

It takes a long time to stop shivering. I've drawn the curtains around my bed, I am swathed in a thick nightgown, I lie curled beneath blankets of heavy wool; even so. The cold has seeped to the core of my bones; when the midnight chimes toll at last, the tremors have barely ceased.

Frigid air blasts my shrinking flesh as I throw back the blankets. I'm shivering again in an instant. By the time St. Mary's tolls the twelfth stroke, I have donned dressing-gown, stuffed my feet into slippers, hurried to the door. I can open it, step through, without making a sound, and there on the threshold I wait.

He is silent, too, when he comes, silent and dark. Shadows

shroud the passage beyond my chamber, the crimson carpet all but black; there's no light to herald his approach, but I know he is there. There's a change in the air. My skin prickles with it, heart races, eyes strain against the night for some sign, some warning—

A soft sound, a *click*. Mother's chamber is next to mine; the latch scrapes when it's opened, closed. He's gone in.

I close my own door, swiftly, silently, and lock it. Tomorrow, perhaps, he will pass Mother's door and enter mine, but for tonight I am spared.

I close the curtains around my bed, tight against the world, and cocoon myself in wool.

It takes me a long time to stop shivering.

The stitches of Dora's sampler wander drunkenly over white linen. I take it from her, set a line of long running stitch to guide the slowly emerging words.

Miss Deverill watches me, though she tries to seem intent upon her work. She has set me a French exercise to complete, to test my ability; while she marks it, I assist Dora and Bella. Neither has said a word, yet, this morning. Dora's sampler speaks for her, works words in large, red letters.

I WILL STRIVE TO LEARN AND BE OBEDENT EVER

I unpick the last seven letters, stitch the missing *i* into place. Obedient. Bella sits on my other side, mute and diligent. There are no words on her sampler, no letters; she is stitching a house into the linen in black and grey.

Miss Deverill has given up asking questions of them. "Your grammar is very good," she tells me. I wait for criticism, for condemnation—my script is poor, or I have blotted the ink, or my vocabulary would disgrace an infant—but none comes. She looks instead at my face, and I cannot read hers.

"Are you tired?" she says, and I am too surprised by the question to answer it. "I thought I heard you come out of your room in the night," she continues. "It was very late. I hope you were able to sleep?"

I don't know how to reply. She is on the floor above mine, and Mother's, her room near to the nursery, and the twins. How she could have heard my footsteps, the opening and closing of my door, even if I had made a deal of noise—but I didn't, I know I didn't.

I don't know why she is asking. I expect to be scolded—"You will catch your death, getting out of bed in the night"—or perhaps I will be pushed, questions fired at me—"What were you doing? Where did you go?" But she says none of this, only waits for me to answer her.

She has asked only if I slept. "Yes," I say. "Thank you."

She studies my face, looking for a lie, but it is true enough: past midnight, with my door locked tight, I have no difficulty sleeping.

"Good," she says at last, and I wait, again, for a fresh barrage of questions. But she only hands me a book, a little clothbound thing. A story-book, in French.

It takes some time for me to focus on the small print, to make any sense of the words. I am too aware of her, the alien presence in our space. I watch her face, her movements, but I find nothing in them to disturb me, nothing to justify my wariness of her. She has stopped smiling so much, when Father isn't here. I think her a wolf, still, but she is a wolf at rest.

I read effortfully. *Cendrillon ou la petite pantoufle de verre.*

Luncheon is served to us in the nursery. Cold chicken and ham, thick slices of bread, and a tray of small cakes. Bella takes two cakes at a time, passing one to Dora; soon they have finished most of them.

I pick at a sandwich, crumbling bread in my fingers. It is as I have at last filled my mouth with ham that I hear a soft, slippered tread approaching. And—Mother comes in.

"Evangeline," she says, upon seeing me. "My girls,"—this to Dora and Bella. There is something like relief in her tone, as though she had thought to find us gone.

I take the hand she offers to me, hold it carefully. Her skin is paper-thin, cold, the bones of her hand too delicate; bird-like. She's thinner than ever, translucent-white, her hair a faded gold halo.

She smiles vaguely upon Miss Deverill. "You have the charge of my treasures," she says, and the vagueness vanishes; her stare is too-intense, fixed on the governess. Relentless. "It is a charge of the gravest importance."

"I know it, ma'am," answers Miss Deverill, gently, but with a strange grimness to her words.

"I cannot protect them as I would wish," says Mother. She sets a bone-white hand upon Miss Deverill's shoulder, gripping it, hurting her. "Please," she says.

"I am doing all I can," says the governess. She does not ask what it is that she is to preserve us from. A long look passes between the two of them; *she knows*, I realise with a start. She has no need of asking what fear it is that brings the frail figure of Mother out of her bed, climbing the stairs to her children's nursery in search of the new governess.

"If anything should happen to them—" says Mother. I cannot tell if it is a threat, or a cry of despair. She makes no very intimidating sight, frail as a fallen leaf, bloodless, pallid as death, but her faded blue eyes seem to burn.

I wait for Miss Deverill to reassure her. *"Nothing will happen to them,"* she'll say, for what else could she reply, in the face of a mother's fear?

But she doesn't. She looks to me instead, and Mother gives a low cry of denial.

I wonder what it is in my own face that carries the truth so clearly. Am I bloodlessly white, like Mother? Am I too thin, too delicate, brittle. Fading.

Mother clasps me in trembling arms. She is sobbing, shedding cold salt tears over my neck. "Not my Evangeline," she says, over and over. "What *use* am I, if I cannot keep you safe?"

Miss Deverill rises from her seat, gently disengages my mother from me. "Madam," she says, steadying Mama, who trembles in her grip—with cold, with rage, with terror. "You have kept them safe as long as you could. You must trust them to me, now."

Mother's feverish eyes painfully search her face, as though she might read safety there, truth, hope. Perhaps she does, for she permits herself to be led, by slow degrees, to the door. "You are not well," says Miss Deverill. "Do you return to bed. I will see to your girls."

Mother casts a last, longing, bitter look at me, at Bella and Dora. Then she is gone, and Miss Deverill returns to us.

I wonder if she has lied to Mother. If she has, she has done it very well: even I cannot find duplicity in her face, though I search for it. The wolfish power of her is nowhere in evidence, today. I realise, dimly, that she is different, when Father is near.

She regards me in brief silence, and I wonder if she will ask.

Am I safe, in the dark hours of the night? Shall it be my fate, to turn thin and drained and weak, like my mother? I wonder what I will tell her, when she does, but she only says, "Cendrillon, Evangeline."

I return to my reading, though I do not absorb many of the words. I am seeing Mother's face, stark with a nameless fear. I am feeling the silent distress of my little sisters, frozen presences beside me.

I cannot comfort them. Their fears, and mine, are all too real.

Midnight, and I am slow, this time, to rise, slow to don my layers against the cold, and present myself at my door. Perhaps it is mother's bloodless countenance that has done it; I may offer myself, but rarely have I spared her by doing so.

She would never wish it of me. That I know. But what else can I do? Mother is so frail, now, and I am young.

Still, I arrive at my door before the midnight chimes have long died away. Someone is already out there, in the shadowed hall: I hear the faint current of someone's breath, a soft, soft swish of a slipper against carpet.

Not Father, then, not yet. It must be Mother, but I shrink from speaking her name into the spellbound silence. It is a heavy, palpable stillness, there in the darkened hall; I wait with the breathless intensity of a hunted animal.

A whisper reaches my ears, so slight I might almost have imagined it. It's my name. *Evangeline . . .*

Miss Deverill's voice. My heart patters, bile rising in my throat. Was I right, then, is she like *him*? My panicked thoughts spin uselessly—I cannot shield Mother *and* the twins, not from two of them—I want desperately to flee, for all of us to flee, but there is nowhere to run to.

A shape drifts nearer, a deeper, darker shadow, then a glimmer of faint white: Miss Deverill, still dressed in her day gown, her face reflecting some soft glimmer of moonlight. "Return to bed," she says to me, gently, so softly I can barely make out the words.

"But," I protest. "Mother. And the girls—"

"They will be well," she whispers. "I will see to them."

I have stopped listening. Another presence lurks there in the dark: my heart begins to gallop with a jolt of fear, and all the hairs rise on my skin. *He* is there, coming nearer.

Miss Deverill says nothing more, merely pushes me, firmly, into my room. The door closes before I can object; I stand on the wrong side of it, heart palpitating, waiting breathlessly for—*something*. A sound, a voice. An altercation.

Silence meets my straining ears, endless silence. I try the handle of my door, but it is locked, she's locked me in. For a wild moment I want to pound on the solid oak, and scream and scream.

I master the impulse. Had Miss Deverill meant me harm, she has had time enough to accomplish it. I fear for Mother, for the twins, but it is not Miss Deverill who threatens them. She is a sentinel against the cold and the night; perhaps she can hold them at bay. For a little while.

A full hour passes before I return to bed, and not a sound has occurred to frighten or reassure me. The house beyond my chamber door lies still as death, and I—I must wait until morning, and the return of the light.

Dora droops over her sampler, shrouded in a heavy silence, thick as wool. She's curled in the window-seat in the schoolroom, hair tumbling in a thicket of gold about her face. The thin morning light turns her skin sallow and wan, the snow's glare casting deep shadows under her eyes.

Bella sits as near to her twin as she can; they're two birds in a nest, huddled together for warmth. I watch Dora, unease clawing at me. Nurse deemed her "out of sorts," forced a tonic down her shrinking throat. It hasn't helped.

Mother has made no appearance yet, nor Father either. Even Miss Deverill is late. The house is hushed, bound in snow and silence; I could almost believe it empty, apart from the three of us, spellbound and shivering in the schoolroom.

"Dora," I say, unable to bear the terrible stillness of her. "You're unwell?"

She only looks at me, a listless, hollow stare, as though she is seeing through me to somewhere else. I rise and go to her, brush back her fall of curls, hardly daring to look for fear of what I might find. But her smooth young throat is white, still, untouched as the snowfall beyond the glass.

Her wrists are concealed behind long sleeves, the cuffs of her neat green dress tightly buttoned. Nurse has dressed her, fastened those buttons with her own hands; surely she would have noticed, if . . . ?

I'm reaching for them, heart pounding in my throat, when Miss Deverill comes in.

"Dora's sick," I say. "Or—" I cannot finish the sentence. What madness she'd see in me, were I to speak the truth. A child's fancies, nightmares, spite. I hear Father's voice echo in the shades of my memory. Foolishness—rampant nonsense—liar.

Liar.

I will not watch the smile fade from Miss Deverill's eyes, see her turn from me in disgust. I avert my gaze, return to Dora; I fumble as I work at her cuff, clumsy with haste and fear. A smooth white wrist, veins marking a tracery of blue.

"She is weak," I tell Miss Deverill. "Because—I fear she—he—" I've wrenched a button from her left cuff in my distress, and it clatters as it falls to the floor, wood on wood.

There. My head spins with horror; for a moment I fear I will faint with it. Something has punctured her fair young skin, torn at it, bruised it. I stare, blinking, as though I could will the truth away.

"'You stopped him," I say, dully. "Last night. You kept him from mother, and from me, and so he—"

Miss Deverill is at my side, lifting Dora's wrist in gentle hands, inspecting the damage. She will blame the scissors, say that Dora had been careless at her sampler. Have I not said the same myself, often enough, when no one could hear the truth?

"I am sorry," she says instead, so softly I barely catch the words. "Nurse sleeps there; I thought that—"

That a nurse, sleeping nearby, would be proof against monsters? I had thought the twins safe in their nursery eyrie, removed from the spaces where monsters roam. I had thought it, because I needed to, and I had been right—until now.

I look at her, the governess, the stranger. There's more than one creature wandering the midnight halls at Bellfield, now, she's one of them. And she's a monster, too, I know it in my bones, see it in the controlled, feral stillness of her. She's a stalking wolf, poised to strike, and for a terrible, suspended moment I know in my bones that we are her prey. A clear, crystalline rage blossoms in her pale eyes as she looks at me, and I think: he has brought her here, she is his.

But she is a statue, fury etched in marble, in bone. When at last she moves, she only fastens Dora's sleeve again, tenderly, hiding the mess of her wrist.

My heart flutters in my throat. I swallow fear and bile, and venture: "It's Father."

She turns those eyes on me again, and they are a frozen lake. "I know," she says.

I was older than Dora is now, the first time. Not by much, a year perhaps, or two. No stout child either; I had been fretful since infancy, had sobbed and trembled through seven years of life, my world confined to the nursery at Bellfield. I had a bird's bones, wrists like brittle twigs; Nurse spoke to me softly, shaded with sorrow, as though, already, I was all but gone.

I saw little of Mother, nothing of Father. He came as a stranger in the night, a demon of the darkest hours; I woke, afterwards, pallid and shivering, my paltry strength drained away drop by drop, convinced I dreamed—or had run mad.

I learned my error, in time. Mother took to her bed, rarely rose from it again; she had not strength even to lift her wan face from the pillow. If he had not turned to me, he would have killed her, soon enough. He still might.

But he has me, now. I am old enough, strong enough, I can bear the toll, if Mother cannot. He has no cause to touch Dora, or Bella—my fists clench at the memory, her infant's face white as chalk, the bewildered misery in her clear child's eyes, and the world turns red with my rage.

He shall not have them.

I prepare carefully. I must appear as usual: there must be nothing to cause him any alarm, no sign to be read in me of my purpose. I wear a grey dress, simple, like Miss Deverill's, though it is silk-sewn. I fill my pockets, careful that they lie flat, concealed. My hands shake, a little, for my heart's thundering, terror turns me sick, but it shall not make me weak.

I go softly downstairs. The day has drifted past in a state of odd suspension: Mother, Father, Miss Deverill all hidden away, silently employed in their separate pursuits. Nurse tends to Dora and her clinging, anxious twin: the door to the nursery stands firmly closed.

The light is fading now, lengthening shadows sliding into the corners, across the floor. I go first to Mother's room, find her silent in sleep, her silvering hair spread limply over her white pillow. She was strong, once, vital and shimmering: the memories fade more with every passing year.

She wakes, looks at me, sleep-fogged. "Evangeline?"

I grip her hand, too tightly: she winces. "Why did you bear it?"

"Bear what, my love?" she says, by rote, and smiles, but it is a thin thing. There are only lies behind it.

"Father," I say, distinctly. My eyes bore into hers, and I know I am frightening: rage has made a monster of me, too, she sees it, feels it, stirs uneasily in her blanketed shroud. I dare her to deny it, I am tense and shaking with the knowledge that she will, as if a thing unspoken cannot be truth. When she does, I will shatter, a thousand jagged shards.

But the lie drains out of her face, her simulacrum of a smile vanishing like mist. I have never seen a person more tired, I think: she is a wraith, barely breathing.

"I had to," she says, a whisper.

"You didn't," I return, fury rising in me, a storm about to break. "You could have—" I stop, brought up short by my own lack of words. "We could have run," I say, but it's a feeble thought, lacking substance. Don't we both know it? Know that we are watched, always, that he is aware of us, each of us, a spider's awareness of the meal struggling feebly at the edges of its web.

"I am his wife," says Mother, simply. "You are his daughter."

She does not need to say that we are property, that we are owned. We are here to succour him, to nourish him, to benefit him in any manner of his choosing. There is no escape.

"He hurt Dora," I say, flatly, like steel.

Mother feels the words like a blow to her face. She flinches as if struck; I watch her mind reeling with shock, with horror. "No," she says at last. "He cannot—have not I been—he cannot!"

"You thought that if you let him, if you bore it silently, then you would be enough," I say, and I am brutal, my words like thorns, like nails hammered into the soft places of her, but I cannot stop. "But you did not protect me. And I haven't protected them. We are not enough, Mother. Nothing ever can be."

I watch the truth dawn on her faded face, the horror of a thousand wrong choices, of helplessness, of hate. I wait for her anger, a fury mirroring mine, but she has none. She is too far gone: for her, it has been too many years, too many midnights, and she has nothing left.

"Lock your door tonight," I tell her, my nails digging into the soft tissue-paper of her skin. "Promise."

She swallows, and nods. "Evangeline—"

I do not wait for her remonstrances, for her fears. I am already out of the door, walking on soft, silent feet up the stairs to the nursery. Night has fallen, and no one has yet lit the lamps; I walk in darkness, unafraid. There are no horrors hiding in the shadows, not yet.

The nursery is dark, too, and silent. The twins are already abed, but not asleep: they shift as I enter, the uneasy stirring of frightened creatures. Prey.

I go to Dora first, touch her hair, let her feel me, catch the familiar scent of me. She calms, Bella too, and I turn from them— and freeze, a cry strangling itself to silence in my throat.

There's someone else here. Someone waiting, preternaturally still, in the corner where the deepest shadows are. My heart races like a trapped animal, and I'm shaking, almost sobbing with shock—

"Evangeline," comes Miss Deverill's voice. "It's all right."

It is not Father. That fact sinks slowly through my turmoil, but it cannot steady me. There is a monster hiding where my sisters sleep. "What are you doing here?" I hiss, drawing myself up; if I have to fight her, I will not shrink from her, she must not see me, too, as prey.

A light flares: she's lit a lamp, turned down very low. Her face appears in the wash of gold, reassuring: she is calm, resolved, though a rage I recognise lurks still beneath. Her eyes meet mine, and some of her calm reaches me, stilling the tremors in my limbs.

"I am here to help," she says, and I believe her.

"Why?" I ask her. I could ask more: who are you, what are you, where did you come from, why are you here.

She answers some of them. "You called me."

I think, suddenly, of one of those midnights, a week ago, perhaps. The snow came in overnight, white drifting out of a black sky, and I sat shivering at my window with my face pressed to the cold glass, weak and bloodied and hurting. My lips had not spoken, but oh, my heart had.

I did not ask how she had heard me.

"I shall keep watch, tonight," I tell her. I do not add that this is the last midnight; that by some means, any means, there shall be no more.

She knows. "So shall I," she answers.

She turns out the lamp, and we wait. The darkness is our ally, now, the silence, too. The hours pass slowly, St. Mary's bells the only sound to mark their waning. Eleven sombre chimes—twelve.

There is no warning. He moves soundlessly, like a spirit, wrought not from blood and bone but from night itself. There is nothing there—and then I see him, a shadow among shadows, bent over Bella with his white fingers reaching.

It is over quickly. He has reigned here so long, he is a king, an emperor, a god: none can challenge him. He sees his governess, his daughter, vassals, slaves: when Miss Deverill's claws—talons—rip through his dead white flesh, splitting him apart like rotten fruit, he makes only a sound of surprise.

He has scarcely registered my presence when he falls. His gaze alights on my set, furious face; I see my name form on his lips, Evangeline? He cannot grasp that I might hurt, that I might kill. I have been a thing all his own, docile, meek; he thinks I will save him.

When he falls, it is by my hand. He lies there, gaunt, shrivelling, crumbling to ash; moonlight glints, cold and pale, upon the engraved silver handles of my stitching scissors, the blades sunk deep into his heart.

Miss Deverill doesn't stay. I had hoped that she might, but when I come downstairs in the morning she's waiting by the door, a carpet-bag set at her feet.

"You're leaving," I say, and run to her. "But I—must you go?"

I am thinking of her presence beside me through the night, our vigil against the dark. I think, also, of the darkness in her; I look at her hands, but there is nothing to see there, now. She's wearing dark gloves against the winter, her fingers slim, graceful. I could almost have imagined the knives they had become, save for Father's face in my memory: split, scored, striped with gore.

"I must," she says, but kindly. I am struck by the thought that there is more for her to do: that there are more men like Father.

Too many midnights.

I say nothing, for there's nothing to say, except thank you: but my face has already said it, she's already smiled, moved away. A blast of cold wind whirls into the hall as she opens the door; then she's gone, taking the winter air with her.

I run to the window. I want to watch as she walks away, sear this last sight of her into my memory. But I see no one. I wait ten minutes, half an hour, but the world outside is still as death, and as cold. I see only an unbroken blanket of snow, thick, noiseless, a perfect, dazzling white.

Ace, autistic, and a passionate history buff, Charlotte E. English grew up in isolated farmhouses in the English countryside, with no heating in winter. She knows all about monsters that lurk in the cold and the dark, and sometimes they make their way into her stories. She now bakes and reads her way through a much cosier life, writing funny, upbeat fantasy novels and short stories, and an occasional dark and wintry tale. Her published works include *The Malykant Mysteries*, *Modern Magick*, and the House of Werth series.

FOOTPRINTS IN THE FOREST

CATLYN LADD

When I find the footprints it feels like fate. Like I knew they would be there.

I kneel, feeling the cold ground through my snow pants, and place my fingers in the frozen impression. The print of the sole crumbles beneath my fingertips and I look at the icy residue on my mitten. Standing, I place my own boot next to the print. It's the same size. I follow the tracks through the eerie silence of the woods. Of course, there are few animal sounds in winter but I often hear geese calling, wind in the branches, the crunch of snow and leaves underfoot. Now there's nothing.

The tracks lead me into a hollow and up the ridge on the other side. With the leaves off the trees, visibility is good, especially with the light from the low sun reflected off the snow. I am not cold, though I feel the air on my face.

In the distance, a dog barks and my heart leaps. I know that bark. Beck has been with me since I was seven, my companion and protector. Sometimes he runs off to track an interesting scent, but he always circles back and finds me.

"Beck!" I call.

Then, when the bark comes again, I call even louder.

I stop, listening. But he does not bark again. I begin to feel afraid. The light has dimmed and I don't want to be out here at night. I tell myself that's the reason for my fear.

93

Following the footprints, I top the rise and look down across a long, wide valley. The trees are thin and I see towering cliffs in the distance, marking the path of the river far below. If I can get to the river, I can follow it out. I know these woods, have spent my life exploring them. But they look different under snow, the landmarks muffled, the trees strange with no leaves. I don't know exactly where I am but I know that going downstream will lead me to a road. Safety.

The tracks lead straight on and I call for my dog again. But all is still. I pull my hood tighter and start down into the valley.

I don't immediately recognize the cabin as a building. It's set back under dark evergreen trees, and their fronds cast deep shadow across the sagging front porch. I see the glint off glass, and a window materializes out of the gloom, the lines reconciling into a square façade, steps, a low eve.

I stop and listen. The cabin doesn't look occupied but a girl alone in the woods can never be too careful. I'm young but not that young. I hear the stories.

Nothing, not even the soft *plop* of falling snow. I could be in a painting it's so still. I wonder if Beck could be up under the porch; it's close enough to the one at home that maybe . . .

I walk closer. It is colder under the evergreens. Darker, too.

I expect the step to creak under my foot but it's solid. Pine needles are piled in brown drifts next to the wall. The door has a window that opens on darkness. The knob turns smoothly.

I hesitate on the threshold. Inside is very dim—I make out an open front room and the entrance to a hall but there the shadows swarm.

"Beck?" I call. My voice feels like an invasion and I hold my breath, hoping nothing answers.

Nothing does. But the house doesn't feel empty.

I tell myself it's my imagination. Too many horror movies at Jenny Wade's house after school. I need shelter and this is it. I step inside.

I wait for my eyes to adjust and see a stone fireplace swim out of the murk. I've never had to start a fire from scratch but I know the mechanics; I'm a girl scout. I make my way across the front room and down the black hall. I want to be absolutely sure this place is empty.

The door at the end is closed and I push it open, eliciting a squeal from rusty hinges. Beneath the dirt-streaked window, a hump of shadow leans against the wall, and I freeze. But nothing moves.

I force myself to step closer. I can't immediately make sense of what I'm seeing: a red coat, puffy like mine, legs stiff, ending in boots. I catch a glimpse of hair, dark, against the front of the jacket. The tip of her nose peeking from beneath the hood is frostbit.

"H . . . hel . . . hello?" I whisper, though I know whoever she is, she is past hearing.

Knowing she is dead makes it easier. I'm careful as I approach; I've seen CSI. But I need to be sure so I can tell the authorities whenever I make it out of here—staying the night is no longer a possibility.

Carefully, I kneel and push the hood back, using only my fingertips. I don't understand what I'm seeing: my face, my curling hair, my black eyes, squinted in death. There are ice crystals in my eyelashes.

Movement in the corner of the room sends me scrambling backward. It's Beck. He barks at me.

I scream, and stumble back. I trip on my shoelace but make it to my feet, running, tearing through the cabin, down the steps and into the forest, blind with panic.

The trees flash by.

It feels brighter.

Eventually I slow to a walk. I can't exactly remember why I was running. I look around for landmarks but don't recognize any.

When I find the footprints, it feels like fate.

Catlyn Ladd grew up in the Ozark Mountains, where she occasionally got lost in the snow. Catlyn worked as a stripper before becoming a professor of philosophy, religion, and women's studies. Her fiction has been published in over a dozen magazines and anthologies including ones by Black Hare Press, Dark Lit Press, and Skywatcher Press. Her nonfiction book, *Strip: The Making of a Feminist*, is published by Changemakers. Her debut novel *As Those Above Fall* is from Winding Road Stories. She lives with her partner and cats in Colorado. She can be found at www.catlynladd.com.

MORFAR'S NOKKEN

BRYAN MILLER

My Morfar Olaf rarely spoke to me, except on the last day of his life.

He probably wouldn't have said much more even if he'd lived longer. Morfar Olaf was a man of few words, and whatever words he did have he sure didn't waste on his family. He was a different kind of grandpa than me, with all my crazy stories your mother tells you not to believe. Before that day I don't know that he'd said more than a dozen sentences to me, even though me and my older brother, Anders, stayed with Morfar and Mormor up here in the north country in their old farmhouse for a few weeks every summer, just like you do now.

Mormor Ulrika looked after Anders and I like we were visiting dignitaries. She cooked us lefse and kolaczki and went out to the field behind the old barn with us to pick blackberries we'd eat with sugar and milk. We'd play Uno and Rummy and sleep on pallets she laid out in the living room. Morfar spent his nights alone at the round kitchen table with the red-checkered tablecloth, smoking Parliaments and watching a little black-and-white TV set. He ate potted meat and stiff little sardines from a can. Anders and I had a code for Morfar—not even a word, just a gesture like a pitcher communicating with his catcher from the mound—a quick pinch of the nostrils like you were trying to hold off all those old man smells.

The worst year of my life, when I was eleven, I went to Morfar and Mormor's house alone, and in the winter. My parents dropped me off so they could spend their anniversary in Minneapolis. It was their first weekend alone since Anders' funeral in June.

Mormor tried extra hard to entertain me. We put up the Christmas decorations early, and she made her lefse, rolled up tight like a cigar with cinnamon and sugar and crushed pecans. But it was a northern Minnesota winter outside their runny old windows. No blackberries to pick, no fields to play in, no lake swimming—not that I ever wanted to go near Lake Mara again after what had happened to Anders there.

On the third day, Mormor came down with a flu. She was too sick to get out of bed. And for the first time in my life, I found myself alone with Morfar.

I was downright startled when he said, "Get your coat on, we're going ice fishing." He'd never asked me to do anything.

Outside, the snow was blowing sideways across the colourless field. I didn't want to go ice fishing and I couldn't imagine what we'd say to each other in that little ice shanty. I'd seen it in the summers, squatting next to the barn on a dead patch of grass where it lived in the off-season. The ice shanty was jerry-rigged out of mismatched planks of dark wood and sheet metal. It looked like an improvised outhouse. I'd seen the old hand-cranked ice augur too, hanging from the wall in the barn like hell's own corkscrew.

I knew if I could talk to Mormor she would help me find a way out of the ice fishing trip, but there was no time. Morfar brought a microwaved bowl of Campbell's chicken soup into her room, and then he was back in the living room, putting on his coat and nodding at me to do the same. We climbed into the freezing-cold cab of his old brown-and-yellow pickup, which got my hopes up for a moment when it threatened not to start, but he cursed at it in Swedish and it sputtered to life while I just sat there with his old khaki rucksack between my feet on the bare metal floorboards.

I knew from the first few turns he made on the slick country roads that we were going to that lake. Lake Mara. The drive took less than ten minutes, even with the roads near unpassable, while a Cool Whip tub of minnows slid around on the bench seat between us.

The shanty looked even more stooped and pathetic out there on the lake ice. A snow drift had gathered along one end of it, knee deep. Morfar snatched the rucksack from between my knees, shoved the Cool Whip tub of minnows into my hands, and clambered out of the truck. He still hadn't said a word since, "We're going ice fishing."

I was nervous to step on the cloudy ice. I couldn't help but think of Anders down there in the lake with the frigid fish. He hadn't fallen through ice. Lake Mara was 75-degree bathwater when he drowned. Of course, he wasn't still down there. I'd seen him lowered into the ground at St. Sebastian's cemetery myself, wearing his black confirmation suit.

I followed the crunch of Morfar Olaf's steel-toed Red Wing boots out into the middle of the lake to the shanty's crooked door. He keyed open the rusty padlock and jerked it free without bothering to put gloves on his bony old hands.

The only other furniture of any kind in the ice shanty was a pair of short, hard-topped stools and a homemade wooden rack for a trio of bamboo fishing poles. The wind was frigid blowing through the door Morfar left open for a moment while he got the two oil lanterns lit. He fired up the wick on the kerosene heater until it glowed red. The only other light inside glowed up green from the hole in the ice where the water caught some of the daylight. Once there was enough light, he used a hammer and chisel to chip away the scar tissue of ice that had grown over the pie-sized hole he'd cut into the lake with his rusty augur.

The smell inside was a combination of noxious fumes from the kerosene heater, the loamy breath of the lake wafting up out of a pumpkin-sized hole in the ice, and the piss-stink of a small portable potty in one corner, which I immediately vowed to myself not to use no matter how badly I needed to.

I sat on my stool while Morfar tied hooks to the lines and skewered minnows on them. He ran the prong through one oilspot eye and out the other. Then we lowered our minnows into the greenish water and sat quietly while the lake sloshed beneath us.

After about an hour of catching nothing, Morfar Olaf dug through the rucksack for a tall metal flask. He started nipping at it. Whatever was in that flask added one more scent to the sour-smelling air.

Speaking of which, do you want a beer? You're old enough. I need a fresh one myself. Have a beer. One beer never hurt anybody. Besides, didn't you ever hear the rule? There's no drinking age out on the water.

"Brothers are tricky business," Morfar said, unprompted. It was startling as a gunshot.

I hadn't heard him utter a word about Anders, not even at the funeral. He'd clapped a hand on my father's shoulder, squeezed it once, then shook his head and looked at the floor. To be fair, this was about as eloquent as anything anyone else had to say about an athletic fifteen-year-old boy drowning in a lake on a sober summer night swim.

"I had a brother, Ove, back in Eskjo. Older'n me. Always I wanted to tag along. One day he says come with me, help me in the field. A sheep needed tending to. Ornery sheep. He had me go in the pen, and that damn sheep chased me. Chased me all over. I was seven, eight? The sheep, he caught me, bumping me with its head. I was crying like a flicka. Ove got it from behind. He had a knife in his hand. Cut the balls right off. The sheep stumbled away bellowing. Ove threw the balls onto the ground for the dog to come and eat up. I said, 'What'd you bring me here for?' and he said, 'Bait.'"

I couldn't believe what I'd heard. Not the sheep story, but any story. It was the most Morfar had ever said to me. His eyes were getting wet and pink and his whole face was sprinkled white with beard stubble. I never saw him with a beard and I never saw him clean-shaven.

I asked what happened to Ove.

"Happened?" he asked, like he didn't understand the question. "Nothing happened. He lived out his life in Sweden. Maybe still is. Wouldn't know."

It never occurred to me that you could have a brother and then not have a brother without something happening. Something like him disappearing on a late-night swim he couldn't be bothered to bring you along to, something that would make your mother and father stop talking to each other for months.

After a few minutes of more familiar quiet, Morfar stood up, turned half away from me, and unzipped his pants. He kicked open the lid of that stinking little potty and started to fill it. The sound and the piss smell filled the space and made me long for the scent of kerosene and lakewater. It also gave me a tingling sensation low in my belly. I'd been holding it in the whole time, hoping we'd leave before either of us had to use the thing.

Morfar kicked the lid shut, sat back on his stool. I pushed the door open a little to get some fresh air under the guise of taking a look at the sky.

"Letting out the heat," Morfar grumbled.

Outside, the snow was falling hard. The sun had just about given up.

"Really coming down out there," I said as casually as I could, the way I'd heard a hundred other Minnesotans say it.

Morfar took another long pull from the flask.

"You want to know what really happened to your brother?"

Morfar wasn't looking down into the hole in the ice anymore, he was looking right at me. Those wet, red eyes bulged over his long, crooked nose.

"Others don't want to know. I'll tell you. Time for someone in the family to be a man."

I didn't know what to say to that.

Morfar sighed. "People know about Nokkens in Sweden. Spirit of the lake. They live down there, deep, where the light doesn't go. In the stories, the Nokken plays music to lure the children from the shore. It sounds like a beautiful woman singing, or some say a fiddle. The Nokken's what lured your brother into the lake. That's what dragged him down to the bottom."

Morfar took another swig. His pale face was blotchy from the cold and the booze, redder still in the light of the kerosene heater.

"A strong boy walking past a lake, going under in fresh water, no tide? Sober as a pastor's wife? Nonsense. I have a feeling, pojke. Was a Nokken he heard."

Morfar let his head droop. Nothing tugged at our hooks. The wind made the walls of the shanty tremble. We sat there a long time, so long I couldn't hold it anymore. I finally had to step past him to use that horrid little potty. He didn't so much as stir. I couldn't tell if he'd passed out or not. While I was standing there with my cold little kuk in my hand, trying to do my business, I glanced down into the open rucksack and saw a pistol. It was the oily black .45 he kept mounted on two nails in the little bedroom where he slept down the hall from Mormor Ulrika.

Oh, hey, look, another beer is open. Guess you'd better drink it then, huh? Yours is looking empty. You'll want a fresh one for this next part.

At some point I realized that Morfar Olaf had fallen asleep. He slumped forward on his stool with his head hung low and his eyes closed. His line still dangled into the water. I kept my line in the water too, mostly because I was afraid of what he'd say if he woke up and saw me doing otherwise. We hadn't gotten a bite all day.

The wind had picked up and caused the whole shanty to shudder. The thread of light I could see underneath the door kept getting dimmer. It seemed unlikely we'd even be able to get back to the truck, much less make the drive back to the house where Mormor was sleeping all alone in her warm sickbed.

Eventually the tension of waiting there in the falling snow and dying light became greater than my fear of rousing Morfar from his slumber. I reached out to jostle his knee. He snapped awake with a phlegmy gasp, his eyes went wide and his right hand dipped into the rucksack. He took two more rattling breaths before he realized where he was, and then that startled expression faded away.

"Morfar, it's snowing real hard outside. Mormor will be worried if we don't get back."

He spat a wad of yellow into the ice hole.

"Worrying is women's business."

He sounded tired. It occurred to me that if the old man keeled over out here, I'd have to spend the night with his body in the ice shanty. Like an upright coffin built for two.

Morfar drained the last of his flask and dropped it into the rucksack. I heard it clatter against the pistol.

"I was thirteen when the Great War started," he said. "Didn't go, of course. Sweden stayed out. Neutrality. When WWII came around"—he pronounced it the Swedish way, V-V-two—"I was almost forty. Couldn't have gone anyway with my svag knee. Again to do nothing. It grinds on a man's soul to do nothing. To see people around them being taken and to just sit by. To be useless. It grinds."

He dragged the back of his hand across his whiskered cheek. Was he crying?

The wind picked up and made a howling sound in the little gap beneath the door.

"Didja hear that?" Morfar said. He sat up straight, and his watery blue eyes shone clear.

I said I thought I just heard the wind. I hoped that was true.

"I heard it," he said.

Morfar stood up, pulled his line out of the water, leaned his pole against the tin wall. He stepped over the ice hole to lay his hand on the door's latch.

"I need you to go outside," he said. "See if something is out there."

I thought I was cold before, but now I was frozen. From the inside.

Morfar flipped the latch and pushed the door open a few inches against the force of the wind, which slurped all the heat from the shanty. Snowflakes spurted through the opening and whirled in the air.

"What?" Morfar said. Now he was looking directly at me, his whole face crinkled with irritation. "Just step out and have a look around."

The wind shoved the shanty door closed, sucked it a little ways open again, slammed it. It squealed against the frozen branches of the trees along the shoreline and turned them into the reeds of a thousand warped instruments.

Morfar scowled at me as he stepped back across the ice hole to rummage around in the rucksack. I expected to see him fish out the flask to drain the dregs, but instead he came out with the gun. He didn't point it at me, just let it dangle by his side. With his free hand he hauled me up by the hood of my coat and gave me a little shove toward the door.

I wanted to tell him my father would never make me step outside in a blizzard. My mother would be furious. Mormor would pull me in close to her and wrap me up in her soft, flabby arms. But there was no higher power to appeal to. It was just me and Morfar.

I pushed the door open slow. Morfar shoved me harder from behind. I put one foot in front of me to keep from falling, and then another.

The little bit of light that leaked through the clouds was refracted through a blur of flakes blowing in circles. The whole world looked like TV static.

Morfar growled "Farther" and gave me another shove. I stumbled a few steps forward and slid to a stop. The wind was blowing so hard there wasn't much snow on top of the ice. When I spun back around, I could barely even see the shanty's crooked silhouette.

Then the moan of the wind changed. The droning swelled into a howl. It seemed to be coming from all around me, like the snow was absorbing sound as well as light.

Those curtains of snow began to part around a shape, some blotch in the twilight. It darkened as it moved toward me, stretched taller. Taller than Morfar for sure. I didn't move. It kept growing. It was coming toward me.

Whatever it was, I could smell it too. There was a stench of low tide, of snapping turtles crawling through the hollowed-out carcass of a dead carp. It smelled like the breath of the lake through that hole in the ice, but after a thousand-year sleep.

What I saw through the fog of the snow looked like a tall woman, naked there on the frozen lake, dripping with muddy water that was freezing in little rivulets on her scaly white skin. Her body was matted with tangles of seaweed and ridged with black mussel shells, and she held a fiddle made out of a femur and a cradle of tiny rib bones.

Before I could muster a scream, a flash of light turned the snow to sparks, and I heard a crack so loud I thought it was the ice splitting beneath me. I fell to my knees, expecting to feel the gush of icewater around my legs. Instead, I bounced off the hard ice while Morfar pushed past me, pulling the trigger of the pistol again and again. I pressed my face between my knees and covered my ears against the screech of the wind and the clapping of the gun.

Then I felt Morfar's gloveless hand snatch my hood and drag me to my feet. He shouted, "Back to the shanty!" and pushed me in what I thought might be the right direction.

A few feet forward and I couldn't be sure. I couldn't even see Morfar's silhouette behind me anymore. If I kept walking, would I be moving closer to the safety of the shanty, or further out into the snowy oblivion? Or, worse, toward that shape I'd seen in the dark?

I looked down at my numb feet and realized if I squinted, I

could make out vague bootprints in the snow, although the wind was wiping them away fast. I pointed my frozen toes in the opposite direction of the boot prints and followed them like an astronaut lost on some distant moon.

Over the sound of the wind, I heard a *bang! Bang! Bang! Bang!*

The slamming shanty door.

I headed toward the noise. Just a few feet closer and I could see the shanty's squat outline. A slender strip of reddish light expanded and contracted as the door blew open and shut. I fell forward towards it, crawled toward the glow and into the kerosene-and-piss-scented cocoon. The heat had all been let out, but just being out of the direct line of the wind felt like warm sunlight spreading across my face.

All at once it occurred to me that the door was still open. If I closed it, Morfar might not be able to find his way back in. But if I left it open, absolutely nothing stood between me and the Nokken with its terrible bone fiddle. Even a flimsy tin door between us was better than nothing but snow.

I yanked the door closed, slammed the latch down. I slumped to the ice in front of the door.

That door bowed in when something slammed into it from the outside. The latch rasped and clacked. I scooted backward toward the far wall. On my way I knocked one of the stools into the hole in the ice. The seat of it caught on the edge of the ice and it hung there, half submerged in the murk. I kept scooting until I felt the burn of the kerosene heater against the back of my neck.

Morfar screamed outside. I couldn't tell if it was wordless shouts or mangled Swedish. The door latch shimmied.

Was he screaming at me through the door? Or screaming at whatever was trying to open the door?

The door went still. The screaming stopped.

That calm lasted for a few minutes. Maybe three, maybe five. Or maybe it was thirty seconds.

Then something collided with the wall of the shanty, like someone trying to knock it over. The wood creaked and the tin bowed a little before it snapped back into place. Then again, *crash!*

Whatever it was hit the shanty from another angle, as if to crack open the wooden shell and scoop out the soft meat inside.

Me.

Bang! The bamboo fishing poles clattered to the ice.

If it was Morfar out there, why wasn't he saying anything? Although could I even hear him over the sound of my own screaming? I had been screaming for so long.

The banging against the outside of the shanty stopped. My throat was blood-raw by then. Over the wind, I could hear it—I'm sure of it—I think I'm sure—the sound of a strained musical note, rising in intensity, the sound of something sharp dragging across the strings of an instrument made from a blunt-ended femur.

The note was eventually lost in the wind, or the wind and the note harmonized together. I can't be certain which. I stayed there on the ice, all that cold rushing up through the hard floor of ice, as far from the door as I could get without touching one of the walls, which might crash in with a blow at any moment.

I sat and waited. For Morfar. For something.

Eventually the tension became unsustainable and my panicked thoughts began to gather themselves. For now, I was secure in the shanty, which was sealed—except, I realized, there was one point of entry into my shabby little fortress. The hole in the ice. If the Nokken came from the lake, what would stop it from slithering up out of the murk, hoisting itself up onto the ice, locked with me inside?

I pushed the second stool down on top of the first one so that their legs crisscrossed over the still water. Then I grabbed one bamboo fishing pole and another, threaded them through the crossed legs of the stools half-jammed into the ice hole. It was a kind of makeshift lock, not so much weaker than the little latch holding the door closed. Although I tried not to think about that.

I pulled my knees up to my chin, wrapped my arms tight around my legs, and watched the hole in the ice. I stared at it all through the night. Eventually the light of the kerosene heater dimmed, and then it began to cool. The lantern lights faded to pale yellow. At some point, one of them flickered out. I had to squint at the hole. A little later, the second lantern sputtered and left me in the dark. Then I just listened for the splashing sound of something trying to push its way up through the hole in the ice.

The police found me there the next morning. Mormor Ulrika awoke to find us missing and called the sheriff. Three deputies kicked in the shanty door far enough to stretch a pair of bolt cutters inside and snip the latch off the hinge. Or so I was told. I was passed out by then, near hypothermia. I didn't really wake up until I was snug in my hospital bed, wrapped in electric blankets, roused by the sound of my mother and father crying.

The police found no sign of Morfar Olaf, or of anyone else. The searchers determined that he must have been lost in the snow. One of the deputies sombrely told my parents that they'd find the body come the spring thaw.

They never did.

Hey there, now, don't get sleepy on me. You drifted off for a minute there. Floating out here on Lake Mara will do it to you. I know, it's a long story and you're not used to beer.

Hey, no, ssshhhh. Don't struggle.

I had to tie your hands. No way around it. Had to be done.

It's just for show, though. Trust your old Grandpa. This boat's not gonna tip over. Hush now.

Come to think of it, holler away. Make all the noise you want. We gotta lure it in.

Thing is, boy, I'm getting old. I don't know how many nights out on the water I've got left in me. I didn't come out here to Lake Mara for years after what happened to me and Morfar. Then I started taking the occasional fishing trip out here in the summers with your father. A little part of me always thought, maybe this will be the time I see it down there. But I never have.

Maybe that means the Nokken never was here. It was just some sad old Swede's delusion, and he passed it on to me like a heart condition.

The older I get, the more I need to know and the less time I have to find out. I have to know, even if it's the last thing I ever learn. The weight of sixty years, not knowing what happened—to Anders, to Morfar, to me—it's too heavy. It's like Morfar told me. Losing people and doing nothing about it, it really does grind.

I said stop your struggling, boy. I won't leave you in the water long. And I won't let go of the rope.

If it comes, I'll go down there to meet it. I'll not hand you over to it, not my own flesh and blood.

I just need some bait.

I've got this rope tied nice and tight. The water's still summer-warm. I just need to lower you in there, just for a minute.

Hold your breath.

Here we go.

Bryan Miller is a Minneapolis-based writer and comedian whose fiction has appeared on *The Drabblecast*, in the *Bombay Literary Magazine*, *Shadowy Natures*, and several other journals and anthologies. He's performed on the *CBS Late Late Show with Craig Ferguson* and has released a pair of standup comedy albums as well as a half-hour special, *Panic Room*. He regularly tours clubs and theatres throughout the United States. When he's back home writing in Minnesota, his thermostat is set to a toasty 73 degrees.

THE END OF A CYCLE.

RENEE CRONLEY

They always tell women like me to never go back,
but I always do.

The black-capped chickadees stopped singing
their cheery song a mile ago,
to watch me stoically from spruces
covered in shrouds of white feathery frost
as I trod up the trail to the cabin
he built with his bare hands.

Our escape, a place of healing
where purples, blues, and yellows
could fade back to flesh tone
yawns before me,
but I am careful not to let those memories
swallow me when I enter.

A cold draft of air slips between
the timber logs,
breathing life into spaces
carved out for the unspoken.

A cloud of mist leaves my mouth

and quickly dissipates
like all other invisible things
that try to make themselves known.

I visit the attic,
where I kept the best parts of him
so we could reunite in scrapbooks,
old concert tickets, and movie stubs.

The wind beckons me outside,
with remnants of his jaunty whistles,
and hits my cheeks with familiar slaps
followed by cool caresses.

I walk past our fire pit
where we made S'mores with Oreos,
to the clearing behind the woodshed.
I don't feel angry anymore,
so I don't see red—
just a soiled history buried
under a clean sheet of snow,
like a blank page
ready for me to rewrite my story.

I feel strong enough to leave again.

The chickadee's eyes follow me home—
too tiny to betray any emotion
and black like the newspaper ink
spelling out his name as a missing person.

Renee Cronley is a writer from Manitoba. She likes taking long walks in the woods and sharing her deepest, darkest secrets with the winter birds. She studied Psychology and English at Brandon University, and Nursing at Assiniboine Community College. Her work appears in *Chestnut Review*, *PRISM international*, *Off Topic*, *Love Letters to Poe*, NewMyths.com, *Weird Little Worlds*, *ParABnormal Magazine*, Black Spot Books, and several other anthologies and literary magazines.

ICE LAMP

EC DORGAN

I sit with a heavy plunk on the sofa, and for a moment, my stomach turns. The floor lamp looms over my head, and the failing window seal behind me blasts ice. I should close the blinds, keep in the heat. It's not yet four, but outside, it's already dark. I turn on the lamp, and the light hurts my teeth.

It's the sixth day of the cold snap. Today's the first day I'm feeling it—probably helps that I've stayed at home. Can't fathom stepping outside—nostrils freezing together, lungs burning from ice. The thought, alone, chills me. On the side of the house, something squeals. It's the gas meter—the colder the air, the louder it sounds. My smartwatch says it's minus forty-eight.

I lean back into the sofa and stifle a shiver. My eyes fix on the wood stove in the corner opposite me. Ten steps to reach it, maybe less. There's kindling and scrunched paper right there by the wood box and beautiful, seasoned birch. Yesterday's embers are probably still hot. I could have a fire going in minutes.

Ten steps to divine, dry heat—if I could only get up.

Ice is forming on the window behind me and under the front door there's creeping frost. I muster the strength to close the blinds, and flop back down to the sofa. My eyes lose focus.

I wake to the sound of yipping—coyotes. My nose is ice, and the cold from the window has moved down my back. The lamp makes a long shadow on the wall.

I shiver and look around for a blanket—there's one folded on the sofa across from me. Three steps, maybe less, to reach it. But even looking makes my skull ache.

Somewhere nearby, I hear scraping. It takes a moment for me to realize it's outside—something brushing against the house. Could be coyotes, they get close in this cold. There's another scrape, more yips—and something else. Can't tell if it's inside my head, or outside of it. Then I have it—the gas meter. It's going so fast, the squeals have merged into a single, shrill scream. My arms are goose-bumps, and when I shiver, the room shifts.

When I open my eyes, the wood stove is watching me.

My teeth are chattering. I'm ten steps to a warm fire, less to a blanket. My watch says it's after 6. I remember the hamburger soup in the fridge, and my stomach roils. Outside, the yipping turns to howls. I lean back, and the shadow of the floor lamp moves.

I have the thought I need water, but it takes another ten minutes, maybe forty, to consider getting up. Six steps to the sink, I can see it from here. Or I could make tea, warm myself over the stove while the water boils.

When I sit up, something hot and acid rises in my throat. I turn my head toward the bathroom—it's a mistake. My gut moves with my eyes and both sides of my temple tighten, like a vise. It reverberates in my spine and molars.

The coyotes howl louder, but there's no more scraping—maybe I imagined it. I wait for the living room to stop moving before I stand.

Somehow, instead of six paces to the kitchen, I'm god knows how many steps to the bathroom. I didn't count, but now I'm here, head in the sink, hair in all directions, cheeks flushed, fighting whatever's coming up my throat.

There's a thermometer to the left of the sink, acetaminophen to the right. I have the feeling either or both could save me but I can't will my hands to reach them. And the thought of that tamper-proof seal . . .

I return to the sofa on hands and knees, not sure if I'm going to faint or vomit.

When I fall back into the sofa, the lamp shadow's different. There's something coming out of its neck, reaching out from the wall like a finger. Funny, there's nothing like it on the actual lamp.

My teeth stop chattering and somewhere in my spine a memory flickers. Should have checked my temperature—for all I know, I'm delirious. Can't even think of going back for the thermometer now, even on hands and knees. The gas meter and howling are too much—I cover my ears.

The world is red and black and grey and thrashing. I'm five and in a different kitchen, cooking stove burning. I'm knee-to-knee with cousins, we're sitting in a circle around Grandpa. He tells us to come closer, to listen to the winter story.

I'm cold and the coyotes are louder—they might be in the house. My teeth won't stop chattering. Grandpa's telling us about the wehtigo. Even the adults have stopped playing cards—they're listening too. I can barely hear the story, my teeth are so loud. Grandma slices bannock to go with hamburger soup and, for a moment, I feel warm. Then my teeth return to chattering and the wehtigo howls, or else it's the gas meter.

I open an eye and the wood stove taunts me—ten steps away. Something's wrong with my vision, everything looks like a moving photograph, or an old film reel. Frost is inching from under the window to the sofa. On the wall, the lamp shadow lengthens with each frame, forming a long, frigid hand.

It occurs to me that I am very, very sick. My head throbs in time with the gas meter and I fix my eyes on the wood stove—it pulses with my head. The vise tightens when I blink. I'm ten steps to kindling, just a few more to acetaminophen. I could crawl . . .

The floor lamp shadow creeps closer.

I have never been this cold.

I curl in my clothes and shudder.

For an eternity, there's only thrashing. I open my eyes once, the photographs moving with the gas meter—lower quality now, grainy, more shadows than colours. There is frost on the sofa, it's a whisper from my toes. My eyes might be open, and the lamp shadow hand is close. My spine thinks, wehtigo.

The coyotes are yipping too fast. I'm deathly thirsty—and steps away from the sink. I'd see if I looked—are my eyes open? The floor lamp looms over me. Its shadow moves and it's cold, cold. I scream or else it's the gas meter. The wehtigo bends over me, and I have a sudden, inappropriate fear for my soup. I clench my teeth and thrash.

I wake thirsty, clothes sweaty, a kink in my neck. The gas meter is silent and somewhere outside there's a chickadee. My mind is clear. I touch my forehead—cool. Smartwatch says minus seventeen, cold snap lifted. I sit up, recall last night's obsession with steps. Haven't been that sick in years. Or that cold. There's a blanket folded on the sofa across from me. I could have reached it if I stretched.

I open the blinds to streaming sun. No frost on the window now, and I probably imagined it on the floor. It could never reach the sofa. I get a glass of water from the sink, then another. The hamburger soup is untouched in the fridge and I warm it on the stove, the smell making my mouth water.

In the sun, the lamp casts a long shadow.

I bring my soup to the sofa, shake my head at the fever dream, and take a famished bite. Somewhere outside, a bird sings. I sit back, and the lamp shadow moves.

EC Dorgan writes dark fiction stories on Treaty 6 territory near Edmonton, Canada. Her gas meter screams all winter, and on cold nights, coyotes brush against her house and frost seeps in through the windows. She has recent stories published in *Augur*, *The Dread Machine*, and forthcoming in *Northern Nights*. She is a member of the Métis Nation of Alberta.

BLOODTASTER

ADRIA LAYCRAFT

Four men confirmed dead, slaughtered while on guard by blades they couldn't see coming in time to even draw their own sword, and now the morning watch hadn't reported back in. Bordan tensed to hide his shiver as the tent opened, admitting the howl of the wind and Holt with it. The man's face, cheeks reddened and blistered above his fur-lined collar, wore a fresh, wide-eyed fear.

Sensing bad news, Bordan surged to his feet, scattering the papers on his table and causing the candle flame to waver. "Double the guard and tighten the perimeter. Do not send any men beyond the line of sight."

Holt nodded, but continued to stand there instead of promptly leaving to do as he was bid. "We must hold this pass, Holt," Bordan said, his voice snapping like cold canvas in the wind. "By the king's orders!"

"Yes, sir!" Holt said, his body straightening into salute stiffness. Then he blurted, as if he couldn't believe it himself, "There is a lady to see you, sir."

Bordan blinked. "A lady?"

Holt looked like a jackrabbit trying to decide between stillness and flight. "Yes, sir, a lady. She's waiting outside. She insists on having a word with you, sir."

After a long hesitation Bordan's mind unlocked and moved on

past his surprise. "Well, let her in out of the storm!"

Holt hurried to obey while Bordan sloshed more wine into his cup. Before he could swallow his drink, or even begin the thought process that would explain a woman here in the mountain pass during a horrible winter storm, she entered on a swirl of snow.

Bordan gulped his mouthful of wine, choking. Holt's expression should have warned him.

She cut a lithe figure, tall as him yet easily half his weight. She was too small to be of the Sholgeer. Even their women warriors were giants, and usually as bundled against the cold as they were. This woman seemed oblivious to the weather. Her pure white hair tumbled to her waist, wisps of it curling to caress bare cheeks and throat . . . which swooped down into a revealing neckline, also naked to the winter wind. She lifted a petite chin, bringing his gaze back up to see her eyes droop close and her nostrils flare, as if revelling in the blast of frigid air she rode in on.

With his own eyes watering and breath short, Bordan pulled out his stool, swung it around, and set it on the other side of his camp table.

"Please, my lady," he said with a haggard voice, gesturing for her to take a seat.

A tiny smile touched her lips, but did not part them. She let drapes of her fur robe slide from pale shoulders to reveal more flawless skin beneath.

Bordan hoped she didn't see the shake of his hands.

Holt edged backwards to leave, but Bordan gave a slight shake of his head. By his understanding of the Sholgeers that they fought, what stood before him now was one of their myths, a being that could read your thoughts by a taste of your blood . . . even after death.

She did not sit on his stool, but instead stepped up to him, so close he could feel her cold breath on his face as she sniffed him and then sighed.

"I can help you find your men." Her voice made his flesh crawl, hair on end, as if winter spoke through her. "Come with me and I'll show you."

He backed away, unable to hold his ground. "You want to go now, in this storm?" he said, scrambling for time to think.

"If they are still alive, is not time of the essence?" She pinned him with her gaze. "Well, to them. It matters little to me."

Bordan wiped a hand over his face. Damned storm seemed to lend strength to the Sholgeers, and stealth to their killing ways. He *did* need help.

"At what cost?" There was always a cost.

"One drop of your blood, no more."

"Not mine," Bordan bargained. He was privy to the king's full plan; if she really could read minds, she would learn everything. "You may taste the men we find, if dead, and tell me what you learn, that is all."

She considered, then drew her fur mantle back up over her shoulders and gave him a little nod. "Fine."

"Holt, you have command," Bordan said as he took up his cloak. "Keep everyone close, within the line of sight, no matter how tight that is. String a rope between you if you must."

Holt's eyes were round like coins. "Yes, sir."

Bordan carefully wrapped his neck in furs and pulled the cloak tight. He glanced at the woman, at the flesh so pale it seemed tinged with blue. He shivered again.

They walked out into the blizzard. Bordan peered at each dark patch in the blinding white, straining to see details, his eyes stinging from the sleet. He glanced back. He could no longer see the camp, or the men posted around it, though they couldn't be but fifty paces away. He had learned, up here, that even when it stopped snowing the wind continued to toss it around like a child in the cook's flour. How were they to defend such a place?

While he slogged through thigh-high drifts, she led him as if the way was cleared for her, and soon crouched to brush away snow and reveal her find.

He stared in dismay at the back of his fifth dead man.

The woman rolled the body over to reveal a frosted face and a fresh sword wound. To his horror, she dipped her fingers into the wound and brought them to her mouth. She watched him as she did it, her lips parting to accept the taste and closing over the digits as she drew them out slowly. Her nails were filed to points, each a tiny dagger. Bordan shuddered and looked away.

"What can you tell me?" he somehow found the courage to shout over the howl of the wind, but she moved on and he had to stagger after her before all sight of her was lost. Could she truly tell him something of value . . . or was she the reason his men were dying? No, he knew a sword wound when he saw one, and this woman did not carry a sword. Bordan thanked all the gods for small favours.

He followed a path of crimson drops that dotted the snow. Soon, they stood over another body and he fell to a knee, overwhelmed with grief and helplessness.

"They pleaded for mercy," she said. "They longed for their loved ones at the very last. But they knew their jobs; hold the pass!" Her voice caressed his ear as if she leaned against him, though she stood six strides away.

What sorcery was this?

He surged to his feet but swooned with light-headedness. His own blood raced through his body, his heart thrashing within his chest while the blood of his men coloured her lips.

Bordan staggered away, falling to his knees once more. Up came his meagre ration of breakfast. He plunged his bare hands into the snow. When he could hold them there no longer for the pain, he pulled them out and put shaking, freezing cold hands to his hot forehead. His stomach heaved again, and he swallowed the bile and fear and emptiness.

When he finally rose, she stood waiting for him. She turned and led him to the last missing soldier, this one closer to the camp than any other. A black-hilted short sword protruded from his back, fresh blood oozing forth as the man exhaled red vapour into the snow and died. Bordan tore his gaze away, scanning the bleak landscape for the weapon's owner. He looked back to find the Bloodtaster kneeling by the body to dip long slender fingers into the fresh wound. Her lips parted in a sigh, and the bright blood stood out in sharp contrast to her pale skin and bluish nails.

"What can you tell me about the Sholgeers?" Bordan did not bother to raise his voice. She heard him, somehow, despite the screeching wind.

Her hair tossed in the wind, and he saw her lick her lips. The wind gusted again, and she rose to turn her face into it. He realized she smelt the air, tasted it, as a wolf or hound would. She looked back at him through lowered eyelashes. "There is little you can do against them. We've struggled for years to stop their advance over the mountains, but they are too big and too stealthy. They understand this land much better than your kind, though not near as well as mine. Shall I taste your blood now?"

He shied back, hand going to his hilt. "No, that was not the deal. Besides, I have learned nothing of value, nor saved my men. Why did you come?"

"I found your men, as promised."

"And you tasted them, as promised."

"It is no fault of mine that the blood does not tell me what you want to hear."

Sadly, she was right. He would send a report. The pass was compromised, of that there was no denying. They must fall back. It would be all he could do to keep the few men he had left alive while they awaited new orders. The Sholgeers had them at a severe disadvantage in this icy landscape.

"What do they want from us?" he said, more in frustration than in any expectation of an answer.

The wind quieted around them, the snow drifting straight down for a change.

"It's not about you."

"Pardon?"

"The Sholgeers want us. They always have."

He studied her, all too aware of the cold numbing his toes and fingers, of the sensation of solid ice packed in his gut, and the fact that she seemed at ease in the terrible cold.

"Why do they want you?" he asked, though he had begun to suspect.

She tilted her head at him and narrowed her eyes. "Do you find me desirable?"

"No," he blurted out. *Yes.*

She laughed, and the sound chilled him worse than the weather ever could. "The Sholgeers find us desirable, at least in the fact that we do not feel the cold the way most do. They would like to breed that into their own bloodlines."

"Why kill us, then? If it's you they want . . ."

"You're in the way." She gave him a ghastly smile, her brilliant white teeth stained with red. "You protect us and do not know it."

Now his report became even more important. The king had a plan, and holding this pass was a key part of it. Now there might be even more reason to stay . . . or, perhaps, more reason to go. Was she friend, or foe? Would what Bordan knew now change the king's plans?

"What happens if we retreat and leave you to them?"

Her gaze snapped to him, as cold as her laugh. "You won't,"

she said, but for the first time he saw uncertainty in her. "Your king commands you to stay here. It was on every man's mind. It was what gave them courage in the face of death."

Bordan gripped his hilt and drew on his own courage. "If you cannot help us, then we will continue to die. Maybe we should let the Sholgeers have you. Maybe they would leave us alone."

"Fool," she spat. Little droplets of blood sprayed the pure snow, and she seemed to grow taller. "They would only become something worse, and take you even in your own valleys and forests. You must not let them have us."

That had a note of pleading to it.

He stepped up to her. "Then help us make the killing stop." His breath clouded the air between them, and she parted her lips, tongue darting in and out, tasting.

"That is beyond me."

Frustrated, he turned and stalked back towards the marginal safety of camp, his uncertainty about her like a stone laid across his shoulders.

The wind shrieked to a new pitch, stealing his breath and buffeting his body. He staggered to one side. At the same moment a massive figure dressed in white furs loomed before him, and sword steel sliced the space his neck had only just vacated.

He dropped and rolled, drawing his sword with one hand and his knife with the other as he came up onto his feet again. He slashed aside the next thrust, aimed at his belly, and threw the knife into the gap.

It connected, sinking into the throat of his enemy above the thick frost bear furs and battered armour painted with whitewash. They were invisible, dressed so. Bordan scrambled backwards to be clear of any final strike, but the giant fell back, useless fingers scrambling as lifeblood spouted. Bordan scanned about for the Bloodtaster.

She stood as if a statue of ice. He looked back at the gurgling goliath now laid out in the snow and wondered if there were any soldiers left alive at camp, wondered how many enemies filled the surrounding landscape, wondered . . .

"Taste him!" he ordered, pointing at the dying hulk. A dark stain grew in the snow. "Tell me his secrets, and we will stay and fight to protect you!"

She only stood staring at the Sholgeer. Did she not hear him over the wind? He went to the corpse and retrieved his knife from the enemy's throat, then closed the staring eyes. "Come," he cried again, waving his blade at her as he stalked back, still buffeted by icy gusts. "Tell me what he knows."

She gave a small shake of her head. "Sholgeer," she said, distaste wrinkling her slight nose.

"I don't care if he's a piece of turd!" he cried. "Taste him. It is not just my men's lives at stake—you said so yourself." He was yelling over the wind, yet, like before, she did not raise her voice for him to hear and understand.

"It will solve nothing."

Fear-born rage burned through him, making him rash. "For you, maybe not. For me, maybe so. Taste!" And he shoved the gory blade towards her.

She stepped lightly to the side, turning and guiding the thrust away and past her. Then, with a little push, he lay in the snow, blinking away snowflakes. *I'm going to die in this pass.*

"You lot taste much nicer than Sholgeers," she said sweetly. "Couldn't we work together?"

He shook his head, gasping as she pinned him down with her foot. "Not without consulting my king first . . . without knowing you better first."

"Ah, yes, I too would like to know more." She leaned over him, her smile terrifying, the metal smell of blood overwhelming.

"Not me," he protested.

Panic surged through him as she pushed a nail into the flesh of his cheek. He lashed out with his knife, slicing in one great arc to knock her arm away. A howl erupted from her, an unearthly sound that echoed from the surrounding peaks.

He closed his eyes in horror, awaiting death, certain he had little or no recourse. When he didn't die, he opened his eyes to find her gone.

He scrambled up, gripping his knife with numb fingers. Had his strike missed? Was he glad for that?

He returned to camp flustered and breathing hard. He touched his cheek, and his fingers came away spotted with red. If she had tasted him, he must change every plan he carried in his head.

Before he reached his tent he began barking orders. "Pack for light trek immediately, survival gear only, leave the tents, leave the kitchen kit, let's go, let's go! We march in ten minutes."

Holt appeared, his mouth open, the question already in his eyes: what of the king's orders? Holt shut his mouth at the sight of him. Chaos grew around them as men shouted against the snapping canvas and howling blizzard.

Soon they were marching, the day like dusk with low black clouds and endless driving snow. True night fell and they staggered on, Bordan's voice the whip to drive them. He stayed at the back of the column, Holt at his side. The storm raged on, making casual speech impossible, and that suited him just fine.

When the tempest rose in pitch, changing into the Bloodtaster's howl, Bordon bared his sword to the darkness behind them.

"What is it, sir?"

"Do you hear her?"

Holt did not reply for a long time. "I hear only the wind. It plays tricks on your mind."

Bordan shook his head. She was angry at him, he knew it. The Sholgeers would follow, just as they had for the previous three countries they had conquered. Was the Bloodtaster honest with him? Or were they in league with the Sholgeer?

He should never have let her get close. He should never have left her alive. She knew the King's plan to come from behind, through a lesser-known pass to the south. Would she tell the Sholgeer?

He should never have left.

He drew Holt to a stop.

"Take them home," Bordan said, weariness thickening his voice. "I must turn back."

"I'll go with you, sir," Holt said immediately. Bordan grabbed both his shoulders and put every ounce of command he could muster into his voice.

"I let her live. Now I must hunt her. Better I go alone. Get the men to safety for me."

Holt stared at him. The mesmerizing line of moving torchlight drew away. Bordan heard the hiss and spit of snowflakes striking Holt's lantern as the man handed it to him. He took it with a nod. "Set camp on the other side of the river and tell the king to pray he can hold it."

Holt's brows locked together as he shook his head. "But why?

You know the king will send us back up there. He will never give up on that pass, and we can't back down before the Sholgeers—"

"She read our dead, Holt. She read me. She knows every detail of the king's plans. I must do the unexpected now. Tell the king that. Tell him to do the unexpected."

Holt's mouth worked. His gaze lingered on Bordan's scratched cheek. "But—she was to help?"

"A ruse." Bordan spit into the storm. "They want their pass back—"

"And you just gave it to them," Holt finished for him.

Bordan stared in cold silence at his best man. When Holt looked away, Bordan relented and said, "I'm going back, aren't I?"

A curt nod, only a hint of suspicion.

"Tell the king what you witnessed. Tell him I say to hold the river crossing as the new border and stay out of the pass. Follow his orders when they arrive, but for now, my orders stand. In the pass we will only die."

"You might die. Sir."

"I might." He turned and walked away from Holt.

Soon he was climbing again, the wind cutting his cheek, leg muscles screaming for rest, but his mind was far away. Not on the war, or the border, not on the weather or the Sholgeers or his king's plans. No. He thought of nothing but a white-haired woman as her fingers trailed warm blood over blue lips.

Adria Laycraft earned honours in Journalism Arts in '92 and has worked with words ever since. She co-edited the *Urban Green Man* anthology in 2013, which was nominated for an Aurora Award, and has two published novels, *Jumpship Hope* and *Jumpship Dissonance*, with the third and final book, *Jumpship Freedom*, coming soon from Tyche Books. When it comes to winter weather, hoarfrost, and freezing spindrifts, Adria is no stranger to life in The North, and this call for submissions was an easy one to answer.

DARK RIVER

BRENT NICHOLS

Pay attention. This story has a moral, and it's important.
I'm not your High School English teacher. You don't
have to read between the lines and make up some
psychological bullshit to get an A. I'll tell you what the moral is,
straight up.

Don't text and drive.

If there's a secondary moral, it's keep your snide judgments to
yourself. You weren't there. It was snowing like God meant to blot
the world out. I couldn't just pull over. Even if I could have found
the shoulder it wouldn't be safe. Visibility was about ten feet. If I
stopped, some yahoo might have rear-ended me.

And the message couldn't wait. I was trying to talk to my son,
and I was screwing it up. I had to fix things before he got pissed
off and blocked me again. I wanted to say, I messed up. Bad. I
want to make amends.

What I actually texted was, *Quit being an idiot and listen for
once.*

So I had no choice. Apologize fast or wait another ten years for
him to give me another chance. I slowed down as much as I
dared, and I tapped the *S*.

And the road curved. Twisted back on itself like a politician. I
looked up, saw nothing but trees, and had time to turn the wheel

about five whole degrees before the first impact. The seatbelt hit my chest like a mule kick and pine branches slapped the windows. The car kept going, knocking over little trees, making a noise like Satan cracking his knuckles. I had my foot jammed down on the brake pedal, but by that time the car was going sideways. All I could hear was splintering wood. Then water splashed across the windshield and I finally got around to being scared.

The worst part of a really good accident is the disorientation. It took me a solid thirty seconds to figure out the car had stopped. It took longer to figure out which way was up. I hung from my seatbelt, hands locked on the steering wheel, with the engine still roaring and my heart doing its best to jump right out of my chest.

My sunglasses were at the far end of the dash, and my briefcase lay flat against the passenger door. I stared at them for a while and finally figured out that the car was tilted sharply sideways. By that time, murky water was seeping in around the edges of the door. I stretched an arm toward the briefcase, couldn't reach it, and then forgot all about the damn thing as the seriousness of my situation finally hit me.

Moron. You've only been driving for fifty years. What made you think you could do it right?

No situation is ever so bad that you can't make it worse with self-flagellation. I squashed the accusing voice and breathed deeply, taking stock.

No one would miss me for a depressingly long time and no one had seen me leave the road. Fat flakes were stacking up on the windshield and the window beside me. They would fill my tire tracks, cover the trees I'd shattered, and obscure my car. I needed to get out, drag myself up the bank, and get onto the road, or I was going to die.

What makes you think you deserve to live?

My foot, I discovered, was still jammed against the brake pedal. In fact, my leg was rigid with strain, doing its best to push the pedal through the floorboards. I shifted the car into park, then forced my leg to relax. I reached for the ignition key, then hesitated. *Best to leave the engine running. Keep the heater going as long as possible.*

It was twilight outside, but the car grew quickly darker as snow accumulated on the windows. I turned on the interior light.

There was a pool of water several inches deep on the passenger side. Worse, I could see a line of water against the windshield. It sloped from the roof, where it covered only a couple inches of glass, to the dash, where it was a foot deep.

The car trembled, and the line of water rose an inch.

If you've never tried it, hanging sideways from a seatbelt is damnably uncomfortable. I reached for the button, but I didn't press it. I didn't fancy sliding down to thump against the passenger door. I especially didn't like the idea of landing in all that cold water.

You survived the crash. It's hypothermia that's going to kill you.

I didn't have the healthiest relationship with my inner voice. Inner Me was, frankly, a bit of a dick. At the moment, though, he spoke sense. *I need to stay dry. And call for help. And get a message to David.* My hand went to my breast pocket, which was empty, of course. *Shit. Where did I drop the phone?*

I spotted it all too soon, beside my briefcase, under almost a foot of water. I swore, braced my feet, and popped my seatbelt. I tried to hang from the steering wheel with one hand, but my fingers slipped and I fell sideways. My right hand hit the passenger door, pain shot through my shoulder, and before I knew it my face was under water.

It was cold, so cold I gave a shriek that cost me most of the air in my lungs. I pushed against the door, didn't move, and spent a bad moment wondering if I was going to drown in a foot of water. It took forever to twist around and get my legs under me. My feet burned with cold as I stood, wiping water out of my eyes. I squatted, fumbled around, and found my phone by touch. Then I braced my legs against the dash and got my feet out of the water.

The water line on the windshield was a good six inches higher. I imagined the current tugging at the car, edging it ever deeper. I was absolutely frantic to know if the phone still worked, but I was terrified of dropping it again. So I checked that my numb fingers still had a good grip, and I pressed both hands against the heater on the dash.

A chunk of floating ice bounced against the windshield. It was a trifling impact, but the car shifted and slid a couple inches deeper. And the engine died.

"Shit!" I stared at my hands, still pressed against the dash.

They're as warm as they're going to get. I brought the phone up near my face, held my breath, and hit the power button.

The screen lit up. Relief crashed through me, lasting for all of half a second. I caught a glimpse of my last text, the words scorching themselves into my brain like an accusation. Then the screen flashed white and died.

I couldn't see the smoke, but I smelled it. The phone slid from my fingers and vanished with a splash.

You let the magic blue smoke out. That's what makes it run. It won't work, now that the smoke escaped. I couldn't remember, now, what it was I'd been trying to fix. Some piece of stereo equipment, with Davie, all of fifteen or sixteen years old, handing me tools and trying to help. He beamed, delighted with his joke.

And I, embarrassed and frustrated, back-handed him across the face.

I'm sorry, Davie. I stared in the direction of the cell phone. *I'm so sorry. And I have to find a way to tell you.*

The interior light went out. The headlights died in the same instant, leaving blurred after-images dancing on my retinas. That, more than anything, spurred me into motion. Some warmth still lingered in the car, after all. It was shelter of a sort. But the darkness made it unbearable. The air tasted thick and stale, the roof and doors pressing as close as a coffin lid. I pushed down my fear, grabbed my door handle and shoved.

It was as if someone drove an enormous nail into my right shoulder. I screamed, and the door clicked shut. I tucked the arm against my stomach, whimpering and swearing with my eyes squeezed shut.

When I opened them, they had adjusted to the darkness and I could see the water outside, a black line past the middle of the windshield. Inside the car the water touched my feet. I stepped down, standing once again on the passenger door. My feet were dead, unfeeling things, but a fresh band of ice seared my knees. My briefcase slid under my foot and I scuffed it aside, getting my footing right.

Letting my useless right arm hang, I braced my left shoulder and the side of my head against the door. Then I popped the latch and pushed with everything I had.

The door rose, and cold air swirled against my face. Fat snowflakes blew in. I raised the door maybe eight, nine inches, and held it there, straining, wondering what the hell to do next. I lifted one leg, thinking to blindly climb upward. My other leg promptly buckled.

The door slammed shut.

Jesus Christ, what's wrong with me? I'm as weak as newborn colt. I stood a moment, shivering, then fumbled at the door above me, finding the window controls by touch. I shoved the buttons back and forth, cursing when nothing happened. I hammered the heel of my hand against the glass, then made a fist and punched it.

The glass didn't break. I felt a distant twinge in my wrist, but no pain at all in my knuckles. *I'm even colder than I realize.*

I panicked. Raw terror hijacked my brain, and I honestly couldn't tell you what happened next until the cold water engulfed me, jolting me and breaking the vicious twisting cycle of my thoughts. I coughed, shook my head, and discovered I was staring at the backs of my hands. They were pale silhouettes against frozen mud. I was clinging to a steep, snowy slope, and I was sliding downward.

I climbed. It was something out of a nightmare, my shoes getting no purchase, my fingers too numb to feel the mud they scrabbled against. I slid as I climbed, and I couldn't have said if my overall progress was up or down. But the frantic exercise warmed me, and terror of the water below kept all thoughts of fatigue at bay.

There was no railing at the top. A curve that steep should have something, if only to give an old man something to cling to in that final, exhausted moment as he pulled himself onto flat ground. The jagged stump of a young pine tree gave me a place to brace my foot, and I crawled at last onto the edge of the road. I wanted to stay on hands and knees, but the cold drove me to my feet.

I shoved my frozen hands into my armpits. My suit jacket was wet, and I wondered if it was doing more harm than good. Still, I kept my hands there as I staggered down the road.

No tire tracks marred the snow. People with any sense were indoors. It might be hours before another car came along. It might be days.

The road made a long pale line curving away into the distance. There was cloud from horizon to horizon, grim and grey and glowing ever so faintly with the last of the evening light. There were no stars.

Except one.

The distant point of light was so faint I thought I was imagining it. With no better option I headed toward it, my feet silent in the ankle-deep snow. I figured I was crossing the road at an angle, though it was impossible to be sure. I shrugged. Getting hit by a car was the least of my worries.

The light brightened. It had to be closer than it looked, obscured by trees. I quickened my pace.

My feet hit a downward slope, and I stumbled. I'd reached the edge of the road. The light was a rectangle now, rather than a point. That meant a window. A building. Shelter, and glorious warmth. I took my hands out of my armpits, extended my good arm to help with my balance, and plodded into the ditch.

What makes you think you'll find shelter? For all you know, it's a power transformer or something.

"Not helpful," I said, then flinched as an invisible twig scraped my cheek. I stretched my arm in front of me, warding off branches my frozen hand could barely feel.

The light vanished periodically as I fought my way through the trees, but it always reappeared. It grew, faster than I'd dared hope, until it looked as big as a billboard. I told myself to look away, to preserve a bit of night vision so I could navigate. But I stared at the light as I stumbled forward, my steps jerky as the cold stiffened my muscles.

I fell, betrayed by feet gone numb. I pitched face-first in the snow, and panic washed over me. I pushed myself frantically to my knees, clumsy fingers swiping snow from my eyes. And I searched for my window, suddenly sure it would be a phantasm, gone forever once I looked away.

I saw nothing but darkness.

"Shit. No. Oh, God, please no."

What makes you think God is listening? For that matter, what are you whining about? Cold? Darkness? Despair? How is this different from your life most days?

I heaved myself to my feet, stretched out a hand, and hit something solid. My skin was too chilled to feel texture, so I slapped with my palm, moving my hand up and down, back and forth. It was a tree, a good thick one, invisible in the dark. I kept a hand on the trunk and circled the thing.

And my window appeared.

I could make out details now. A vertical line divided it into two panes. There were curtains, gauzy things. The light, golden as butter, poured right through them and lit a wide expanse of snow.

"Thank you. Sweet Jesus, thank you." I left the trees and hurried across flat ground. The snow became deeper, and I brought my knees up with every step. It was exhausting, and if the building had been much farther, I don't know if I would have made it.

It was a cabin. An honest-to-God log cabin with a door next to the window. I didn't see the front step until I stumbled over it. I landed on my knees with my shoulder against the door. I knocked, then pounded the door with my fist.

The door opened, and I sagged across the threshold. I saw floorboards, the edge of a rug, and a pair of feet encased in fuzzy slippers. I tried to tell my story, babbling and stuttering as someone grabbed the shoulders of my jacket and dragged me inside. The door closed behind me and I lay there, forehead pressed against the floor, trembling helplessly.

"Sorry." It took some time to get the word out. I could see a fireplace off to my left, flames dancing merrily across thick split logs. I wanted to crawl toward it, but as my despair drained away, some sense of dignity returned. I couldn't feel the floor when I pushed against it with my good hand. My muscles still worked, though, and I shoved myself up into a sitting position.

The cabin was like something out of a frontier storybook. It was tiny, one open room with a couple of padded chairs and a futon sofa with a log frame. The fire was the only source of light, but it seemed like plenty after the darkness outside.

A man stood over me, studying me, his mouth turned up in a sardonic smile. I smiled in recognition. "It's me!" When he didn't reply I said, "I know you from . . ." My voice trailed off. Where did I know him from? What was his name?

The sense of familiarity faded, and I shook my head. "Do I know you?" I heaved a sigh, then began the painful process of rising to my feet. My leg muscles didn't have much left to give. "Sorry. I'm pretty cold. Pretty shook up. I thought I recognized you . . ."

"You look kind of rough." He sounded more amused than concerned, which I took as an encouraging sign. "Better sit down before you fall over."

I took the chair closest to the fire. The warmth didn't seem to touch me. Well, it would soak in soon enough. In the meantime, all that lovely yellow light was comforting.

My host took the chair across from me. He was middle-aged, with craggy, weathered features. He folded blunt, callused fingers across his stomach and examined me from head to toe.

I wished he would be more solicitous. Maybe offer me a hot drink. Still, his casual unconcern was good for my frazzled nerves. *There's clearly nothing to get excited about. Which means I'm going to be okay.*

I shivered and made a half-hearted attempt to wriggle out of my wet jacket. Ice crystals glittered on the sleeves, and I worried about soaking his cushions. But my arms felt clumsy and distant, and I quickly gave up. *I'll sit here until I warm up a bit. A little water won't do any harm.*

The shivering grew worse. It scared me, making me realize how close I'd come to hypothermia. The pain in my shoulder didn't seem so bad, and I managed to stretch both hands toward the fire. "Thanks for letting me in. I think you saved my life."

He inclined his head, not speaking.

"My car went off the road. Landed in the river. I barely made it out." I pointed vaguely toward the door. "Just up the road a ways."

He didn't speak, just watched me.

"Dropped my cell phone." I shrugged. "I guess it didn't matter by that time. It was wet. It wasn't working."

My arms were getting heavy, and the fire wasn't helping much. So I rubbed my palms together, then clasped my hands and laid them in my lap. They shook. My whole body shook.

Something popped in the fire, and the wind moaned around the eaves. I sat and shivered and waited for him to speak. When I couldn't stand it any longer, I said, "Do you have a phone?"

His smile deepened. He made no other reply.

"I don't even know who I should call. A taxi? An ambulance? The police?" I shook my head. "What's the playbook for going off the road, landing in a river, and surviving?"

He shrugged.

"I mostly carry the cell phone for emergencies. Now I've finally got an emergency, and it's ruined." I chuckled. "Bricked.

That's what my grandson would say." I sighed. "That's why I got the phone. So I could text with my grandchildren. My son says that's all they ever do. They never talk on the phone anymore, even though they've always got a phone in their hands. They just text, text, text."

The man raised his eyebrows, the biggest sign of interest he'd shown so far.

"It didn't work." I gave a frustrated half-shrug, then rubbed my hands briskly together. Was that a faint glimmer of warmth? I didn't have the energy to keep rubbing, though. "I text them exactly once a year. Two whole words. 'Happy birthday.' Which is twice as many words as I get back." I grimaced. "They always say, 'Thanks.' And that's it."

"What made you think they wanted to text you?"

I looked at him sharply. The look on his face might have been sarcastic amusement, but it might have been an encouraging smile. His voice was flat, neutral. I decided to give him the benefit of the doubt. He'd just saved my life, after all.

"I guess I hoped for the best. Things with my son, well, they aren't as good as they might be." I smiled at this gem of understatement. "But I thought maybe, with the grandkids, it might be different."

"What makes you think you could do better?" There was an ugly edge to his voice now, a hint of nastiness in his smile.

"Hey, now." I leaned forward, squinting at him. "Do I know you?"

The light was fading, obscuring his features. "It doesn't seem likely." He shrugged. "I mean, you don't seem to know much, do you?"

His eyes, cold and ugly, glittered in the firelight. I looked away, then blinked in surprise. The wall behind him was lost in shadows. I looked at the fire, terrified it might be dying.

A log shifted, sending a thousand shining sparks up the chimney. Plenty of wood remained, all of it burning brightly.

"I think I hurt myself." My teeth started to chatter, and I clenched my jaw until it stopped. "I'm having trouble seeing."

"What makes you think you could see before? Perceptive, were you?" He gave a derisive snort.

"Who are you?" Golden light still washed one side of his face, but the other side was lost in darkness.

"Why did you even bother climbing up to the road? Were you worried your loving family would be distraught without you?" A mocking tone made it clear he knew the answer to that question.

"I did it for my son. And for the boys. I had to tell him—"

"Tell him what?" He sneered. "That you're sorry you took a big steaming dump on his entire life?"

"I didn't mean to!" The words, pent up for too long, poured out of me. "I was stupid, and I was so angry. And I didn't know any other way. So I raised him like my father raised me." My hands formed useless, trembling fists. "And now he does it to the boys. I know he won't forgive me." I knew it, but it still shook me to speak the words aloud. "But if I tell him. If I tell him I was stupid. That I made a mistake. That it was wrong, and I regret it."

"He'll tell you to go fuck yourself."

I nodded. "Maybe. But maybe he'll be a little different with Henry and Jason."

A bit of light limned one shoulder and the hair on the side of his head. The rest of him was invisible. He snickered, cold and derisive, and I stiffened. "You sound exactly like my father." I looked around. The fire still burned, but it was strangely hard to see. There were fresh ice crystals on my sleeves. They were spreading. "What's happening? Who are you? Where am I really?"

"What makes you think you'd understand the answer if I told you?"

"Please. You have to let me use your phone."

"What makes you think an ambulance would save you?"

My teeth started chattering again. "Let me call my son. If I'm dying, if I'm losing my mind, let me make amends. Let me fix some of the damage."

He laughed. "What makes you think you can get it right?"

I jabbed a finger at him, suddenly furious. "That's what I did all this for! That's why I climbed out a window and clawed my way up a riverbank and walked God knows how far through snow and forest! So I can give a final message to my son. So I can make up for at least a little bit of what I've done."

"What makes you think you deserve the chance?"

It wasn't easy to speak with my teeth chattering like castanets. "It's the only reason I bothered getting out of the car."

He leaned forward, into the light. His grin widened, becoming the only thing I could see. His voice was barely audible over the clatter of my teeth.

"What makes you think you left the car?"

Brent Nichols is a speculative fiction and crime writer, bon vivant, and man about town. He likes good beer, bad puns, high adventure, and low comedy. He's never been seen in the same room as Batman, but that's probably just a coincidence. He has books with Seventh Terrace and Bundoran Press, and he self-publishes science fiction novels under the pen name Jake Elwood. He does his writing beside a frozen lake in Lethbridge, where he ponders the dark secrets that just might lie beneath the snow and ice.

DARKNESS FALLS ON
CARVERSVILLE

JACOB STRUNK

July 24, 1893

Ms. Florence Harper
Fall River, Massachusetts

My dearest sister,

It's not yet been three months since I saw you, waving from
the window as the carriage carried me away, but it feels like an
eternity. Surely in six months you've grown, made new friends,
advanced in your studies. I feel dreadful missing it. I fear you may
not recognize me next we meet!

Do tell me, how is Mother? I hope you two are getting on. She
can be difficult, I know, but remember that she has your shared
interests at heart. Has Mr. Snyder called on her again? He is
strange, I know, and unusual, but he is kind. Perhaps the two of
them could help mend each other's broken hearts.

I wish I had more exciting news to share, but I'm afraid until
quite recently things have been rather dull. I know I shouldn't
complain. How many girls would love to be where I am, breathing
this clean air, this idyll far removed from the laundry presses and
the foul muck and men of the docks alike? And it is lovely, really!
But there is something about the silence that makes my heart sick

with loneliness. Even the birds sound melancholy. Mr. Morse himself is quiet—as if his presence in a room stills even the mice in the rafters.

Oh, I know I should call him Husband, but even in our evenings alone together I feel such distance—from him, from you, from everything to which I have been accustomed all these years. In time, I suppose, the space between us will warm, even disappear, and the footfalls and laughter of children will replace the silence. Perhaps it is just that I am impatient, ready to start my life, our life together. He is pious, stoic, and in that respect unlike any man I knew in the city. But I do so wish he'd put eyes upon me as I've read husbands do, or wrap me up in his strong arms. Or perhaps these are the fantasies of a child, and I'd best give them up or live swaddled in disappointment.

Of course, I feel silly fretting over domesticities here atop the hill, surrounded by acres of fertile land and sweet-smelling forest, while our friends in the village have faced a hard summer. The rains fell for days. Not forty days and nights, of course, but had the count been eight or even ten, I would not be surprised; I lost track of the number. Here on the hill, I marvelled at bouquets of lightning spreading like veins across the entirety of the sky, at thunder loud enough to shake the house and send dust down the chimney. Below us, the rains swoll the rivers. They coursed through the fields and forests like fat worms, eating the very earth, it seemed. Two cottages were shifted on their foundations, and one was carried away by the current as the lake itself broke free of its shoreline and cascaded past the church.

Sweet Florence, the cries on the morning the rain finally stopped carried all the way up to where I stood in the doorway, hanging herbs to dry from the transom and watching Mr. Morse —Justus, I must practice until it is natural!—watching Justus strap a pack upon his back to carry into town. He brought provisions as he could: flour, bacon, eggs I wrapped carefully in cloth. The news he carried back to me that night was awful. Three dead: the Gowers and their daughter, all asleep when the waters came for them.

Still others lost their animals, livestock numbering in the hundreds lie bloating in the fields. Dear sister, I tell you this not to shock or disgust you, but to impress upon you the gravity of the devastation and to express to you my gratitude for our safety, and for the resilience of our homestead here. The mood, as you must imagine, has been dark in the days since the floods.

I pick flowers each day, arranging them in the dining room, even in my chamber and my husband's. But many days, as the men toil to rebuild, even these fragrant offerings are met by Justus with a sigh.

I do wish he would talk to me, tell me more about how he feels, not just of progress made each day or of the fields lost to the rain. But it is each man's nature to define his own voice, and hardly my place to pry it out of him. The weight he carries must be great, for many crops have been lost, and so late in the season there is hardly opportunity to replant. The responsibility he feels for the village is greater than I can know, for it is his father's land the farmers lease, his name on the deeds of both the gristmill and the sawmill, and with the elder Mr. Morse these many years in his grave, poor Justus must stand accountable for the fates of those who work his land. We are lucky, all of us here, that he does not tire in his work to rebuild stronger than before. And when the time is right, when he is satisfied, he can afford the indulgence, perhaps he will turn some of his attention back onto me, and I may feel satisfied in my duties as a wife.

I must tell you of one peculiar thing, though, if for no other reason than to clear it from my head, where I fear it has been knitting itself into knots of unfounded worry. You see, I am still not familiar with all the ways of the country, and I know there are many old traditions that might seem uncanny to the likes of us, city girls more used to the hiss of steam and squealing grind of the freight engine than the whispers of the forest or the coo of a night wind through the trees.

This was a week ago, the night I want to tell you about, and the Gowers not yet five days in their graves. Justus took his brandy in the parlour with four other men, two of whom I know only by their surname—Coffin, if you can believe it, brothers—an old buzzard named Crauley, who hisses at passing children dare they look up into his face, and another man I hadn't seen before. He must have ridden in from Rutland; his horse seemed fatigued by the time they arrived here atop the mountain. I saw him only briefly, but noted his broad, furrowed brow; shock of grey hair; and dark, deep-set eyes which gave way to fans of chiselled crow's feet. He looked like grim news made flesh.

They spoke in hushed voices for a while, perhaps an hour, behind the closed parlour door while I tried as best I could to busy myself, that Justus could hold some expectation of privacy. After that hour, Justus would tell me nothing but that an errand of dire import required all of them, and that it must be dealt with then, that night. The five of them rode off together, and when Justus returned hours later, colour was already beginning to bloom in the sky to the east. Exhausted, he asked only that I wake him before eight. I did, and nothing was mentioned of it again, but the Coffins seemed in good spirits that week, and even Crauley kept his hissing to a minimum in the days that followed. Whatever deed required their service, they must have completed it satisfactorily, though what on earth or heaven might need attention at that ungodly hour is beyond the scope of my experience or imagination, save childbirth and death.

Please do, darling sister, write to me of your studies and anything and everything else in your world. I miss you terribly— Mother, too!—and will await your word with bated breath. Take care of yourself, and please spare a prayer on Sunday for the good people of Carversville, who do their best at all things, are honourable in the eyes of their God, and remain strong even in the hour of His wrath.

Your loving sister always,
Mrs. Honora Morse
Carversville, Vermont

October 14, 1893

My Dear Florence,

I have not received correspondence from you, and I trust this is because you are so busily involved in your studies. Keep at them. Your mind is your greatest strength, a tool to forge the life you deserve. You always were the smartest in your class. I do hope you'll write soon. But please do put your education at the forefront. Not many of the girls in Fall River have that luxury.

I'm afraid the strange and tragic occurrences continue here. As a girl I read stories of bizarre happenings in the northern woods, of magic and witchcraft, even. Well, I haven't met any witches, but in the evenings when the clouds descend on us, shrouding the mountains and filling the forests, it's easy to believe in spooks, goblins, and any other ancient lore. Oh, it is beautiful country, Florence, as far as the eye can see, and I do hope you can see for yourself soon. Perhaps next summer.

But in the interim, the village is having a dreadful time of it.

The sawmill and gristmill took most of August to repair. They're operational again now, and with a skeleton crew, but with so much lost time and most of the crop gone, the village's stores for the winter are pitifully low and many of the farmers themselves in arrears.

The Gowers were barely in their graves two months when another terrible tragedy befell our beleaguered congregation. The blacksmith, a cantankerous German named Mueller, was nearly killed when the stable caught fire and burned itself down on top of him! His cries awoke three neighbours who rushed to his aid and managed to free the poor soul just as the huge old crossbeams landed on his erstwhile bed. He did not smoke, and so it couldn't have been his pipe; his furnace, he swore, was sound; his wood stove cold, as an Indian summer—in the parlance of the region—lie hot and fat across the entire valley that week. It was only that the windows were open to invite a nighttime breeze that the neighbours heard the calamity at all!

Unfortunately, all six horses stabled in the structure were lost. The grief the townsfolk felt and the reverence they displayed for the beasts was heartrending, sister. What remained of them was carefully collected from the embers, and some of the men buried them on the hill behind the church while the children sang and wept. Truly it was a sight to see.

Mueller, wrapped in field dressings and covered head to toe in soot, watched from across the thoroughfare as his life disappeared into ash, as if it had never existed, wiping at an occasional tear. I've never seen a more broken man, more distraught and utterly alone, even as the hands of his friends and neighbours reached out to comfort him.

After the last earth was shovelled into the mares' grave, he turned and—without a word—began walking east out of town. He did not so much as glance back, even at the calls of the women to refresh his bandages, but trudged off toward Ludlow with a limp, dragging the singed remnants of his pants along the path. I watched him, his shoulders slumped and head hung low, until he disappeared behind the first hill. What happened to him thenceforth, none of us knows.

Florence, I must also share with you the strangest thing yet, though it may sound inconsequential in light of the very real tragedies that seem to lie just behind every storm cloud this year. But I fear if I don't tell someone, the mystery of it will eat me alive. I was in the study because it faces east and has the most spectacular view, all the way to Mount Saltash. Sometimes I'll sit and get lost in the view. This day, I found myself fidgeting with one of my earrings—the jade, you remember?—and it fell to the floor, disappearing behind the ornately clawed foot of Mr. Morse's roll-top desk.

Believe me when I say my fingers could not have been more than a hair's breadth from the stone, taunting me from there against the baseboard, but it was useless. I resolved to move the desk and collect my earring, or to hell with it. Using my weight, I rocked it ever so slightly, back and forth, slowly walking it forward. One inch, two inches, and I thought that would be enough. I let the desk down and something dropped with a clatter to the floor. Well, I got to my knees and put my cheek to the floor. Indeed, there it was, with something resting just next to it. I reached out, cupped both of them in my hand, and stood.

Lying in my palm beside grandmother's jade earring was a tooth. A molar, in fact, fat and yellow like those heat blisters Mr. Knowlton gets when they're infected. Of course, Florence, I shrieked! And promptly dropped both again to the floor, where they went bouncing into different corners. I forgot all about the earring when I stooped to look closer at the back of the desk. There was a small imperfection in the wood that had warped in a corner just enough to allow a small gap, a gap through which a molar had fallen just now out of the darkness and into the light.

The drawer was locked and I searched high and low through the study for the key, but could find no trace. I brought from the barn a long file used for shoeing the horses, but it was too wide. Even the smallest knife in the kitchen would not penetrate the latch. Aha! I plucked a pin from my hair and felt about inside the lock for the tumblers. Remember when Father hired the locksmith to open his office after dropping his keys in the river? You were very young then, when he was alive.

My patience paid off, and I coaxed the latch open. I pushed the pin back into my hair and, taking a deep breath, pulled the drawer open to reveal a horror of teeth, yellow and brown, black and chipped, abscessed. Hundreds of them, incisors and canines and stained buckteeth flat and wide like rusted spades. I stared at them, Florence, for I do not know how long. I was lost in them like I'd been lost in the view. And then my eyes found a cracked cavity, a spiderweb of fissures leading to the snapped root, and I pushed the drawer shut.

I was able to lock the drawer again with the pin despite my shaking hands, and I have not stepped into the study again since that day for fear my curiosity will overcome my sense and have me turning the place apart with an axe. The evenings Justus spends alone in there with the door closed and the fire low ignite a desire in me, a thirst to know more. Heaven help me, I don't want to know, but I need to.

Please keep us in your thoughts, darling sister. Three in the town have taken ill this week. I fear we cannot bear any more loss, not with the days drawing short and winter looming like a storm on the horizon. Write to me soon. I miss you so.

Lovingly,
Your Honora

January 6, 1894
  Sister:
  My heart is full of worry having not received word from you, though my husband grows weary of my saying so. He has seen these letters delivered to the post himself, and has also received the news through friends that you and Mother are well, and even that Mr. Snyder calls regularly. I trust then, that you've been too busy to write and not that you've forgotten your dear elder sister, here atop a mountain, alone most days and pining for the comforts of the city most nights. I'll be sure to deliver this letter to the post myself, to see it accepted with my own eyes.

Justus demands I write less often, as it discomforts the people of the village—particularly the men—he says. Wives in this region, he said, needn't fuss with letters; perhaps this explains the sidelong glances I often feel in the village. Or the wide berth given me when not escorted by my husband. Whispers and furtive glances. Sometimes, Florence, I fear I'm going mad up here, that perhaps there's something in the water or on the wind—or maybe it's just the isolation, the silence—pushing my mind ever closer to the edge of some unknown cliff.

I fear I write with more tragic news, and more bizarre occurrences.

Old Stokes died the second week of December and, the ground already frozen solid, was laid in the town mausoleum until spring. It was consumption, they say, and he was not the last. Three others, all children, were dead by Christmas. Oh, God, the shroud of grief that hangs over the all of us. As if the crushing despair of the grey winter wasn't enough, the hunger and sickness, the unimaginable losses, compound daily. A woman, Mrs. Carver of Cuttingsville, and her child were next to die in the week before the New Year. What an awful way to go, drowning in one's own blood, coughing oneself bit by grisly bit into handkerchiefs to be buried in the privy. I can't bear to think.

But here is where circumstances took an even wider turn toward the absurd! I shudder to write these very words, lest you think me mad. But sister, you must believe me, every word is true!

Two nights ago, a stirring in the house woke me from a fitful sleep. It was a clear, cold night. The wind howled through the trees, ghostly silhouettes bending in the light of a nearly full moon. We haven't seen fresh snow in a week, but the stubborn patches in the meadow, crusted with ice, twinkled like calm waters in bright sun. Something moved in the house, downstairs. I sat up, straining to hear, though my chamber door was closed. And then, still and silent as could be, I saw flashes of white light below me in the dooryard, each accompanied by a sound like a shot! I startled, but then curiosity took hold and I crept closer to the window and peered out, my forehead against the cold glass.

It was a horse I saw, its iron shoes sparking on scars of exposed granite, flashing against the very bedrock of the mountain itself. Presently the horse was brought to a halt, and its rider descended. Still half-delirious with sleep, I thought it the Revelation of John himself, this rider atop a horse black as midnight.

As the rider pushed back a heavy hood and raised a fist to knock against the door, I saw the shock of white hair and immediately recognized the strange visitor of last summer. Almost uncannily, he turned to face his dark eyes directly up at me in the second-floor window. He couldn't have seen me, as I had no candle or lamp burning, but I ducked down out of sight like a scared child and listened as the door below me creaked open and then latched shut again.

I peered over the windowsill and saw Justus join the man and exchange a few words in low, hushed tones. I watched from the window as they saddled another horse, and then the two of them began down the hill toward town, slowly, almost leisurely.

I waited for them to fall below the line of the road and then quickly pulled one of Justus's thick jackets over my shoulders, stuffed my feet into a pair of leather boots, tied a quick scarf, and stepped into the cold night. As the cold sucked the first breath of air from my lungs, I marvelled at the explosion of stars in a crystal-clear sky bisected by the great, bright track of the Milky Way, even as the moon shone so brightly as to mimic the pale light of dawn.

I followed them, hewing close to the tree line along the path and ready to duck into shadow at a moment's notice. I could not discern words, but the men's voices carried to me through the still night, and I presumed their horses' slow gait was to allow some further conversation before they reached their destination. What I couldn't have imagined was where they were headed, and sister, I tell you my very blood chilled in my veins when realization struck me.

I sneaked through town behind them, creeping through shadows, keeping an ever-vigilant eye as I dodged ice and ducked beneath windows. The village was deathly quiet save the echoing hoot of one lonely owl. I watched as they left their horses behind the church and struck off on foot, with a bulky black bag in the hand of the pale rider. Ahead of them I saw, twinkling through the trees, what must be the light of a lantern. But no, I told myself, it can't be. For there beyond the edge of the village, through the wood behind the church, was nothing but the cemetery with its buried secrets beneath ground frozen as hard as the granite beneath it.

The trees in the wood provided shelter for December's snow, and here it remained a foot deep. I stepped in the tracks made by my husband's large boots, carefully elongating my stride to neither leave trace nor betray myself with the sound of packed snow underfoot. I stopped yards from where the trees broke and met the wide, white lawn of cemetery atop the hill. From there I had an unobstructed view of the goings on, though clear understanding of what I was about to witness eludes me still.

Waiting by the crypt, shivering around an oil lantern, were the Coffins and old Cauley. The rogues' fraternity reunited, Cauley pulled a ring of heavy keys from his cloak and unlocked the chain fastened through the crypt's gates!

From my vantage, I saw him loose the chain and step aside. The doors were hauled open by the Coffins, and—dear Florence, I didn't know what to think—my husband and the stranger stepped inside with them!

The four of them disappeared into the tomb and out of my sight, while Cauley set to building a small fire. He must have previously arranged the kindling and even splashed a little lamp oil onto it, for while he struggled to strike a match with his hands in bulky gloves, I saw the flame take to the wood quickly, and soon enough he had removed his gloves and was holding his hands over the flames.

You're surely wondering how I myself was not tittering and chittering in the frigid night, but my astonishment was such that I barely felt the cold at all, and the trembling that washed over my body in waves in the minutes to come may well have been from shock and terror as much as the winter chill.

Movement, then, from inside the mausoleum, itself a contradiction of sense and reason. The Coffins exited first, each of them stepping carefully out with arms holding an end of a wooden casket. Behind them came Justus and the stranger.

Dear sister, you cannot imagine the raging whirlpool of thoughts and emotions I felt then surging within my body. I clasped a hand to my mouth, barely catching and containing a shriek of alarm. No sooner had the Coffin boys set the casket on the ground next to the fire than the stranger reached into his black bag and produced a pry bar, which he quickly set to the lid of the casket, making short work of it.

The men all stepped back as the lid fell open. I could not see inside, thank Heavens, but after a moment of hushed silence, Justus nodded to the stranger, who kneeled beside the casket and reached once more into his bag of evil tricks. Again, my breath caught in my throat, again I stifled some manner of guttural animal noise welling deep within me as I watched the stranger lean over the casket, both hands around the hilt of a long, broad knife, its blade curved like a crescent moon, unlike any I've ever seen before.

He pushed and pulled, sawed, wrenched with his weight, and I heard the disgusting cracks and groans of his devilish work even from where I knelt, hidden by darkness. He hauled the knife free then, and by the flickering orange light of old Cauley's fire, I made out some manner of foulness on the blade. He wiped the blade clean, looked once at each of the men standing over him, and then reached in with both hands.

From the casket, he produced a Cornish hen. That's absurd, I thought. And then the terrible reality struck me, and bile rose in my throat as I saw him move nearer the fire. Its light revealed the hideous truth as Cauley stepped back, and the man in the black cloak placed old Stokes's cold heart atop the pyre.

My husband, Justus Morse, he of few words, of strong convictions, of a demeanour I presumed stoic but now—now I hadn't a clue what to think—watched as the flames lapped at the heart, thawing it. Even from where I was, I could hear it sizzle as the blood flowed yet again, dripping into the embers, where it popped and spat, hissing like old Cauley.

But the abomination that came next, oh my sister; the stranger with the white hair and the black eyes had one last trick in store, one last dread instrument, one final terrible design. He pulled forth from the bag a plier and handed it to Justus.

Without a moment's hesitation, and with a deft and practiced hand, Justus knelt beside the head of the casket and reached in. One by one, he dropped small, pale pellets into his palm. A child knelt at the shore collecting a pawful of pebbles. But these weren't pebbles. These were old Stokes's teeth. And I could control myself no longer.

I collapsed backward and, both hands held firmly over my mouth, could not break my fall. Down onto a large dead branch I fell, with a crack that shot through the forest and cemetery alike. I froze, hands over my mouth, holding my breath.

All five men looked up, their eyes scanning the dark tree line, Justus still with one fiendish hand in the corpse's mouth. A fear unlike any I've ever felt gripped me. And a shock. Such a terrible confusion as I've never known.

There was my own husband, whose bed I have known, wrenching the teeth from the dead, and I here trembling in fright at the thought of being seen by him.

Florence, I haven't the words. I know the cultures here are foreign to us and superstitions run deeper here than the snow in the coldest ravine or the lake after the spring floods. But by Heaven, these deeds . . .

After the longest moment of my life, what felt like three lifetimes, the men made up their minds to finish their work. What that might have been, I will never know, as I loped through the snow following the tracks backward as quickly as I could. I got home and rushed back into bed.

I'd been home an hour when I heard the front door open, heard Justus enter, heard him slowly cross to the study and unlock his desk.

Write to me. I beg you.

Honora

Mar. 26 or 27

F —

I know now my letters haven't reached you. The postman is not to be trusted. None of them are. These wretched people with their wretched, ghastly beliefs. Their rituals.

Eighty-four days ago, the day I heard the postman call, heard their whispered voices drifting up from below, heard the silence as Mr. Morse—surely no use in calling him "husband" now—read my last correspondence to you.

Since then, I've been locked in this room. Escape is impossible. The window has been nailed shut, and while I may break the glass, I'd also break my legs in a fall from this height. I've thought also of using the broken glass to slash my own throat, but what of it? And who then would take my place beneath their boots? Food is brought, set on the floor just inside the door before it is latched again. My chamber pot is taken and emptied every third day. I have not washed, though Justus acquiesced to my howling and brought me some books to read. It is on their flyleaves that I'm writing this to you now.

Their voices come to me up the stair, reverberating through the floorboards at night. "The Outsider", they call me and blame me for their misfortune. First a flood, a fire, an illness. Acts of God? It would be comical were it not so horrible. Imagine such beliefs, curses from beyond the grave, dead old men rising to infect the living, a pox carried to the living through the ill will of the deceased. If all this blame is to be laid at my feet, what then of the fire that tore through Ludlow three years ago, ignited by lightning strike? To what unfortunate soul did they assign that blame? Or my captor's own mother, bled out in childbirth some grey December long ago, her baby stillborn, the both of them laid in the mausoleum until the spring thaw. I wonder now, are their teeth in that drawer in the study?

It will happen soon now. I heard them again two nights ago. A dam failed on the Black River, and many drowned. They've called for him, their avenging angel, and when he arrives, they'll fall in line behind him. Even Justus. Hiding behind faith. Is there anything more cowardly?

My last request of Mr. Morse will be that whatever fiction they invent to explain my demise, my remains be returned to you and Mother, returned to Fall River where I lived and loved. Thereupon may be found folded into the tresses of a befouled dress this letter. I pray that you should read it and believe that every day I thought of you, and that you may set designs to shine the light of truth on the men of Carversville. Show the whole world what has happened here. Let true judgment fall on this damned hamlet, the judgment of Law. And of History. And of lessons unlearned.

I hear him, his horse, and out the window in the gloaming I see an enchantment of sparks thrown by devilish hooves on this cursed mountain's bones. I am ready, save for one question, the answer to which I will never know.

How ever will they explain what's happened to my teeth?

— H

Jacob Strunk was born in the wintery woods of Wisconsin and has been short-listed for both a Student Academy Award and the Pushcart Prize in fiction, as well as the Glimmer Train short story award and a New Rivers Press book prize. His genre-bending fiction has appeared in print for over twenty years, most recently in Coffin Bell, Five on the Fifth, and his 2023 collection *Screaming in Tongues*. He earned his MFA in creative writing from the University of Southern Maine's Stonecoast program and teaches film and media in Los Angeles, where he lives with a few framed movie posters and the ghost of his cat, Stephen.

Don't Wake Up

J. D. HARLOCK

one night, a little
girl I was
building a
snowman with
began to cry

when I
asked her
what the matter
was

she begged me
not to stop
dreaming—because

if I did, she would die

this was right before I woke up

J. D. Harlock is a SWANA American academic pursuing a
doctoral degree at the University of St. Andrews. When not in
hibernation, he writes, and his work has been featured in *The*

Griffith Review, *The Cincinnati Review*, and New York University's *Library of Arabic Literature*.

The Penitence of Ice

LAURA VANARENDONK BAUGH

It was hard to wake in the mornings without light to creep across the blankets and ease him out of rest. It was not that the sun did not rise here; he was not so far north as that, and the snow threw back the rising sun's light in eye-dazzling brilliance. But the hut was built without windows, all chinks tightly sealed against the cold and other things. No light reached inside to wake him, and he slept deeply in the dark.

That would change soon, he thought.

The patchwork repairs in the walls did not match, rendered by two dozen sets of hands with varying skill. One ominous corner had showed a man-sized plaster fill in a markedly different colour, and Alef hung a blanket over it—insulation against the cold and the reminder.

"There's a book of guidelines and practices," the sergeant had told him when they unchained him at the door. "If you can read."

Alef found a thin journal listing first chores and then other notes, but it suffered from ink doodles over the text and several missing pages. He'd given himself one day to despair for the lost advice before resolving that he'd expected to have none, and he would have to make do with what he had.

So each morning he woke, eventually, in the hut's darkness. With his furs clutched about him, he shuffled to the door. If he could discern light through the latch, then he groaned, pulled the furs tight, and went out to the pit that served as a toilet. If it was dark and he had woken in the night, then he used the bucket in the corner. Even the stink of his changed diet was not enough to open the door by night.

They had given him two shirts, two sets of trousers, and three sets of under-trousers—"you'll need more of 'em when you hear it," one guard had snorted—but there seemed little point to changing each day. Who was there to see? Anyway, he did little to stir up a sweat, and he could bathe daily.

That was his sole pleasure, and he bathed a little longer each day. The hut was built around the sacred spring, as it was a sign of the goddess's protection (of the south, at least) and provided a degree of safety for the sacrificed man in the hut.

Now, Alef was that man. He had known, vaguely, of the sacrifice. He had not thought on it much beyond assuming it was both necessary and deserved. He had never supposed it would one day be him.

After bathing, he wrote poetry. He sat for hours, debating each word and phrase, crafting to perfection before committing ink to paper. He knew this was not the best way to write much poetry, nor even the way to write the best poetry, but he had more time than he had paper and ink. Writing materials had been his request, when he could choose his gift into exile, but they would not last. Not like the hours would.

And then, finally, the night would come again. Each night was announced by a growing pressure which intruded upon his poetry, making concentration more difficult, until at last he gave it up. Each night he put away his paper and ink, checked and rechecked his stockpile of fuel, lit the sacred lamps, wrapped himself in layered furs, and braced himself. Each night, he wondered if this would be the night they arrived.

As he forced himself into the chill air for his morning relief, he noticed a patch bare of snow. Elsewhere the snow lay knee-deep, as far as the eye could see. But here, a stone's throw from the hut, a span of bare ground lay muddy and damp.

Alef had his breakfast—three dried apricots—and thought about the patch of ground. There were no footprints but his own, and no wind would have left such an odd hole to the ground. It must have melted, leaving the earth muddy instead of frozen.

That should have been impossible.

He finished his breakfast and went to perform his duties and his ablutions.

First, he must clean the hut. He was neat by nature, but the hot spring made the task more difficult, settling a fine mist of nearly imperceptible film around its stony border and sometimes on his provisions. Still, cleaning did not take long, especially when performed daily. He swabbed the stones set around the spring, and then he checked the hinges on the door and went over the walls. The hut was warmed from within by the ever-steaming hot spring, and according to his lean notebook, they preferred not to enter it, but as the season deepened, they would, just as wolves would try a farm if the winter grew too fierce. The patches bore evidence for the warning.

After the hut was clean, he scooped water from the pool and sat with the bucket upon a nearby stool. There he disrobed and washed himself with the warm water. The discharge ran away across the floor, joining a shallow channel where the pool's overflow ran beneath the wall and outside. They would not enter through the sluice of hot spring water, he had read, so it was important to keep the channel clear and flowing. A few inches beyond the wall, the ice dam began to build; knocking this away was another of his daily chores.

Once Alef was both physically and ritually cleansed, he could enter the sacred spring, or at least the pool it made. First, he brought bushels of snow into the hut and dumped them into the pool, cooling the temperature to something more comfortable for human flesh. Then he eased himself into the steaming water, relaxing beyond what was possible elsewhere. Even during the day, even before the proper onset of winter, some part of him knew he was never truly safe within his furs and hut walls and circles of flickering lamplight. Within the tiny pool, filled directly by the goddess's own lifegiving spring, he was protected.

He had plenty of food. They had left him with a considerable store of dried fruits, preserved meat, pickled vegetables. He had enough food and more than enough. No one wanted the sacrifice to die of hunger.

He had taken two days to inventory his rations and work out a daily menu, to be repeated every five days. This, he hoped, would provide helpful structure. In dire cases of doldrums, he might depart from the scheduled menu for a craving or favourite, but he expected there would be few favourites after weeks of the same. He hoped to live long enough to grow bored of the food.

Gradually the temperature of the pool began to rise again, fed by the hot spring, and at last he got out and dressed. He cut and measured his supper ingredients, and he hung the sealed pot in the hottest part of the pool to cook. Then he took out yesterday's lines of poetry and set himself to finishing them.

It was a long day, leading toward a long night.

The danger had not always been this great. Long ago, the sages said, the winds had been cooler in Omlapi, and the sun less fierce on the stone-paved streets. Alef could imagine such days, for still in spring there were times when the narrow streets were cooled by breezes and when the overarching awnings and flowering trees were pleasant features instead of necessities. In those days, too, the sages said, the northlands were not so brutally cold, merely snowy, and the caravans could pass with reasonable care for ice and freezing temperatures.

But the plains had grown hotter, an anvil to the sun's strokes, and the breath-sucking gales of the far north had twisted south and into the trade passages. The sages said man's sins had done it, though the exact explanations varied, whether it was greed for treasures or ingratitude for their natural gifts or lusts and gluttonies of all sorts. But the winds had changed, hotter and colder, and then *they* came on the north winds.

Some said they were ghosts of men who had died in the northlands, seeking vengeance on those who yet lived. Some said they were spirits of the ice, yearning to extinguish all warmth and happiness. There were other stories, too, but Alef did not think the explanations mattered much. Ghost or spirit, once-man or once-snow, they were implacable predators, and knowing the right name to call them would not make death kinder.

Whatever they were or had been, they were nearly mindless. Their attacks upon the trade caravans were vicious, but they could be distracted. Like a fish in a bowl or a bird in a cage could hold a cat's attention, the snow beasts could be drawn away from the trade routes by a single man in a hut. A condemned criminal, safely exiled and trapped by hungry frosts, could be made useful again to his city by drawing those hungry frosts away from vital trade routes.

This year, Alef was the condemned man. He was expected to survive long enough to allow any late-moving caravans to finish their season, and then at last to die sometime in the deep winter. They would bring another man the next year.

His crime had been to love. He was a coppersmith, burnishing warm metal to a glow, and his work had supplied a fine house, which boasted a fine daughter, whose heart had warmed to him and glowed. But she had been promised in a political match, and her senator father could not afford to break an alliance.

Alef had been afraid, and he had told her that she was brilliant, she was beautiful, she was beyond him in every way, and he dared not court her against her father's wishes. She'd cried, and then she'd told Alef she would elope with him, though he had not asked it.

She must have told her father the same, after Alef had left alone in his cowardice, for guards burst into his workshop and seized him with accusations of housebreaking and seduction. His trial had been quick, his sentencing efficient, and he had lingered in the prison barely a week before being conveyed north.

His quick conviction, so late in the season, had probably relieved some other condemned man scheduled for the sacrifice hut. He wondered if that man thought of Alef. He wondered what crime that man had been guilty of.

They came for the first time while he was asleep.

The hut's temperature dropped, making him shiver within the furs even beside the pool's heat, and the wind slammed into the wall like a thing of flesh instead of air. He sat up at the sound, wondering if a mountain beast had come down to the plains or if something else lurked outside, and then he heard.

He understood then what the sneering soldier had meant about hearing them.

They cried in the voices of the wind, their shrieks almost a shriek of agony but not quite, their moans almost the moan of ebbing wind but not quite. It would have been better if they sounded more different, he thought, so that he could be sure of what he was hearing. The wondering, the arguing with himself whether he heard wind or ghost, was somehow worse.

He did not sleep again. When at last the voices ceased and they left off pounding on his walls, he still sat upright, waiting for them to return and imagining again and again that he heard them in the wind. In the morning, even in the light, he needed long minutes to ready himself to go out to his toilet.

In the future, he need not listen in the dark. He had plenty of oil for his lamp. The sacrifice was not meant to despair in the dark, lest he run into the night to end his torment too soon. He could light his nights all the winter.

As if that would help.

The caravan route was not so far from the sacrifice hut. The hut had to be near enough to tempt the creatures (or ghosts) from the route, after all, until the season's last trade had ended.

If a sacrifice survived until spring, the senators promised, he could hike out to the caravan route and obtain free passage using the badge that hung on the wall as an enticement to survive. Once returned safely to Omlapi, he could claim from the Senate a fine house and a small fortune. It was a bribe to keep men from surrendering to fear and despair too early. It was an easy promise for the Senate; no one had ever claimed the prize.

The first night had been only the discovery of the sacrifice, perhaps by a ranging scout or three. The next night, it brought the others, louder in numbers.

They shrieked at the hut, battering it with wind, clawing at the chinks and tearing at the timbers. Alef huddled in his furs, blanket over his head, knees drawn to his chest as if conserving warmth might defend against them. For hours they raged, making the oil lamp flicker even inside the hut, and Alef stared at it breathlessly, terrified it would go out. The light and the warmth kept them out, he thought. That was the purpose of the sacred lamp. He'd laid his ember box nearby, in case of need, but it took long, long seconds to coax an ember into enough flame to light a lamp, and instinctively he knew it would be too long.

He did not sleep that night.

When he went out the next morning, there was still frost upon the door, a single large patch with five tendrils spreading across the planks. He held up his hand, his spread fingers making only a third of the reach.

The patch of muddy ground, to the north of the hut, had

widened. Now he could have lain down across it, fur-lined boots at one side and wool-wrapped head at the other. When he returned to the hut, he browsed through the book of instructions and notes. No one had mentioned a patch of melted snow before, or it had been lost in the missing pages.

He wondered at times about those missing pages. Had another sacrifice written of his terror and then torn out his admission in shame? Had an illiterate man destroyed inaccessible advice for spite? Had someone desperate for fuel torn pages to burn one at a time, until the effort had failed before he had worked through the book? Had someone used them for toilet wipes?

He cleaned the hut, washed himself, bathed. He opened his book of half-written poetry. He thought about the senator's daughter, about her copper-coloured hair and her forge-hot promises against his smothered replies. He added twelve words to his page.

The sacred spring had been placed by the goddess near the trade route and discovered by a lost donkey driver who mistook rising steam for campfire smoke. It was possible to drink the water, once cooled, though the minerals gave a strong taste. Sometimes, while Alef bathed, he played with the soft clusters of minerals that floated into the pool, spinning like misshapen flowers in the current.

The water was given by the goddess, yes, but it came from within the earth, rising to fill the pool. What if another spring was rising to the surface outside? If it lay underground, its heat might melt the snow, leaving a bare patch as he'd seen. Was he about to be blessed with a second hot spring?

He was not sure of the purpose of that blessing. Two sacred hot springs could not provide much more than one. But he supposed he was not meant to question divine blessings. And anyway, there was no spring yet, only bare ground.

He slept in the afternoon, to make up for the night.

The next day, the bare patch was wider, and simmering.

Alef stared in fascination. The ground had softened and partly sunk, leaving a sloping pit. At its centre, mud intermittently rose into a small dome and then collapsed upon itself, repeating a hands' breadth away a moment later, a slow-moving parody of the stew he had started for supper.

He crouched a few paces away and watched it, tucking his hands under his arms and shivering. If the pit continued to open, he could imagine it becoming a pool, like the one in the hut. The sacred spring's pool was in stone, however, not mud. Did that make a difference? Maybe this would have been a pool, had it emerged in stone, but now it would be soft mud.

He hadn't really considered the ground around the hut. It was all just snow, grey under clouds and blinding on sunny days. He moved away about twenty paces and dug down through the snow, clearing a small hole to the dark beneath. He scraped at the ground, but he couldn't guess whether it was rock or frozen soil.

After he cleaned the spring that day, he carried a bucket out and emptied it into his hole. The snow melted away, leaving a clear view of the substrate beneath. He rubbed at it, dampening his fingertips, and a thin dark layer smudged. Not rock, but not quite like soil . . . Curious, and with nothing else demanding his attention, he brought another bucket. This one washed more of the dirt away, leaving a small visible patch of smooth pink and white.

It looked like unpolished marble, to his casual eye. Not soil, not the dark stone of the pool, but something like stone.

He had no tools to chip at it. He went inside and set his glove beside the lamp to dry, and he wondered at pink and white stone.

That evening, he dreamt of an underground city, made of marble, buried in snow by unseen beasts of frost. The shrieking in the dream woke him to the shrieking outside his hut, and he huddled in the thin light of the lamp.

The mud was leaping into the air, splattering into the ground and punch-melting little holes in the snow a dozen feet away. Alef watched it, fascinated by the play of water and soil, and by the mystery of what it could mean.

It was too cold to stand outside and watch the mud boil, so eventually he went back into the hut. He did his chores, and he washed himself, and he entered the pool to soak. When he was thoroughly warm, he rose from the pool, wrapped a blanket about himself and slipped his bare feet into his boots, and went out braced for the cold to look at the mud.

The intricate, never-repeating patterns of bubbling mud and leaping spouts held his attention until the cold began to penetrate. He went back inside and slid again into the pool, shivering in the irony of too much heat. Once he was heated against the cold again, he went out again.

It became something of a game, a fresh way to pass the time. He left the blanket and wore only his boots to protect his feet from the ice and the boiling mud, and he counted off the seconds he could last before he began to shiver. He was careful, without the blanket, to stand well back of the spraying mud. He did not need a burn wound to tend in this place.

The mud pit did not heed his spectating nor his increasing duration in the cold. It was making its own increases, first settling to a simmer and then rising in mud-flinging intensity for a minute or two before lowering again.

And then, as he stepped outside the hut, the mud in the pit heaved, like a shoulder about to break a pool's surface. All at once a torrent of water burst upward, high above Alef's head. He shrank back as muddy rain began to pour down, melting dirty pockmarks in the snow and rattling against the roof of the hut.

After a long, terrifying moment, the fountain calmed, and the muddy water eased down to its usual place, a beast calmed from its rage. Alef still waited at the door, though, shivering and cowering in the cold air. He had not respected the new spring; he had taken it for an amusement. If he had stood naked beneath that blast, his skin would have been scalded from his body. He must be careful, from now on.

The next day, he went again into the pool and then into the cold, but he stood nearer the door, ready to seek shelter if he saw the mud mound again. He counted seconds against his endurance, and also for the time from when he saw the mud's first leaps until the rush of boiling water burst upward. The geysers came more often—not regularly, but several times each day. Sometimes he saw it; sometimes he heard it through the wall, a mocking counter-note to the screams of the night.

The goddess's second gift, if that is what it was, served little purpose but to provide a relief of boredom, in tracking its timing, and to give him an additional danger to beware now during the daylight as well. He had to listen carefully before going out to relieve himself, judging whether the pit was in its simmering stage or about to rain boiling mud upon the hut and the surrounding area. He had been taught not to guess at gods' gifts, but it was difficult to see the blessing in this one.

By night, they clawed at the walls and beat at the door, and he wrapped himself in blankets and furs and pressed his hands over his ears, praying for dawn.

He wrote painstaking poems to her. In his poems, he could say what he had not dared to say in the city. In his poems, in hindsight, he knew there was no safety in restraint, no mercy in circumspection. In his poems, he apologized for his fear and promised to be worthy of her love and courage.

He took his time, choosing each word with care to make the most of his limited paper. He took his time, forcing himself to consider what he had surrendered with his hesitancy. If he must be taken for looking too high above a coppersmith's station, he should have earned his punishment more thoroughly. Now he had left her with not only loss, but rejection.

He wrote painstaking poems to her, pouring out his regrets in words he knew no one would ever read.

Tonight, they came early.

He had only just toed off his boots and sat down in the furs, wanting their warmth but dreading the night before him. The first bang against the door, like a thrown ball of ice, made him jump in place. Quickly he lit another lamp, wondering if he'd somehow lost the time.

But the oil, measured out each day, showed that it was only late evening. They were growing bolder, or hungrier. He pulled a heavy fur over his shoulders.

They prowled around the hut, probing, testing, shrieking. He tracked their progress without turning his head, feeling the air chill and shift within the hut, a tiny storm to mirror the weather outside.

Then they stopped circling, and after a moment, Alef realized the sounds had slowed, as well. They still scratched at the wall, but more slowly, and the sound was more like a wind's moaning than a scream of rage. Had they burned out their fury in their frustration? Dared he hope?

But then something in him recognized the fresh danger. This

was a change like a barking dog, raging at a fence, suddenly quieting as he found a hole to enlarge. This was—

He whirled in place, twisting his coverings about him, and stared at the blanket hanging on the wall, now quivering over the patch it hid. The patch had held thus far, but tonight it beckoned as a weak spot, and tonight they were setting upon it, scratching at it with icy claws.

Alef's stomach crawled into his throat, blocking his air. For a long moment he only stared at the shaking blanket, and then he seized his courage and ran to place a lamp at the base of the wall. He removed the blanket, so that it could not catch the flame, and retreated with it to his bed.

This was wise defence, and a mistake, for now he could see the wall itself tremble. Mud plaster flaked from the patch, and gradually it began to darken with moisture, drawing condensation from the steamy air as it chilled.

The lamp's flame flickered at the base of the wall, and no plaster flaked within a span of its dance. But a mere lamp could not hold them back, nor could its heat protect an entire wall, and Alef knew it was only an inconvenience to them. They would come.

Were they vengeful ghosts of men who had died in the northlands? Were they spirits of the ice, hateful toward all warm and living? Suddenly he wanted to know what he would face. But what could it matter, when he was about to die?

I am so sorry. I should have spoken for you.

The damaged section of wall collapsed inward with a triumphant scream of wind. Alef rolled into the steaming pool.

The wind tore about the hut, shaking the walls and throwing his possessions and rations into disarray. Alef plunged his head beneath the water, blocking out the sound. But he could not hide there for long, and as his ears pounded and his lungs burned, he came up to gasp.

Everything on shelves had been thrown down, and his pages were lying on the floor or in the damp channel or escaping through the gap into the night. Cold winds tore at his hair, and he sank as low as he could into the pool.

With the moon's light, he could *see* them. They looked like frosty smoke on the wind, rippling like a banner caught in a breeze but sparkling and shimmering as they moved. They were mostly formless, except when something like a hand or claw plucked at the failing wall or a remaining bag of barley flour or an overturned bucket.

They plunged and swooped about the hut, their cries louder than ever even as he kept his ears below the water's surface. They circled the pool but did not descend to it, and he thought they avoided the steam that now twisted in the admitted wind. He saw one glisten nearby with the moon behind it, and in a sudden fit of daring, he splashed at it. It twisted away and screamed, and an instant later they all shrieked at him, furious at his counterattack.

The pool would protect him from the cold. That was good. But it would not protect him from the heat. He used this water for cooking; he could not stay in it until the morning. His limbs were already stinging, and his heart pounded. He could last for a short while, with the fallen wall admitting the frigid night air, but eventually the pool would be too much.

The irony of it—dying of heat to survive the cold . . .

He braced his feet against the side and rose from the water, splashing to scatter the beasts. He lifted only his torso out, gasping with relief as the cool air struck him. But he could not spray all around him effectively, and one struck him from behind. Icy chill shocked through him, making him gasp, and he fell forward into the water. For a moment he could not move, and then he twisted upward and broke the surface, coughing. His lungs ached as if he'd been in a night blizzard.

It had been good luck or the goddess's blessing that the creature had knocked him into the pool instead of to the ground. He could not risk sitting on the pool's edge, rotating limbs in for safety and out to cool.

There was a bucket on its side, just a few feet from the pool's edge. He did not know what use it might be, as he could not reach snow to cool the pool. He thought giddily of snagging a frost beast from the air and dragging it down into the water, cooling it, and he knew he was on the edge of madness from fear or heat.

Outside the broken wall, the mud pit burbled and sputtered. The whole night seemed bent on killing him.

A rime of ice was forming on his blankets and sheepskins beneath the shattered wall. The coolness taunted him, illusive relief. He was growing dizzy, and he would soon pass out and drown if he did not climb from the pool into their reach.

He was going to die here, cooked in the sacred spring or sacrificed to the frost beasts, and his poetry and his love and his life would be gone. Tears of pain and rage and despair mingled with the steam and sweat. Alef splashed at the creatures, and they twisted away and descended again, cautious but relentless.

Of course. They had always gotten their prey before. They were confident and hungry. Outside the mud pit burbled and spat, and a spray fountained into the air.

An idea came to him, desperate and insane. But what had he to lose?

He tested his footing at the edge of the pool. Between his failing fingers and the creatures' predations, he could have only one chance. He took a breath and lunged from the pool, reaching across the black stone to snatch the bucket. A frosty claw snagged his sleeve, but he threw himself back in time, and the creature recoiled from the water.

Clutching the bucket, he paddled to the side of the pool nearest the open wall. The pinpricks of ice stinging his face felt good against the heat. He thought of how many seconds he had counted in the cold, warmed by his plunges in the pool, and hoped it was enough.

The mud pit began to spiral water and steam into the air, little spurts about the height of his knees.

He dragged the bucket across the water and climbed from the pool, screaming his defiance among the wind's shrieks. He swung the bucket, throwing an arc of steaming water over and around him, and icy smoke twisted and howled, battering the walls. He dropped the bucket and ran, snatching up a frosted sheepskin and leaping through the broken wall.

They swept after him, catching up and raking at his steaming clothes. Cold stabbed through him, piercing and deadly.

The boiling fountain heaved into the air. Alef dove to the warm mud at its edge and rolled into a defensive ball, the ice-rimed fleece over him.

They descended, a cacophony of frigid death.

The geyser erupted, blasting steam and boiling water. The sound was greater than Alef remembered, rising with their predatory cries. The creatures' shrieks turned to screams, and the claws vanished as hot water rained down upon him.

The eruption continued a long time, longer than he'd seen

before. It was perhaps a minute before the boiling rain stopped. He lay gasping in the mud, listening, waiting. At last, he pushed back the steaming sheepskin and sat up.

Nothing soared in the moonlight. No claws reached for his unprotected head. They had followed the bait into his trap, and they had been destroyed.

He stood. All around the bare pit, the snow had melted away. Cold began to seep through his wet clothes, cooling the hot layers and chilling his skin.

Outside the ring of geyserfall, something moved in the snow, twisting and glistening. Alef went into the hut and scooped another bucket of steaming water. He returned and emptied it on the writhing shape. The snow melted away to bare ground, leaving nothing.

He was shivering now, with the cold hardening the wet clothes on his body and with the realization of what he had done, and that he had survived. He went back into the hut and fumbled the cold, wet clothing off, shaking with chill and relief. Then he fell back into the pool, gasping with the shock of it.

He stayed until the sting of frostbite changed to the sting of heat, and then he rose and dug through the debris for his remaining clothing. Then he wrapped himself in blankets and furs, at the pool's edge with the steam drifting over him, and he waited.

Nothing more came that night.

In the morning, he piled snow high against the broken wall to stop the wind, and he hung blankets again on the inside. He treated his raw and blistered skin with the little physick he had. He righted his overturned rations, recovered what he could of spilled oil and cleaned what he could not, as he could not risk spilled fuel in his only shelter. He collected a few dozen pages of the hut's notebook and of his poetry. Then he slept.

In the evening, he set the bucket beside the pool, placed himself in the steam again, and waited.

Nothing came. The wind howled, but it was only wind.

When morning light came, a sense of relief rolled over him greater than any previous morning had brought. He sank onto the black stone and drew deep breaths for the first time in two days. He laughed aloud, the sound frightening to his ears.

He got up and made a curry pot to put into the pool to cook. Then he knelt to thank the goddess for her blessing of the muddy pool.

He spent the rest of the day assessing his inventory. He had lost supplies in the attack, but if he was cautious, he could last until the equinox. He finished by writing out a new schedule to maximize his resources, and then he savoured the finished curry, his last full meal for the winter.

But lean meals were a small price to pay for a fine house, a fortune, and the chance to apologize to the woman who had loved more bravely than he. He pressed the badge of transit in his hands, and he thought about walking out in the spring sun to wait for the first caravans.

Laura VanArendonk Baugh writes fantasy of many flavours as well as non-fiction. She has summited extinct, dormant, and active volcanoes, and has visited one active eruption, but none has yet accepted her sacrifice. She included geothermal activity in this story anyway. She lives in Indiana where she enjoys Dobermans, travel, fair-trade chocolate, and making her imaginary friends fight one another for her own amusement. Find her award-winning work at LauraVAB.com.

NEITHER RIME NOR REASON

J. M. TURNER

Shadows summoned forth from the setting sun dripped from the branches and needles to pool on the frozen forest floor. Wreathed in this cloak of gloaming the humble village of Caernarfor glowed with the golden light of hearth fires; a defiant candle in the mighty sea of conifers. It was at this murky hour, when the only signs of life among the small cluster of homes were the men bringing in extra logs for the fire, that Donnan, with face red from wind and cold, found himself outside of the glorified shack that served as Caernarfor's inn. A breath of warm air that drove the chill from between his shoulders greeted him when he stepped through the door. But the reprieve was short-lived, for the cold of evening was replaced by the icy stare of the townsfolk within. Donnan averted his gaze and found himself a seat in a lonely corner that the candlelight did not touch.

Though Caernarfor was under nominal rule of the noble house of Cearfoss, it possessed none of the hospitality that Donnan had become familiar with while traveling these lands. Even the young woman who came to serve him thin stew and hard bread did so without a word.

Donnan had often heard that those who dwelt in the northern reaches of Horinthal, beyond the peaks of the Winterbliss Mountains, had a wild, almost feral, way about them. Few southerners spoke of their northern brethren, and fewer still bothered to travel beyond the frosted fringes of the Winterbliss foothills. Donnan, never one to judge, dismissed most of what was said regarding the north, but once he had left Cearfoss Hall, the last bastion of true civility, he found that the rumours held true. Superstitions, old even before the kingdom formed, were upheld in religious fashion, and the rugged highways were lined with shrines for dozens of demigods and spirits. Each unpleasant night that Donnan had spent on the road was filled with the distant chanting of cults and the sporadic lights of witchfires.

Donnan ate his meal in silence and did his best to ignore the sharp glances and furtive whispers from the other patrons. Invoking his father's name for favourable treatment would do him no good this far north. When he had finished, he took his bowl to the hearth where the serving woman tended the cauldron of stew.

"I beg your pardon, but have you seen a man that looks similar to me?" Donnan asked, indicating his own square jaw and dusty hair. "His name is Cillian and he would have come this way some months ago. He likely had a lute with him."

"Ah, the bard," the tavern maiden said, only the slightest form of recognition gracing her flat voice. "He was here, yes. Just the one night though."

"Did he say where he was going?"

The woman regarded Donnan with a hooded stare. "The song stones, like every other southern fool."

So, he did not have a change of heart, Donnan thought. "Have you seen him since?"

The woman shook her head.

"I mean no disrespect, but more than like he is dead. No one comes back from the wastes these days. If the cold doesn't take them first, the curse swallows them up."

"Curse?" asked Donnan. "The madness, you mean?"

"The madness," the woman said with a nod. "You intend to follow in his footsteps?"

"I do. I know the chances are slim, but I hope to find him alive," answered Donnan, fishing in his pocket for some form of coinage. "Is there a room available?"

"Up in the loft." The young woman jerked her head in the direction of a ladder. "There are blankets and plenty of straw for bedding. Sleep wherever you like."

Though there were only sheets hung in intervals to provide a semblance of privacy, the loft proved to be far more comfortable than Donnan had expected. Wrapping himself in a fur blanket, he laid back into a pile of soft straw and tried to put the worries of the road ahead out of his mind. It took some doing, but exhaustion eventually got the best of him and he tumbled into a deep sleep.

A fresh coating of plush snow covered the forest when Donnan left the inn the next morning. The shafts of rising sun illuminated the ivory landscape such that his eyes watered and he was forced to squint. With stumbling steps, he made his way to the shade of a towering pine and consulted his map before he struck out onto the ice wastes. His map was little more than a tattered bit of parchment with a few scrawled landmarks copied from a proper map he had seen at Cearfoss Hall. He traced a finger along the route he intended to take. The journey to the song stones would take him just over a week. With only a handful of shelters along the way, the first of which being a humble hole dug into the leeward side of a boulder, he would need to keep a steady pace lest nightfall's vicious winds catch him in the open. Donnan rolled his map with a sigh and stuffed it into the pocket inside his fur cloak.

"Best get on with it," he said, striking out without sparing Caernarfor a parting glance.

He walked for little more than half an hour before the forest gave way to the flat and vast plain of ice that stretched north for untold miles. While feathery grey clouds spotted the leaden sky, they were sparse and spare and would do little to impede the blinding morning sun.

Eyes screwed shut against the glare, Donnan fumbled through his pack until his fingers found the smooth wood of the sun mask he had purchased from a wandering peddler. The mask was carved from pine—the sweet scent of the conifer still permeated the wood—and unadorned save for a series of narrow slits cut into the rough shape of eyes.

Donnan slipped the mask on and received a pleasant shock at how much his vision had improved. Filled with a comforting confidence, Donnan took the first of many steps onto the ice.

The layer of powder snow that rested atop the ice crunched

beneath Donnan's boots, a constant rhythm like the beat of a marching drum. Having no trees or hills to slow its pace, the wind ripped about every which way, screaming as it whipped the dry snow into whirling devils and nibbled at him with sharp and frigid teeth. *Is there truly a curse here on the wastes,* Donnan thought. *Or is it this damned wind that drives men mad?*

By the time the sun had ceded the sky to the moon, Donnan swore the wind was speaking to him—ghosts of words whispered just out of earshot. Before he could convince his weary mind to attempt interpretation, he spied the hulking shadow of his destination through the swirling snow.

At twice his height and thrice his arm span, the boulder was an oddity in the surrounding nothingness. A field of smaller stones circled it, giving the scene the look of supplicants praying to a giant. Erected among the smaller rocks were cairns, no doubt housing the remains of fallen travellers. The presence of the dead gave the possibility of words on the wind a touch of the sinister, but Donnan was too tired for any significant fear to take hold as he passed the graves.

While he had known it to be fruitless, Donnan had prayed to every god he could recall that this shelter would be more than just a depression carved out of the ice, and he groaned as his hopes were dashed. Shelter was a generous term for such a sorry hovel, but the interior of the hole was lined with bark and branches to stave off some of the cold, and there was a pile of rocks assembled into something of a hearth. The most curious feature of the place, however, was the figure lying in a corner on a bed of furs. Though their face was turned toward the wall, the absence of the scent of smoke told Donnan all he needed to know. They were dead.

Donnan made to approach the remains, a knot of worry tightening in his bowels, but when he spied a tuft of auburn hair poking out from beneath the figure's hood, he sighed and settled himself down near the hearth. It was not Cillian.

He lowered his pack to the floor and retrieved a bundle of birch bark from within. In the span of a minute, he had achieved a flame and began to feed it with twigs.

While the fire grew, Donnan rummaged through the ash pile for any leftover fuel and found an oddly shaped bit of wood. Rubbing away the dust, he found that he had discovered the remnants of some stringed instrument. Runes from old U'ssar were carved into the lacquered wood, and though Donnan had forgotten much of the instruction from his youth, he could interpret these symbols to be a blessing to imbue the notes of the instrument with clarity and power.

"So, you were a musician as well," Donnan spoke to the back of the deceased. "I suppose that should be no surprise."

He pocketed the remains of the instrument and added more kindling to the fire; its warmth melted away the wariness he felt towards the dead bard. "I will finish your journey for you, and take what's left of your instrument with me to the song stones.

"But I am afraid you will have to spend one more night here, friend. I will keep you company. In the morning, I will make a cairn of sorts and you will be able to have a proper rest."

Sensing the conversation was drawing to a close, Donnan produced a generous log from his pack and laid it on the fire. Satisfied that the flames would catch on the timber, he unfurled his bedroll and settled in for the night. As he drifted off to sleep, Donnan thought he heard a chord of faint, discordant notes float by on the night's breeze.

Her unseeing eyes bored into him with the cold weight of eternity. Donnan wanted to move, to scream, but he was pinned in place as if frozen to the ground for the corpse had, somehow, rotated during the night to face him. He forced himself to sit up though his swimming head brought him to the brink of nausea, and took a long series of deep breaths. Try as he might, Donnan could not find an explanation for the corpse's movement. *Madness.* The word oozed through his mind leaving a slimy trail of fear.

His appetite suitably ruined, Donnan stowed his bedroll, collected the remnants of firewood from the hearth, and donned his hat and gloves. The greater part of him wanted to depart with all due haste, leaving the dead bard where she lay, but a glimmer of his honour shone through, and he approached the body with tentative steps. "She's only sleeping. You've lifted sleeping women countless times," Donnan whispered as he stooped and hoisted the corpse into his arms. The cold had prevented any form of decay from taking hold of her and were it not for the dullness of her eyes and a chilling pallor he might even believe the lies he told himself. "Yes, she is only sleeping. She is . . . a very stiff sleeper."

Donnan trudged out of the shelter. A fist of cold air hit him in the face, as he placed the bard's remains near a large number of the scattered stones and set to work constructing a tomb. It was a more arduous task than he had anticipated, and he was soon damp with sweat as he stacked the rocks around the deceased.

While Donnan worked his mind wandered, and he was reminded of a day many years ago when he and his brother Cillian built a miniature castle out of stones found beside the family pond. Once their construction had been finished, Donnan had grown bored of the little castle and shattered it while pretending to be a giant. He could still recall Cillian's face twisted in a hideous scowl.

"You were the responsible one, Cillian," Donnan murmured to himself. "And I rash. So why now have you decided to act so reckless?"

It was only when Donnan was setting the last stone of the cairn in place did he realize that there were tears in his eyes.

There was a moment after finishing the bard's burial that Donnan considered spending another day and night beneath the boulder, but thoughts of his brother dashed that prospect. He stole a final look over his shoulder at the distant black blot before securing his mask and continuing into the foreboding white expanse.

Donnan plodded forward, stopping every now and then to drink from his waterskin or nibble on a bit of hard biscuit. The only breaks in his monotonous world were the waist-height stacks of stones that served as trail markers from shelter to shelter. Some of these constructions had bits of coloured cloth wedged between the stones that whipped about in the wind to better catch the attention of passing travellers. So thoroughly had the grey of both sky and snow seeped into Donnan's eyes that the sight of such vibrant colour burned his eyes.

Time crawled ever onward with the only sign of its passing being the almost imperceptible movement of the sun overhead. Though the hours advanced at only a trickle, they still outpaced Donnan and he could feel the icy breath of evening on his neck. A night spent out on the ice was out of the question—with nothing between him and the wind and darkness, he would freeze long before the first pale gasp of dawn. Donnan used this fear to banish the strength-sapping cold. He gritted his teeth and forced his legs to work. His muscles burned in protest, but he urged them on until he saw the looming shadow of trees in the distance. Donnan allowed himself a moment to suck in a fortifying breath before he plunged ahead for the last stretch.

The vagueness of the wastes had so dulled his senses that the gentle groaning of ice-laden branches was as fine music, and the sharp aroma of pine a salve to his lungs. His legs were quaking, struggling to hold his weight, and his head was swimming by the time he had passed through the forest and stopped at the entryway of the shattered keep.

It was a squat tower, nearly as wide around as it was tall, and crumbling from the weather's constant abuse, but compared to the boulder from the night before it was a luxurious thing. Despite the snow and disrepair, the structure reminded him of the keep that occupied the high hill at the centre of his family's lands down south.

Memories of home flooded his mind as Donnan staggered into the shelter of the redoubt with only his willpower keeping him from collapsing into a heap onto the cold, stone floor. He managed to wrestle his pack from where it had frozen onto his fur cloak and spill the final log and last bit of kindling into the hearth. Unlike the boulder, the keep had a proper hearth and even a small bundle of tinder leftover from the last guest. As he set to lighting the tinder, Donnan knew that he had not enough wood to last the night. Loathe though he was to return to the frigid darkness, he would need to harvest wood from the conifers if he wanted to pass the night in any form of comfort. He decided he would allow himself to rest his weary legs and warm his numbed fingers before returning to the biting cold.

With the fire well enough along to tend to itself, Donnan took stock of his surroundings. Any furniture or furnishings had long turned to dust, but the keep's floor was littered with loose stones and masonry from part of the second story that had collapsed. A small wall erected from the rubble formed a half circle about the hearth to trap some of the warmth.

Donnan laid back against the wall of rubble and watched the tongues of fire swirl and dance. He felt sleep tugging at his eyelids, luring him into its calming oblivion, but he fought the temptation and rose to his feet. He fetched his hatchet from his pack and set out into the forest.

The wind had increased in ferocity since his arrival and brought with it heavy flakes of snow that clung to his furs and pelted the exposed portions of his face. Donnan positioned himself on the leeward side of a large pine and began to chip away at the layers of snow and ice in search of fallen branches. The work was taxing, but the effort kept the cold at bay and proved worth his while when he uncovered a sizable bough. His spirits high, Donnan made to bring the wood back to the tower when he saw movement among the trees not twenty paces away.

At first glance, he thought it was simply a branch stirred by the gusts of wind, but a second shifting of the shadows proved him wrong. The motion was too fluid, too human. He thought for a moment it could be another traveller, but the figure's movements were furtive and sinister, unlike the trudging steps to be expected of an ordinary pilgrim.

And if not a fellow pilgrim, then what?

Nothing mortal could survive out in the wastes.

Without removing his gaze from the direction of the interloper, Donnan made his way back toward the keep. He saw no additional movement, but just as he was stepping past the tower's threshold, he thought he saw a shock of auburn caught in an errant ray of moonlight.

Back in the keep, the smoke from the fire rose to the stony ceiling where it writhed along until finally curling under the entryway to disappear into the night. Donnan pulled his furs tight about his shoulders and turned a fearful eye toward the cold darkness that lurked just beyond the firelight. If he kept the fire burning low, he would have enough wood until morning but even were the fire to gutter out, Donnan dared not set foot in those woods while the moon ruled the sky. He would rather suffer the frost than face whatever entity stalked those trees. He wished the keep had a door.

Donnan awoke to the wind snarling outside. Ferocious gusts swirled about carrying powdered snow and bits of ice. Some of the gales found their way into the keep, stirring up ancient dust and ash and stripping Donnan of what little warmth remained. The cinders in the hearth flickered with their final bits of flame, occasionally flaring when a whisper of wind invigorated them.

Aside from a handful of tinder there was nothing left to burn.

I can't travel in these conditions, Donnan thought, shrugging his blanket from his shoulders. He stood at the threshold and stared out into the maddening whiteness. *I'd lose my way the second I lost sight of the keep.*

The trees that had been only paces from the tower were now completely shrouded by the driving snow. Even stepping out to gather wood was a massive risk, but with no indication that the storm would calm, and the burning numbness worming its way back into his limbs, Donnan knew he had to take the chance. He held his hands over the dying embers before scooping up his hatchet and delving into the woods once more.

The wind hit him like a hammer blow and nearly knocked him off his feet. He walked in as straight a line as he could manage, wavering only when the wind buffeted him. Terror almost got the best of him when he lost vision of the keep and there was still no tree in sight, but he steeled himself, pressed forward, and walked directly into a large pine. He scraped enough bark from the tree to fill his pockets, keeping watch for the creature he had seen the night before, and then began chopping away at some of the branches within reach. Once he had collected an armful, Donnan made an about face and lurched back toward the tower. His face burned and his furs were wet and heavy as plate armour, but a bundle of kindling was not going to last him very long.

"Damn you, Cillian," he growled, fanning his anger to fuel his exhausted body. "We told you not to travel north. We warned you!"

Donnan returned to the storm, the heat of his growing rage staving off some of the bitter wind that beat in his ears like a massive, tuneless drum. Instead of heading straight out of the keep, Donnan turned right in hopes of finding some deadfall or a freshly descended bough that he had overlooked during the night.

"And mother and father think of *me* as the family disappointment?" Donnan shouted to the wind. "I may not be able to carry a tune, but at least I never followed an imaginary song into a frozen hellscape!"

He stopped at the first tree he stumbled upon and, finding nothing useful on the ground, cut all the branches he could reach and piled them for collection on his return trip. With his rage emboldening him, Donnan stomped on to the next tree, and the next, until his sweat was freezing onto his forehead and he was wheezing from fatigue. He placed a hand on a cedar's trunk to steady himself and get his bearings. To his dismay, he found that his footprints were already near imperceptible due to the heavy snowfall. He sank against the cedar, pulling his scarf down so that he could take deeper breaths.

It was then that he detected a hint of sulphur in the air. He stood and took a long, deep breath. His lungs tingled with the telltale odour of the wretched mineral. *There can be only one source of such a smell this far north,* he thought.

A newfound strength surged through him and Donnan took off into the storm to find the source of the mephitic scent. Wheeling sheets of snow soon gave way to tumbling clouds of steam. Donnan inhaled deeply, allowing the warm vapours to soothe his frigid lungs. He heard the bubbling of water over the wind, and the hard packed ice and snow turned to bare rock just as the piping pool—its water clouded, almost white, from the concentration of minerals—came into view.

Donnan pulled off his furs as quick as he could manage and threw himself into the water's invigorating embrace. For the first time since setting out from Caernarfor he felt true warmth. The choking grasp that winter had held him in loosened and melted away like snow beneath the spring sun. For a glimmer of time, he forgot about his fear and anger and lost himself completely in the steaming waters.

Splashing from the far side of the spring shattered Donnan's relaxation and he jolted to his feet. He peered into the steam, eyes sharp for the slightest movement. As the steam drifted in the wind, it revealed a motionless shadow looming in the waters not far from where he stood.

"Is someone there?" Donnan asked, his voice more confident than he felt. "Who are you?"

There was no response; no sign that the figure had even heard him. He lowered himself chin deep into the water and crept forward, the unnatural chill on the nape of his neck growing with each step he took. It was when he saw the colour of the figure's hair that the supernatural cold dropped down the entirety of his spine. Auburn. He recognized the figure for the bard he had buried back at the boulder. But now, without furs to obscure her form and face, he knew her to be more than that.

"Mirren?" asked Donnan in a whisper drowned by the stirring of the spring.

The woman turned to face him with sad, tired eyes. She was as beautiful as he remembered, with skin clear and healthy and hair a sheet of luxurious red silk. Had he not buried her the day before, Donnan would have believed this mirage to be the Mirren he had known. The Mirren he had beguiled and stolen from his dear brother, Cillian. He averted his eyes from hers as shame swelled up in him.

The recollection of that night almost two years prior took hold of his consciousness. Donnan saw himself working his charms, tightening the puppeteer's strings he had fastened onto the poor woman's innocent heart over the years. Mirren had proven elusive prey, her guard requiring far more subtlety to slip through than most of the women Donnan had encountered. It was her loyalty, the iron clad devotion she had for Cillian, that made the manipulation so difficult. That and his own misgivings about such a cruel betrayal of his brother's trust. In the end, however, Donnan's jealousy and lust had conquered his honour and love. It was a balmy summer night, after one of Mirren and Cillian's frequent spats, when Donnan made his move. Made vulnerable by whatever musical disagreement she had had with Cillian, Mirren allowed herself to fall sway to Donnan's advances. But come morning, whatever passion they felt had curdled into regret.

When his awareness returned to him, Donnan was standing alone in the spring. Had Mirren heard the same siren's song that had lured Cillian to these frozen wastes? Or was it something more human that had drawn her north?

He looked to where she'd stood just a moment before, but only steam and sorrow lingered there now. Guilt and disgust began to well up within Donnan, and the spring's warmth lost its comfort. The water seemed to thicken, becoming feverish and purulent like the discharge that seeps from a wound. The scent of sulphur soured and morphed into the offensive odour of a charnel house. None but Donnan were to blame for Mirren's death, his brother's grief-fuelled quest, and his own current sufferings.

A crushing weight pressed down on his chest, and he

staggered toward the shore. He was tempted to simply walk off into the distance and let the icy claws of the blizzard bring him to justice but he hoisted himself out of the spring and pulled on his clothes. *Now is not the time for cowardice,* Donnan thought as he began his trek back to the tower, collecting the bundles of branches as he went. *No, now is the time to make things right.*

The storm was settling to little more than a discordant chant rather than a raging symphony when Donnan rose the next morning. He had slept in far more comfort than the night before, and even had some wood leftover for whatever poor soul sought shelter after him. He warmed some dried meat over the coals for breakfast and then struck out northward.

It was one of those rare moments when the snow-covered earth and the ever-sour skies did not coalesce into a single, colourless entity—there were strokes of blue coming through the overpowering grey. Curse the clouds though he did, Donnan preferred the ineffable grey to the sun and its savage rays which bounced off the mirror sheen of the snow and pierced his eyes like a flaming arrow. Even with his wooden mask in place he struggled to see. Every time he lifted his head to find the next guidestone, tears burst from his eyes and streamed down to his cheeks where they froze into glittering cascades. His head throbbed long after the heavy sheet of clouds once again dominated the sky, the pain only beginning to abate when he arrived at his next source of a shelter.

The cavern of ice seemed to be the creation of two waves crashing into one another, with frozen spears jutting out every which way so that the whole structure took on the appearance of an urchin. Too exhausted to ponder its origin, Donnan passed through the mouth with its icicle teeth, lit a fire in the pit he found in one of the alcoves, and fell into a heavy slumber.

As he was stowing his bedroll the next morning, Donnan caught a glimpse of colour play over the ice beside him and turned to see Mirren reflected on the frozen wall. She stood motionless, skin once more the colour of death and eyes sightless and eternal. When Donnan whipped his head about to look up on her directly, she was already gone. With neither time to waste on sadness nor courage to reflect on past misdeeds, Donnan gathered his things and departed at a brisk pace.

Wake, march, sleep. Such was Donnan's existence for the next week. The monotony of his journey wore away at his awareness so that his mind hardly registered the increasing oddity of his nightly waypoints. One night he slept amongst the ribs of a colossal and long dead beast, another was spent in a log cabin that lay within a desolate copse of wind stripped pines. He did not see Mirren, or whatever phantom had her form, again, though part of him wished she would appear once more, if only to give him a shadow of company.

With only the occasional clump of deer moss or troop of rimeling mushrooms to supplement his dwindling rations, Donnan was forced to endure the pangs of hunger in addition to the weight of exhaustion. So sorry was his state that when he beheld the song stones reaching toward the distant steel sky he very nearly wept for joy.

Then he noticed the bones.

Hundreds, thousands of bones made a path toward the stones. Cloth and fur still clung to some of the more intact skeletons, but the brutal winds had left most of the remains bleached and scattered. Donnan passed through this graveyard with sombre steps, eyes alert for any sign that his brother rested among the fallen.

The closer he drew to the song stones the more concentrated the bones grew. Strained notes carried on the wind struggled to form into a cohesive melody, their grating tones grinding his ears. Donnan pushed the discomfort aside and approached the stones. Only standing in their shadows could he fully appreciate their sheer size. Though they all varied in height, each of the stones was a monolith in its own right; fingers of a god if the legends were to be believed. Hundreds of holes had been bored into each of the five stones so that their sonorous voices sang no matter which way the wind blew.

Tearing his attention from the queer spires of rock, Donnan became aware of half a dozen kneeling figures that were just visible through the swirling powder snow. Emaciated and weather-beaten though they were, the musicians played their instruments with trance-like dedication to the tune of the song stone's daemonic moaning. One of the bards, a sandy haired man plucking at a battered harp, slowly raised his eyes toward Donnan.

"Cillian!" Donnan fell to his knees beside his brother and

pulled him into an embrace. "Gods, it is you. Here, eat. You look famished!"

Cillian turned his gaunt face from the offered food. "How can you think of food when surrounded by such wonderful melodies?"

"Take a moment to eat something, please. You're withering away."

Cillian raised a finger to his lips for silence and continued to coax the wretched noise from his harp.

Donnan surveyed the bleak scene around him and sighed. "Cillian, I am tone deaf . . . but even I can tell that you're off-key."

"The root of your apathy runs deeper than your pedestrian ear," Cillian stated, his voice devoid of emotion.

Donnan ground his teeth but maintained a level tone. "Cillian, you are not well. Look at your fingers . . . blistered and bleeding. And your own ears are black from the cold! Come, we need to get you someplace warm."

Cillian wretched his arm away when Donnan attempted to lift him to his feet. "You would dare interrupt our performance?!"

"I would dare save you from whatever devil has you under its thrall."

Cillian ignored Donnan's words and proceeded to draw a string of frayed notes from his harp. Donnan pulled at his hair and released a guttural snarl. He wanted to cuff Cillian over the head and drag him off into the wastes, but he knew that would prove futile. If the horrid sound of Cillian's own instrument was not enough to draw him from whatever enchantment clouded his mind, then nothing Donnan could say would convince his brother to leave the song stones.

But perhaps there was another way.

Donnan dropped his pack from his shoulder and took his hatchet in hand. He strode towards the smallest of the stones, an obelisk no less than thrice his own height, and swung with all the strength he could muster. The impact left an ugly gouge in the blade of the hatchet but succeeded in biting into the rock.

One of the bards cried out and made an effort to confront Donnan, but after two feeble steps he collapsed onto the ice and grew still. Donnan struck again and again, sparks and bits of stone spraying him in the face until a fist sized chunk of the spire fell away, altering the pathway of one the holes that wormed through the monument.

Instantly the wind changed tune, becoming a shrill howl that made his skin squirm. Cillian and the rest of the bards ceased their playing and shrieked in pain and terror. Their wails were inhuman, like the cries of a dark beast from the depths.

There was a low moan from the abyss under the ice and then Donnan felt the ground beneath him shift and crack. Vapours from the ocean that lay far below belched forth with the rotten odour of ancient life. Horrid sounds formed unbidden in Donnan's mind and echoed off of the inside of his skull, rising with a gradual cruelty until his consciousness was dominated by the cacophony. Donnan felt his chest heave with silent screams as he tore at his ears in a desperate and vain attempt to silence the daemon choir. Warm blood trickled down the sides of his head and coated his hands. He was sure he was going to drift out of consciousness when the noise ceased just as suddenly as it had begun. His head swam and his ears were mutilated ruins, but Donnan felt close to himself again. He blinked hard, shook his head clear, and could once again perceive his surroundings. The first thing his recovering ears heard was Cillian calling out for him in a panic. His brother raved, pounding his head and wailing like one in mourning. "I cannot hear, Donnan!" His screams carried out over the scarred ice to be lost in the infinite and obscure. "My ears! It has taken my hearing!"

The homeward journey was sorrowfully silent. Though there were many things Donnan wished to speak of, Cillian's new affliction made all but the simplest conversation tiresome. Even were the brothers able to develop some efficient method of communication, Cillian showed little interest in talk. Most of his focus and energy went into putting one foot before the other, and more often than not Donnan had to act as his crutch. Half-starved and fatigued to the bone as they were, Donnan decided that Cillian did not need to know about Mirren's death. That revelation was likely to prove fatal for his already crumbling mind.

So, the days passed at a slow and weary pace. Hunger bit at them with teeth just as sharp as the cold. Donnan's conventional rations were spent by the morning of the second day of travel and the brothers were forced to subsist on whatever fungus or lichen they could find. The grove of barren pines that sheltered the log cabin provided them with what passed for a bounty this far north, and they boiled the moss and mushrooms into a sort of sloppy stew. The flavour was unpleasant, the stench even worse, but it kept them on the living side of things.

There were a dozen times on the return trek where Donnan came near to throwing himself onto the ice to let the cold meld him into the landscape. It was Cillian's quiet and dogged persistence that kept him from giving in to his weakness. *Even in your sorry state you are the one carrying me,* Donnan thought, letting his brother lean on his shoulder for a moment of rest. *I do not deserve you, Cillian. I never have.*

It was when they were in the tumbledown keep sitting by the hearth after a tumultuous night of sleep that Donnan reached his decision. It was a long time coming, but with half a water skin and a handful of foraged foodstuffs between them it was an impossibility that they would both reach Caernarfor alive.

"Cillian," he said as he tugged on his brother's sleeve. "Look at me."

Cillian turned to face him. His eyes were bloodshot and speckled with rheum, but they were as keen as Donnan could remember.

"There is not enough." Donnan exaggerated the movement of his lips and indicated their supplies. "You will go on."

Cillian furrowed his brow, not understanding at first, but his eyes soon widened with comprehension, and he shook his head violently. "We go together," he said with the amplified volume of a man newly deaf. "Or not at all."

The discussion devolved into shouting, though Donnan knew not why he bothered. There were threats and accusations; old wounds laid open to sting anew. In the end, it was a lie that settled things.

"Mirren," Donnan said, his lips curling over every letter. "Mirren is waiting for you."

Cillian turned his gaze back to the fire and was silent for a long time. Donnan could see memories, good and ill, swirling with the reflection of the flames in his eyes. Finally, just when Donnan was about to press him for a response, Cillian nodded. "Fine."

The two men rose and embraced, the first genuine gesture of

affection shared between them in years, and then Cillian packed his supplies and departed quickly. Probably, Donnan thought, before he changed his mind. Donnan watched his brother's form until it vanished in the desolate grey swirl and felt a strange sense of peace pour over him; a calming assurance that the proper course had been taken. He sank onto his bedroll, too exhausted to concern himself with his fate, and was soon drifting off to a dreamless sleep.

A warming presence roused him from his drowsing. He lifted his head and saw the shade of Mirren sitting beside him, watching the glow of the embers. He pushed himself to a sitting position and joined his old lover in observing the dying fire.

"Oh," Donnan said, patting at his furs until he found the piece of Mirren's instrument that he had carried since that first night in the wastes. "I forgot to leave this at the stones. Forgive me."

Mirren's shade reached for the bit of instrument, her hand lingering on his for the briefest of moments, and then tossed the memento onto the coals. Together they watched the flames consume the bit of carved wood as the cold and darkness circled about them one last time.

J. M. Turner is an author of the weird and fantastic. Turner believes the bleak cold of winter is the perfect setting for fantasy tinged with the eldritch and he loves writing in worlds of blood and ice. Drip by drip, like an icicle hanging from the eaves of a long-abandoned house, Turner's portfolio grows. He has short stories published in *Swords and Sorcery Magazine, Bewildering Stories, All Worlds Wayfarer*, and *Lovecraftiana Magazine*. He has also self-published his debut epic fantasy novel, *The Fine Edge of Dawn*, on Amazon. You can join Turner on his writing journey by following his Instagram:
www.instagram.com/jmturner.author/.

MILE ROADS

CHADWICK GINTHER

The way John flew over the gravel roads, I was pretty sure we'd never live to see the new house—new to me, old to him. Our Taurus bounced over washboard ruts sliding edge to edge on the icy gravel. The white was all-consuming. I had no idea how I'd survive out here. No idea how *anyone* survived out here. The prairie stretched forever, occasionally interrupted by shelterbelts and farmyards. The car's defrost couldn't keep up with the cold, and frost crusted the windows, shrinking our view and our world. Our passage stirred snow behind us, making the way back disappear, as if we'd appeared from nothing, and had nowhere to return.

"We're going to hit the ditch and we're going to freeze to death."

"We won't hit the ditch," John said, as if talking to a child. "I know these roads better than my own dick. I could drive them in my sleep."

"I'd rather you pay attention to them while you're awake."

John laughed as my nervous eye found the speedometer.

I wouldn't be comfortable doing fifty kilometres an hour down this road *in summer*. In fact, even calling this a road was being generous, but John was doing eighty—ninety at times. He rode the beaten gravel's contours effortlessly.

Nerves aside, one thing I loved about John: I *did* trust him. He drove just as wildly in the city when we'd first met and started dating, and I'd never felt the vehicle was out of his control.

Even when he scared the shit out of me. *Especially* when he scared the shit out of me.

"I have no idea how you can find this place after so many years."

John looked at me as if I told him he'd grown a third arm. He pushed his dark hair past his eyes—his beautiful brown eyes—and shot me a shit-eating grin.

"Jack, I grew up here."

"Fine. I have no idea how *I'll* ever find my way without you."

"Simple. Seven miles south of the old town sign. Four miles east."

John loved giving directions according to where things *used* to be. "How many kilometres? Our car uses *kilometres*."

"There," he said, pointing with his driving hand. "You see that road?"

I saw the crossroad, and nodded.

"That's a mile road," he said, as if he was revealing the secrets to nuclear fusion. "Whole prairie's built on them. One mile grids. It's how they laid out sections of land for the farmers. Makes it convenient to give directions too."

"I'll bet."

"We're headed south, that's mile three. We're almost there."

He was so excited his grin took in his entire face. I'd never seen him happy to think of this place. There'd always been a shadow when he'd talked of home, and I had the impression growing up out here hadn't been easy for him. Mort Cheval was *a* city—now—but to everyone in Manitoba, Winnipeg—where we'd met—was *the* city. Despite being the third largest centre in the province, Mort Cheval hadn't lost its small-town nature—good and bad.

"Got called 'John Queer' a lot at school, whenever I wore green, or wore a John Deere hat," he'd said. "'Nothing runs like a queer,' they'd yell if I didn't stay to get my ass kicked."

That story, and others like it, always made my heart ache for him. Living in Winnipeg and coming out to my family had been hard enough—I had similar stories—but I couldn't imagine doing it out here in the land of gun racks, corn, and wheat.

John listed off the families belonging to the farms we passed. Houses hidden behind rows of trees, red barns, metal sheds, circular granaries. The occasional rusting vehicular hulk pierced the snow like yard art. The names all had a similar flavour.

Friesens, Klassens. Dycks.

"Lots of Dycks in Mort Cheval." It wasn't a new joke for us, either.

There was a truck oncoming; the snow swallowed its path, too. Houses on the horizon gone. Nothing in any direction but churning snow. John slid us to one side.

"Motherfucker," John grumbled.

"What?"

"He's not moving over."

We had no shoulder to ease onto. Only a snow-filled ditch. John laid on the horn. The truck didn't budge from its path. I squinted, trying to get a look at the driver.

"Doesn't he see us?"

"Oh, he sees us," John said. "He's just an asshole."

"You know him?"

"Probably."

"What if he doesn't pull over?"

John strangled the steering wheel, smile and jokes gone. "He'll pull over. He's fucking with us."

The truck maintained its collision heading. Out the passenger side window the snow-filled ditch looked ready to swallow us.

"Just pull over and stop. Or at least slow down."

"There's nowhere to pull over," he shot back, hotly. "If we do, we'll get stuck. We'll have to walk to the farm and hope a tractor will start so we can drag the car out."

I didn't like the sound of that. John rode the ditch's edge. The truck was right on us. I didn't like *that* either.

"*Shitshitshitshit!*" I yelled.

The wheels slid into the soft snow at the peak of the ditch. Time slowed as the truck passed us, inches to spare on our driver's side. The driver turned, smiled coldly. He looked familiar. Which was impossible. I didn't know anybody out here except for John and his mom. I banged my head on the passenger window as the car accelerated, snow flying in plumes as the tires spun, and John fought to wrestle us under control.

"C'mon, c'mon," he muttered.

Sweat slicked his forehead as he tried to will us out of the ditch. Finally, the car veered from the event horizon and we lurched onto the road, fishtailing. No trace remained of the truck that'd almost run us off the road, only loose snow kicked up in his wake. The way back still hidden. The way forward too. For a moment, a complete white out. Snow and loose gravel peppered our windshield.

John slowed a bit once he had the car steady, but he muttered the rest of the way to the farm.

At the end of what I assumed was a lane shrouded by snow, about a half kilometre away, I saw the farm yard. One house, the newer, was more in the open. A second, the old house from John's tales, peeked above a maple tree shelterbelt. Three tumbledown wood granaries, an old barn, and two large sheds—one of which appeared to have been built in the current century completed the yard. Here and there rusted metal poked from the snow drifts.

The buried lane brought John's anger to the surface again.

"Bill promised he'd have the fucking lane blown out for us."

"What a Dyck," I joked. Then, needling him with an impossible challenge rather than let him stew in impotent fury, I asked, "You can't drive through that?"

"I could," he said. "Just not in this."

I tried to place John's stories of his youth as we walked. Hiding from a tornado in the old house's cellar, praying for safety with his grandmother. Building a tree fort behind the machine shed with his dad and brothers. The boys fixing up vintage cars his grandfather had collected with their dad in the barn once the livestock were sold off. Those men were both gone now and I'd never met John's brothers, only his mother.

I sensed the ghosts of John's past in every building, in every tree. I didn't know if they'd welcome us here. John hadn't shared any stories of the new house, which appeared to be 1960s vintage, the house which was now our house. I hoped that was a good thing. Hoped we could make it our own. Make it a home. I hoped his ghosts would let us have that much, even if his living family didn't seem to want to.

John's relations had both wanted to keep the land in the family, and not wanted it to go to us. They'd kept the furnace running at the bare minimum to keep the pipes from freezing while they'd tried to find somebody else—anybody else—to make an offer.

We made love the moment we crossed the threshold, John's wire stubble rubbing my face near raw. Making love—fucking—making the house ours—*taking* it. We leaned against the bare wall and lay there, content for a time, John kissed my temple where a bruise bloomed from my bump in the car, drawing lazy circles on the small of my back.

The house felt . . . odd. Still. Nothing of us was here yet, besides us, and, I supposed, John's memories. None of the family would live on the farm after his grandmother passed. They'd moved further away, into town, back to the Old Farm near the U.S. border. John had taken me there a time or too, when we'd made day trips to Mort Cheval. It hadn't been any more welcoming than this cold, empty house, but it was more picturesque.

John came back from the basement where he'd been examining the furnace, holding a worn deck of cards, apparently the only thing left behind. He held them as if he knew them. "Wanna see a magic trick?" Tentatively, he shuffled as if his fingers were remembering how, and drew a card, holding it to face me. "Ace of Spades," he said, not looking. I saw him release a long breath—in relief, disappointment, I couldn't quite tell—when I confirmed. "I know every fold and crease on this deck."

"As well as you know the roads?" I winked.

He laughed. "Only one way to find out."

"You a magician now?" I asked. "My magic Mennonite?"

"Magic." He smirked and drew out the word with his best faux-spooky voice as he palmed the card.

"Well, at least your family left us *something* as a housewarming gift."

He chuckled. I loved his laugh. And his crooked smile that'd won me immediately. "I'm gonna see if I can get a tractor going," John said.

"Okay."

He smiled. "And then?"

"Round two?"

He dug out around the steps, and just when I'd thought he'd try and shovel his way down the entire lane to our car, he returned from the new shed with a snow blower. We'd bought the farm as is. All the junk, all the scrap. The houses had been emptied, but not the barns. He waved at the house window from time to time as he appeared and disappeared in great clouds of snow cast from the snow blower.

After, he managed to start a tractor and we crawled inexorably towards the car. I'd never been on a tractor before, let alone one with an open cab in January winter. *Not* the experience I wanted. Not that I had much choice—someone had to steer our car while John towed it in. I imagined there'd be more rides in my future, and smiled, thinking of the implications for summer.

When the car was parked and plugged in, John returned to clearing snow, and I to cleaning. Dust had gathered everywhere in a greasy film. The floor creaked under my feet and the walls shuddered under slamming winds. Frosted windows blurred John against the white of the snow.

Echoing emptiness answered my every step. In John's few photos, this farmhouse had been cluttered, full of antiques and animals, and people. Now there was just me. Just us. The moving truck wasn't here, wouldn't be here for a few days yet. Nothing to do in the meantime but explore.

The house needed updates. Carpet in the living room, flooring in the kitchen. New cabinets and appliances for the kitchen, the bathroom should be gutted. Everything *definitely* needed fresh paint. I couldn't abide white walls—they seemed to stretch out into the winter outside, and I shuddered. I didn't go into the basement. I've seen that movie.

I know how it ends.

A knife of cold sliced through a window and the cutting breeze made every hair on my arms stand on end. I shivered uncontrollably. A shadow on the lane crept into my vision's edge. Someone was here. A neighbour? John's family? The house groaned. A clicking sputter came from the vents. I thought I heard John's voice from outside. Then, nothing. The shadow moved swiftly, a speeding car glimpsed, then gone. An animal at the treeline. A dog, it had to be a neighbour's dog. The shape gone, too.

I shuddered watching John out in the cold and I turned the heat up. Chill still permeated the house too, warm only in comparison to the January wind. The furnace would have to work for a long time to banish all winter that'd settled into the house's bones. I rubbed at my arms and hoped John would come in soon. I stared at the cards on the kitchen counter, where John had left them. I'd never been much of a player. The last time I'd played Solitaire had been on my parents' computer when I'd still lived at home. John's grandmother had always told him cards were the Devil's game, I remembered, as I dealt my first hand in over a decade. Devil or no, a hand or two would pass the time. I could almost hear John's voice whispering to me, telling me where to move the cards, but his advice didn't seem to help. After five tries, I hadn't won once, and bored, I abandoned the sixth game unfinished to make supper.

I planned where the dining table would go. Imagined our family sitting around it. I'd always wanted kids but John had been ambivalent. Claimed he'd make a better uncle than father, and he was a shitty uncle. He never gave himself enough credit; most of his "deficiencies" as an uncle were from not being welcome in his siblings' lives.

I trailed a finger over the frost at the living room window's edge, carving a heart for John to see on his way back in from the cold. I'd like to replace those windows, too. I sighed. Another thing for the list. I'd have to tack sheets over them until we could hang proper curtains. The furnace kicked in again, and I couldn't believe my relief when it did. Warm air radiated from the vents, the frost fairies seemed to melt and move, as if retreating from the meagre heat. Lingering in that thin vein of forced air, the cold didn't seem so bad.

I had no idea how I'd survive out here. We weren't John's grandparents. If something went wrong, who cared to help? If we had no power, if the car wouldn't start, if the tractor wouldn't start, we'd have to walk. If we died, how long until we were found? Would anyone miss us? Seven miles south and four miles east to Mort Cheval. It may as well have been across the ocean. I wrapped my arms around myself and shuddered again, picturing Jack Nicholson at the end of *The Shining*.

I'd known life would be different out here, but I hadn't counted on feeling so . . . *alone*. Everything felt brittle, as if a wrong touch could shatter it all. You had to be self-sufficient on a farm, and I was in way over my head. John was handy. At least I had John.

What if I didn't?

I looked at the blanket of white.

In the summer I'd ride my bike into town.

A gust of wind sprayed the window with snow.

Summer was a long time from now.

A lifetime.

When I woke in the morning, back aching from our air mattress bed in the centre of the empty living room, snow and wind had buried us again. I could barely see the car. The old house, only two hundred feet away was gone. There were no other farms. Just us.

John was in the kitchen. He'd cleared my half-played game of Solitaire and shuffled the cards, dealing himself a fresh hand. He didn't greet me when I woke and made us a pot of coffee. Instead, he played with a mania. Scowling. Muttering about aces and eights, moving cards almost mechanically. He'd never played in Winnipeg but being home made him a different person. I suppose that's true of anyone. It was making John worse. Or different. I wasn't sure which. Both.

"You played." It wasn't a question.

"Yeah."

"Did you win?"

"No, I got bored."

He slammed a palm on the counter. I'd rarely seen John so upset. When he'd finally caffeinated and I could drag him away from the cards, John headed outside to dig us out all over again. There was a snow blower attached to the larger, and newer tractor with a heated cab, but the tractor wouldn't start. That didn't bother John. He hitched some metal contraption behind the open cabbed tractor, and dragged the lane, flattening a path we wouldn't use. Not until the storm ended anyway. I wondered why he bothered. The wind still howled, and we'd soon be buried. Again. At this rate, we'd have to take the tractor into town for groceries.

We'd brought a few coolers of food, I wondered how long it would last. How long the storm would last.

How long would we last?

I busied myself hanging pictures while a casserole was in the oven. I covered a spot where the sun had permanently faded the shadow of a cross onto the wall. The ghosts of John's stories abounded on the farm, but so did the ghost of who his grandmother had been, even in the otherwise empty house. Normally, hanging pictures and art was the last thing we did in a new home, but I needed some piece of before present here, now. I wanted the house to feel like *our* home as soon as possible. The house didn't cooperate. The dry wall gave and the frame fell the moment I turned my back. I cut myself gathering the glass shards. Looking closer at the wall, I spotted mould. Little black blooms that grabbed my insides and twisted. What else waited in this place?

John played Solitaire while the snow fell outside. Didn't even offer to help clean.

I crumbled more of the dry wall with a grunt and looked into the hole. Two glowing eyes stared back. I jumped, heart pounding, and dented the wall behind me. I looked again, more closely. Sighed. Only pinpricks of light from nail holes on the opposite wall. John didn't notice.

Finally, I asked him, "Why are we here? Why *this* place?"

"My family is here. My life."

"*I'm* your life. You're mine. *They* never talk to you. They *hate* you."

"I hate you."

The whisper sounded like John's voice, slightly twisted. I could almost pretend I'd never heard it. I couldn't ignore it, though. The words may as well have been shouted. I *wish* they'd been shouted. I could've hit back then, but I had no riposte for this whispered wound.

"Christ you're useless." The same twisted whisper, then silence, again. The aftermath of another mortar strike I couldn't tell if he was talking to me, himself, or the cards. It had to be me. He yelled at the cards. John muttered something maybe, "Sorry," or, "See ya."

He left without another word. I cried while I set out the plates hoping he'd come back.

John's face was red and his lips chapped when he returned. Ice crusted his beard. For the first time since we'd come together, I shrank away from his kiss but he acted as if nothing had happened, as if nothing had been said between us.

How could he ignore it? How could *I*?

I felt the distance more than his breath hot on my cheek. I shivered as the ice in his beard melted against my cheek and trickled down my chin.

"If this keeps up, you're going to have to help me out there," John said.

"If you keep coming back in reeking, I'll make you walk into town to buy more soap."

He laughed and held me close. In his arms, for the moment, at least, my questions lay buried.

Things felt better, though John's words still twisted at the back of my brain. I'd half convinced myself he'd never said them. The other half feared to confront him and be proven correct. The weather changed in our favour. It didn't warm up much, but the wind died—as good as a heat wave. Without having to constantly clear the lane, John rummaged in the sheds and found an old snowmobile he'd ridden as a boy. He was determined to fix it.

Damned computers, he'd grumbled.

I felt his pain. The wireless out here was terrible. We barely had any bars on our cells. An old rotary phone hung on the wall in the kitchen—not power dependent—but we hadn't reconnected the landline. With money tight, another bill seemed a frivolous expense. John told me how there'd been a party line—three farms all connected to the same line.

No, thank you.

The shadow was back. Peeking out of the shelterbelt surrounding the old house. Closer. Too close. I picked up the heavy green phone. No dial tone. No "party" on the other end of the line. No sound other than my own worried sigh.

John dragged me outside on a "warmer" day—only minus thirty with the wind chill, instead of minus thirty before the wind chill, he joked, "Balmy."

I was no stranger to cold weather—John and I had both grown up in Manitoba—but out here there was nothing to stop the wind except the trees lining the farmyard. Unlike in the city, there were no heated buildings to duck into, no underground mall, or aboveground pedestrian walkways to allow you to avoid the weather. In place of coffee shops and malls, we had an insulated, but still freezing, machine shed, and rundown, bow-roofed granaries.

But while we were outside together, the cards didn't seem to have a hold on him.

John got the snowmobile running, but I eyed it as suspiciously as I eyed motorcycles—I'd internalized too many accident statistics at my old job with Manitoba Public Insurance. John tried to teach me how to drive the tractor. It was both simpler than a car, and more difficult. I ground gears. Stalled it. Flooded it. We abandoned the lessons. The stupid thing started for John immediately, spitefully, after I left the seat, and he parked it in the shed.

Snow returned and the wind and cold roared back with it, swallowing the world outside the house. In the morning, despite being plugged in, our car wouldn't start.

John tried not to act worried, but I could tell it bothered him. Cars were freedom to John. Growing up out here, I could see why. Miles to the next house. More miles to town. Much further to anything resembling a city. I'd found my freedom in my bicycle, or transit, not that either would help us now.

"It's not used to the cold out here," he said. "We had an underground parking spot in the city."

"It's a car. We're not going to 'toughen it up.'"

He ignored me. "I'll look in the shed for another battery. We'll give it a jump. It'll go, you'll see."

He was probably right. I'd been constantly astounded with everything left behind on the family farm. Everywhere but in the house.

"Everything will be fine."

Everything was *not* fine.

The storm worsened. The tractor broke down next, as night smothered us.

John's games of Solitaire picked up frequency. He refused to talk to me. He stopped trying to clear the yard with the small blower. Instead, he muttered to himself as if he were having a conversation, walking through the cards, complaining about the deal, treating me as if I'd hidden cards from him out of spite.

"He's here."

John's voice sounded weak. Small. Two descriptors I'd never applied to John. He was breathing hard, and rubbing at his left arm while he leaned against the door frame with his right side. Sweat ringed his brow, and he looked pale and sallow. I took a step towards him and he fell to his knees.

He murmured, "He found me. He's been waiting for me."

"Who, John? Who?"

"He's here."

The last word barely passed his lips when he collapsed into my arms. It couldn't be a heart attack. John was young. Strong. He couldn't die on me. Not now. Not here.

But he *was* dying. I knew he was.

I called 911. My phone beeped and died the moment the call connected.

"Shit. Shit. Shit."

I scrambled for the land line before I remembered: it wasn't connected.

"Don't leave," John rasped.

"I'm not going anywhere," I said.

I tried my cell again. Again. Again. *Again*. The call connected.

"911, what's your emergency?"

"My husband," I panted. "He's having a heart attack."

"Are you alone?"

"Yes."

"Do you know CPR?"

"Yes. No. I . . . I think so. It's been a long time. I . . . don't know."

"Where are you?"

"Oh, God," I muttered. "We just moved here. Out in the country. Uh . . . southwest . . . east. Southeast of town."

I tried to remember John's directions. Mile roads. The numbers wouldn't come.

I tried not to wail. I wiped away tears and snot with my sleeve. "He's going to die, and it's my fault."

The operator tried to calm me. I barely heard them.

John leaned against the doorframe, breathing hard. "Seven miles south, four miles east from Century Road," he said.

The operator must have heard him, bless her, before I could repeat John's directions, she said, "We've dispatched an ambulance. Help is on the way. Stay on the line."

"The ambulance can't get through."

The furnace died.

The power followed.

Outside, the storm intensified, and took the last of my hope with it.

We were alone in the cold and dark. Me, and John. And John's fevered whispers.

I couldn't ask him to go downstairs, let alone try and fix the furnace. The cold had already insinuated itself into the house. No escaping the slow, gradual freeze. By the time anyone found us, there'd be nothing left to find.

We shivered in our blankets. John didn't look well, but I didn't think he was going to die in my arms.

"There should be an old kerosene heater stashed somewhere," John said. "If it didn't get sold, or stolen."

"Where?"

"One of the sheds . . . the cellar in the old house, maybe." He sighed. "Things are gone. I remembered the batteries being here the last time I was out. When we bought the land. Gone."

"You stay here," I said. "I'll be back soon. It'll be okay."

The snow smothered everything. The silence swallowed me. All I could hear was my heart thudding against my chest and my muffled footfalls. The old house's door was locked. I turned around the wood burned sign beside the door reading: Hildebrandts, and found a skeleton key resting in a groove cut to its size. I took off my gloves to pry it free. My nail bent backwards and I hissed, sucking at the ragged tear.

I tried the door and the hinges squealed. I winced at the sound, but it opened.

Through an empty porch the old house was as barren as the new house. According to John's stories, it'd been crammed floor to ceiling with antiques and auction buys when he was a kid. Had it been cleaned out when the new house had been built, or before we took title on the property out of spite? The floor creaked loudly in protest to my steps. Between the intersecting walls and cupboards there was a hole outlined in the far corner of the kitchen floor. Stark particle board amid worn linoleum with a circular door pull. The door groaned open. I propped it against the wall, engaged a hooked latch to hold it in place, and peered down. A rickety ladder set on a slight incline instead of stairs ended in a dirt floor.

That was some *Evil Dead* shit down there.

The cellar smelled of rot and cold stones. I descended. It was *cold* but at least there was no wind. I worried with each creak that the whole thing would tumble down on top of me. Worried I'd be entombed here with the worms and mouse shit while John froze to death. I steeled myself. I wouldn't let John down. I *couldn't*. *He needed me.*

I whispered the words aloud to reinforce them. To *be* needed. The shadows answered, "*Does he? Does he need you?*"

A shape stepped out of the shadows. *The* Shape.

Up close, he looked a lot like John. Harder edges, eyes a little too bright, a too-wide smile that held no kindness, *but oh, how he smiled*. Bald, bearded; his crisp white suit shining incandescent against the stone walls. He moved with a smoothness I couldn't believe. Practically danced closer to me. He didn't hunch from the cold. Somehow, I recognized him as both the man who'd tried to run us off the road and the shape out the window.

He shook his head. "You really believe he gets to be happy, Jack?"

"He'd be happy if the furnace worked."

It was the bravest thing I could think of saying.

"You'll never keep him. I have plans for him." The Shape's smile widened. He drew a deck of cards—John's cards. Shuffled and removed one before tucking the pack into his suit pocket. He showed me the card without looking. "Ace of Spades."

I ignored his magic trick. "*I* have plans for John, too."

"We'll see. We'll see. He hasn't told you about me? He's been talking to me since he got here."

"Bullshit," I said, believing every word.

"I met him for the first time right in this cellar? There was a tornado. He was here praying with his grandma." He looked at the floorboards above us. "Something had to answer all those fervent prayers."

Some*thing*, not some*one*.

John had told me that story. I'd always felt there'd been something he'd left out. Something he couldn't share. John had lots of stories like that. At first, I'd thought the story was cute; a boy and his grandmother praying together in the cellar. It'd been cute because they'd both survived. The tornado passed over the house. They'd lost nothing. Except John *had* lost something in this cellar. And I worried *I'd* lose him down here too.

"Who are you?" My voice didn't sound right, as if the question had been dragged out against my will. I wanted an answer but I didn't want to hear it.

"You know me. *Everyone* knows me. But today, I'm him. I'm his father. His grandfather. I'm what he was, is, and will become. He can't escape me. Even if he isn't playing my game."

His game. The Devil's game.

"Heater's right here." Long fingernails clacked off metal. "But you won't use it. Ask John about us. We go way back."

I dragged the heater to the ladder. It looked like an oversized camping lantern. It might keep us alive, but we wouldn't be comfortable. I looked at the Shape—the Devil. Somehow real. Somehow here. I doubted I'd ever be comfortable again.

"I'd offer to help, but you know . . ."

The Devil patted his suit.

I set the heater on the ladder. When I looked back, I was alone.

I didn't want to tell John about the encounter. When he saw my face, he knew.

"You need to go," John said. "Take the snowmobile."

"But I have the heater."

"*Go.*"

"What about you? What about . . . *him*? I won't leave you with him."

"I'll deal with him." He shuffled his cards weakly, dropping most.

I knelt and gathered the cards, pressing them into his hand. "I'm *not* leaving you."

"You can. And you will."

His words felt like prophecy. As if any future he could see for himself no longer included me. *Couldn't* include me.

"No."

"Goddammit!" He slammed a fist into a kitchen cabinet, splintering it. "Listen to me! The Devil's chased my family for a long time. Since before I was born. My grandad, then my dad, now me. Always targeting the eldest sons. I used to believe. Then I thought it was bullshit. Thought it died with my dad. Couldn't be me, because I've never felt a part of my own family. But it didn't die. It can't. It never will. God help me, I believe again. He'll keep me playing until the game's done."

"This isn't a game, John."

"You need to go, and be warm. Go to the Klassens'. Go to Mom's. Just *go*. Someone will come for me."

I wasn't so certain. Standing aside while we died might leave their hands clean in their minds. I was less certain I could find my way to their house in a complete whiteout.

I sensed the Devil in our house. His eyes shining through the hole in the wall, his whispers filling my ears, voice so like John's. "What're you going to do, Jack?"

Unseen fingers drew lazy circles on my back.

We left. For once in his life, John was too weak to fight me, and I got him on the snowmobile. The snow swallowed the barn, the house, our dream of a life together here. Those I left for the snow, and the cold, to do with as they willed. Such a simple dream. Making *a* home into *our* home. I'd believed we could do it.

Flashing blue eyes ahead. Ambulance lights, or a snow plow? The Devil in his bright white suit, come to claim John? The snowmobile engine screamed. Inhuman. The glowing lights didn't look like salvation. I slowed, so I could hold John. I so wanted to let go. I couldn't let go.

"Hold on," I said. "Hold on."

When we reached the ambulance, John pulled a card from his sleeve. The Ace of Spades again. John howled a laugh the wind couldn't swallow. I heard another, answering, laugh, familiar, echoing in my mind, drifting in the darkness, glittering like snow against the moon.

Chadwick Ginther has driven through ridiculous winter storms so he could be trapped with friends who played Dungeons & Dragons and has been the only roommate willing to leave the warmth of the apartment in -30 weather for a bag of chips. He is also the Prix Aurora Award-winning author of *Khyber: Sinister Tales of Sword and Sorcery*, The Thunder Road series, *Graveyard Mind*, and numerous short stories. He lives in Winnipeg, Canada where he writes stories full of skeletons, giants, and dragons. Find him at www.chadwickginther.com

The Chestnut Avenue

SAM HICKS

I was twelve, or thereabouts, when my parents sold our house for a larger one, only two streets down. It was the custom in their circle to move around like that, blaming their restlessness on their children's hypothetical demands. They'd move out to rural properties "with space for the kids to run around" and then back to the town "to be nearer to the schools," or like my parents, swap streets because little Jane or Johnny "needed a bigger room." But, as it was, we had some kind of delay in the move and would be renting for three weeks, including, controversially in my opinion, Christmas. A farmhouse, I was told, divided into two, a few miles out.

It was reached by one of those hedge-dark, one-lane roads, where the flat fields spread out on either side, and tractors lie in ambush around every other corner. Then it was a turn onto a tree-lined driveway where the going was so rough that our speed didn't rise above a crawl, and Dad hunched over the steering wheel like a shaky old codger. But even in slow motion it was a shock when the trees stopped and, behind a sweep of lawn, the house sprang into view; it was so peculiarly long and low, and a fading warmth seemed to fall across its whitewashed walls and to ignite soft loops of light in its leaded windows, even though the sun hadn't been seen for several days.

"There's a ghost," I said, when we were almost past. "See, up there."

And Dad, glancing up, saw it too. The image of a face, insubstantial as muslin, semi-transparent, attached to nothing, I thought, behind an upper window's glass.

"Don't be daft. That's not a ghost. Not yet, anyway," he said. "That's very much an old woman. But give it time."

Mum leaned across, too late. "I think the Lewises have an aunt, or something. Probably her."

But I wasn't convinced. I believed in ghosts as a fact of life, and my close reading of *Supernatural Mysteries* magazine had given me a pretty good idea of what they looked like. The grey ladies, the weeping urchins, and the face at window, being incompletely in this world, were all cut from the same flimsy stuff.

We pulled into the yard that served the farm, with its barns and little duck pond, and an immense metal silo for grain I'd already been warned to keep well away from. Two yellow Labradors wagged across the gated courtyard behind the house, bringing a middle-aged woman in their wake.

"Watch out. Here comes the welcoming committee," Dad said, as he stopped the car. "Let's hope Colin's not about. I could do without him droning on about drainage ditches for hours."

"Be nice," Mum said, unclipping her seat belt. "They're doing us a favour."

I'd never met Mrs Lewis, and had no idea how she knew my parents, but as she came across the courtyard to open the gate, I felt I'd seen her before. There were a lot of her around there, these women whose hardy, cheerful natures served as well for wrangling animals and Land Rovers as they did for troublesome husbands. She wore her hair in a coarse, blondish bob, the compulsory country woman haircut, and I imagined her smile was the same she used when she knuckled down for a night delivery in the heat of a lambing shed.

"Come and warm up," she said, leaning down to the driver side, "and I'll get you your keys."

We stood in a big, stone-floored, meat-smelling kitchen, while the Labradors circled us in vain, and Mrs Lewis—Belinda—dug around in an old Welsh dresser for the keys to our part of the house. "Shall I take you over?" she said when, eventually, she found them, and something needy, a hint of dogginess, showed for a second in her small brown eyes.

"No need," Mum said, quickly. "Colin showed us everything last week."

"Oh yes. Of course." She pressed the keys into Mum's hand, like a present. "I wasn't here, was I? You see, I had a—"

"You know you've got a ghost upstairs?" I couldn't hold it any longer. All I wanted was my suspicions confirmed, so I could get on with other things.

"What?" said Belinda. She looked down, seeing me, I think, for the first time.

Dad nudged me in the back. "Sorry. She saw someone upstairs, that's all. Your aunt, was it?"

Belinda threw back her head and gave an extravagant laugh, and the dogs looked up in unison, as if it meant food was in the offing. "You mean Lucy? Colin's great-aunt? No, she's not a ghost, young lady. She's just very, very old. Lucy's always lived here, since a girl. She was here when Colin was a boy, and I wouldn't be surprised if she outlives us all, I really wouldn't. Comes with the house, does Lucy. Technically, it's hers, I mean, legally, you know, but Colin can do whatever he wants, and it'll come to him soon enough, but I suppose I shouldn't say that, should I?"

"Just how old is she?" Dad said, putting his arm around my shoulder, pulling me a little closer.

"Lucy? God knows. Just you try getting her to say. Nineties, maybe? Colin says he sometimes thinks she's always been the same age. But you won't see much of Lucy, not in winter. Her blood's like ice nowadays. She makes it out to the courtyard in summer—oh, she can still get around—and she'll sit there in her rocking chair on the hottest days, all wrapped up in her shawls. We say she's thawing out."

It was a blow, of course, to be told I was wrong when I'd been so absolutely certain. It was entirely possible though, but not worth the arguing, that the ghost and the old woman were not one and the same. But I pretended not to care, looking out the window to the lawn and the fields and woods beyond. It was hard to gauge how far the trees went, but I had the impression they covered the entire side of the first ploughed field.

"Well, I think that's everything," Belinda was saying. "But you know where we are. Oh, and the girl is welcome to explore the garden and the woods, though bits are hopelessly overgrown. Just steer clear of machinery. And the grain silo. And the haystack in the barn."

"Who's that man outside?" I said. He was walking slowly backwards, gnarled fingers knotted around a long wooden handle—a rake or spade I guessed—the weathered face beneath the flat cap deadly serious, a smouldering tobacco pipe dangling against his chin.

"Oh, heavens," Mum gasped.

Belinda turned to me. "He's not a ghost either, dear. That's Charlie. Colin hates leaves on the lawn, so you'll see a lot of him. He chases leaves around at this time of year, like a cat."

There was no connecting door between the two parts of the house, or "wings" as Belinda called them, as though, long ago, some rift in the family had split it into walled-off factions. Our part was like a country hotel, with striped wallpaper, cracked leather sofas and chairs, brass lamps with burgundy shades, and framed hunting scenes everywhere. But in the hallway leading to the stairs, and on the landing at the top, stood two dark oak chests, nearly black, with fascinating flowers and faces carved into their sides, that Dad said were centuries old. The ceilings in all the rooms were low, and they and the small windows lent everything a feel of perpetual dusk.

I was confined, for that first weekend, within this eccentric vision of rustic luxe, since as soon we'd unpacked, the heavens opened. Not that a little thing like torrential rain deterred the trusty Charlie. All the windows but the kitchen's faced the lawn, and his becaped form, like a deep-sea fisherman clearing the catch from the decks, or a waterproofed grim reaper, would pass by at regular intervals, solemnly steering his rake. He did an hour in the mornings and afternoons, and Mum said she felt sorry for him, that it must be some kind of madness of Colin's, to be so obsessed with leaves.

"He's getting paid, isn't he?" I said. "And it looks like he's used to it."

"That's a little hard, don't you think?" she said, like she did whenever I came out with something undeniable.

And I still didn't get the chance to explore outside the house in the days that followed. It was the last week of term before the

Christmas break and dark when Dad drove Mum to work and me to school, and dark again on the way back in the afternoon, and all we seemed to do was shunt back and forth through a state of night to closed-in, stuffy rooms. In the back seat, I'd listen to them talk, and I suppose they thought I wouldn't be able to fill in the gaps of their private squabbles and snips of local gossip, although why they'd underestimate me like that, I really didn't know. But I'd stopped listening while we went along the driveway, because I was trying to work something out, and it seemed to me that it was at about the halfway mark where the trees became a single line, and that the woods at the side of the field must be nowhere near as extensive as I'd thought.

The wind came down from the North on Friday, and on Saturday morning there were lacy whorls of ice on the outsides of the windows, and when I saw the thick frost on the lawn I was as thrilled by the transformation, and the thought of going out in it, as if it had been snow. After breakfast, I told Mum I was going to look around the woods and she made me wear two scarves as well as a hat and promise to be back by lunch. Things were different then; you were trusted to the wild.

I had to go around our end of the house, past a bed of brutally pruned rose bushes, to reach the lawn. My boots crunched satisfyingly in the frozen grass; I could see my footprints when I looked back, and my breath making smoky billows. I came across a few fallen leaves when I neared the other side; curled and crisp and dusted with sparkles, ribbed in glittering white. Rich pickings for Charlie, I thought.

There was a discernible path running into the trees, but with little foliage about, you could still see through to the ridges of the field on the left-hand side. I think I felt, as I walked along, the quiet awareness that all woods, of whatever size, possess, and I kept stopping to track the tree trunks' height and then on to the searching tips of their highest branches, thinking, did they have somewhere that they called a head and could they, in some way, see?

The leaves on the path were delicate and coppery, and their frosting made me think of ginger biscuits, and then I came into a fall of thin, lemony slivers which looked equally delicious. There was a story I recalled, where a starving girl found some cakes laid out in a forest. She remembered too late, as she wolfed them down, the warnings about fairy food, and then they, the hidden folk, came and took her. Serves her right, I thought. Who eats cakes they find in the woods?

Before long I'd reached the turn in the path that would take me back to the lawn, but here I stepped away, deeper into the trees, where the prospect—the dark crossings of the branches, and the scintillant light—was so enchanting, so exactly like one of those glittered Christmas cards where winter seems like a place, not a time. I patted the trees as I passed, scuffing through the leaves, moving across to where I thought I'd meet the other leg of the path. But after a short way, I met a kind of living wall.

I couldn't fit a finger between the weave of twigs and thorns, or see through more than a few inches, and this resistant barrier towered to at least three times my height. I walked down, almost back to the start of the lawn, finding no gap in the growth, no deliberate opening, and then I retraced my steps, following this enigmatic work of nature all the way back to the other side. It took up a good part of the central section of the woods, although, when I stepped back, I thought the same thickness of growth couldn't extend all the way through, since I could see the twisted branches of full-size trees growing up above the top. Nature, it seemed, had made a prison.

Was it natural though? When I walked to the end, I found the corners sharp and square. Charlie, maybe, keeping everything shipshape? Did he do a stint up here when he'd finished chasing leaves? So, was it meant to be some kind of decorative feature, perhaps coming into bloom when spring arrived? But, as I went down along the other side, I felt there was nothing like that about it, nothing ornamental. The branches growing into other branches, the thorns that cut through other thorns, and the ivy that had colonised any remaining spaces, reminded me of the structures that rose out of the mists in the worlds of Frankenstein and Dracula; mausoleums, ancestral tombs and temples, or at least how I remembered them from the few films like that I'd seen.

Finally, after inspecting every side and finding it impenetrable, I regained the last section of the path and started back towards the lawn. The house, across the stretch of glittering white, had the same glow as the wax of a lit candle. I imagined it was moving, not I, as I approached; that it was slipping back through all its centuries. And then I saw her again, the ghost—or as they'd have me believe, Great Aunt Lucy—at the same window as before. The image of a face, blurring as it tried to fix itself to where it was, and then, as it failed to hold onto form, dimming slowly into darkness.

Once indoors, I told Mum and Dad about the enclosure in the woods, but they weren't the least interested, only repeating what Belinda had said about things being overgrown. And when I looked out from the sitting room to where the lawn, the trees, the field, were bright with a moving, skipping light, I wished I hadn't mentioned it, because the chances were, even if they went to the woods, they'd never have noticed it was there.

On Sunday, Mum and Dad left me alone all afternoon while they went into town for something involving friends and cheese and wine. It was raining when they drove off, and I think they assumed that, as I'd said, I'd be keeping myself out of trouble with the television and my books. But the rain cleared after half an hour and I'd had no intention, anyway, of staying stuck indoors. All the frosty magic of the day before had been washed away by the rain, and the wind must have brought down more leaves because when I rounded the corner of the house, I saw old Charlie in the distance, emptying a full wheelbarrow into a blue plastic sack.

The path into the woods was slippery, with the crystalline leaves now turned gelatinous and black, and the breeze was shaking down even more, so all around me was a travelling, pattering sound, like the catching of a fire. I made my way through to the wall of thorn and twig, determined to find a weakness, a place that could be breached with a little initiative. Perhaps I could find some fallen branches and lean them up, as a sort of ladder? At least then I'd be able to see what was on the other side. But after only a few minutes of following those inscrutable limits, I found that no effort would be required.

I remembered, from the day before, the tree stump that sprouted fleshy ears of fungus from its smooth flat top, but now, nearby, was an opening; a neatly clipped passage through the growth, with the cut ends showing white as though their wounds hadn't had time to heal. Was this, as well, the indefatigable Charlie's work? It was wide enough for one person, though only just, and ran for about six feet.

There was no mausoleum, no ancestral tomb, on the other side; instead, I came out into what I instantly thought of as an avenue, like you'd find in a public park. Its length I already knew by the extent of its enclosure, but when I crossed into the central part, I could have believed it was limitless, that it carried on across the lawn and through the house, as far as the horizon. On either side, trees dipped their branches inward, and in making contact, in combining, stole the view's sharpness, so that very quickly it was scraps and snatches, scored lines and speckled light, and where its end point was, or its beginning, was impossible to judge.

The grass was short and regular. Brambles and nettles hadn't gained a hold—Charlie's work again, I guessed. My knowledge of trees was limited, and it's not much better now, but one of the few I knew was sweet chestnut, because there was one not far from our old house. I recognised the prickly shells that lay about, so decomposed that the bared insides had turned to wet black coal. And I recognised the fallen leaves, once like straight spear heads, but now desiccated and drawn up around drops of smutted water. But still some leaves hung, limply attached, like hands with no strength left, and they were umber, terracotta, white.

I walked a little way, in no hurry, and faintly wary of going all the way to the end. They must have been planted long ago, those trees. A place for the local gentry to stroll with parasols and picnics, a tamed piece of nature, a living folly. The trees would have been smooth and straight back then, but now, left to themselves and locked away, they'd grown a little monstrous. Their branches forked at each swollen joint, sharply angling into imitations of violent human movements. Their trunks— massively wide and clubbed at the roots—twisted as though huge hands had taken them and tried to wring them to death.

I stopped at one whose trunk was so swollen by lumps and burrs that it looked as if it were under parasitical attack, and at another with a cracked and sooty core from which the bark drew back like the flesh. I saw, when I went closer, cobwebs, white inside its folds. The likenesses of open mouths, swollen eyes, injured breasts, pressed themselves through roughcast bark, which, when I put my hands to it, I found to be like mud; damp, and quick to turn to mush. I paused, alert. Although the wind had dropped, I could see one single leaf beside me nudging at a breeze I couldn't feel, and although it was that one alone that moved, a sound, a papery fluttering, now filled the air, softly spreading.

As the leaves began to fall, as I knew they would, something happened to me, a mild disorientation that I recall as a slight vertigo, a floating, and a dimming of the light. The overhanging branches, their camouflage, made even fairly close things difficult to distinguish, but I thought I could see something moving to the left of a tree so contorted that it looked as though it had, for centuries, been trying to rip itself from the earth. A shadow, perhaps, but on that overcast afternoon, the shadows were barely there. And when it moved, with a slow sway, out into the open space, I thought it must be an effect of the branches, how they made shapes from nothing. But it became more defined, less a thing of bark and leaf and air, more the semblance of a human being, only without detail, without real life, but owning, even so, I was sure, a kind of awareness. It began to move towards me.

I felt a jolt, at once draining and electrifying; an upturned, drowning feeling, like I was tumbling from a cliff. I scrambled backwards, nearly falling, and began to run, terrified for one mad moment that the passageway might be gone, that I'd be trapped forever. But the white tips of the severed twigs and the needles of the thorns came rushing up to meet me, and I dived inside and tore through, clumsy, colliding, so that I snagged my hair, scratched my hands and lost a button from my coat.

And then I was out, dodging between the trees, and seeing, with relief, the dull brown and bronze of the ploughed field, and then the lawn lying before me, a vision of tranquillity, only disturbed, I saw when I looked back, by the trail of sweet chestnut leaves I'd left behind, as though I'd laid it out for someone else to follow.

Once in the safety of my bedroom, I pushed a chair against the door, and because I was shaking so much, wrapped myself in a blanket as I huddled, facing the window, at the end of the single bed. When Charlie appeared, I moved closer to the glass. He always started his Sisyphean work at the top, nearest the woods, so I didn't have long to wait, and when he came across the trail of leaves, I saw him stop, or rather, experience a sudden interruption in himself, as though awaking from a purely automatic state. But he didn't look up towards our wing of the house, searching for signs of the perpetrator. He gazed instead to the other half, to where the ghost lady lived, and it occurred to me then that I hadn't seen her, or had forgotten to look, when I ran back over the lawn. He stayed like that for a while, as if not quite sure how to proceed, staring up, pipe dangling in puzzlement. And then, pulling himself together, with precise and decisive movements, he began to rake the leaves away.

The comforts, even escapism, of skepticism, were new to me, and I never thought to question why I, normally so credulous, was now so keen to rationalise what I had seen. Had I mistaken a person, an employee of the Lewises, perhaps, for something not quite real? And what if the place was another item on Belinda's forbidden list? Had I been caught trespassing? Had this person, the man I couldn't clearly see, been about to warn me off, and wasn't it only natural that I'd want to run from him? I did my best to persuade myself, adding details to that elementary form, so that now the man might have been very tall, and holding an axe— or at least a stick—and I said nothing about the avenue to Mum and Dad, and for the next few days I stayed inside, apart from a few cold walks along the fields, and I think I'd have kept away from the woods altogether if Natasha hadn't turned up.

Mum had taken our last two weeks in the house as leave, and she embraced this freedom by inviting a succession of her friends over for lunch. The lunches usually led to wine, and in the week leading up to Christmas I spent a lot of avoidant time in my bedroom, reading or trying to do a thousand-piece jigsaw puzzle of a scene from *The Lord of the Rings*. I wasn't bothered by the situation. The friends had usually gone by late afternoon, when I'd descend to assess what state of mild inebriation Mum was in, and if it would be casserole or Chinese takeaway that evening, and I thought it was quite funny, to see her flushed and hiccupping and trying to appear normal. The only hitch in this arrangement came on the eve of Christmas Eve. One of the friends was due for "afternoon drinks", and I'd already withdrawn to my room with a plate of biscuits and my new book on UFOs, when Mum called me downstairs.

They looked like a firing squad, all lined up in the sitting room;

Mum, her friend Dawn—a woman I'd never warmed to because she always wanted to stroke my head—and Dawn's daughter, Natasha, who, it so happened, had recently slipped in and out of my parents' conversations in the car. A nightmare. Running amok. Boyfriends, drinking, shoplifting. I'd last seen her two years ago, in similar circumstances—when she was fobbed off on me by Mum and Dawn. Even then, she'd been a pain, boasting about the pool and riding lessons at her private school, as condescending and derisive as only a precocious twelve-year-old can be; amazed by, and scathing of, everything I said and did. But now, at fourteen, that girl was gone, replaced by someone who looked ready to start a fight, or had just been in one. She had a proper grown-up body now, and a woman's face glowered darkly beneath her yellow spikes of hair; she was a couple of years too late for punk, but to be fair, in those parts, we were all a bit behind the times.

We stood our ground, Mum, Dawn, Natasha, and me, weighing each other up. Oh, I understood. Dawn wouldn't leave this changeling alone at home, in case she started a riot.

Mum broke the stand-off. "Do you want to take Natasha for a walk, dear? While Dawn and I do some catching up?"

I didn't exactly know what I was thinking, what I had in mind, when I said; "Yes. Great! Come on then, Tash." She was actually chewing gum, with classic, almost iconic, teenage insolence.

As we walked together over the lawn, she gave me a snaky look and said; "So you're still wearing those kind of jeans?" and I had to hand it to her, she knew her stuff, because I instantly felt self-conscious, childish, unfashionable, and far too defeated to give her a sound slap. But I was going to take her to the avenue. I knew something she didn't. The man might be there, lurking. He might come after us, but I knew my way around and she'd be at a disadvantage, running scared, whimpering, and that would do just fine. Or if he wasn't there, I'd just make up stories about him, as we stood beneath the deformed trees. I'd make them so lurid, I'd make them so gory, that she'd see him in every looming shadow and every crooked branch. Poor reasoning of course, but, well, that was the only kind I had.

A breeze sifted through the trees as I led us from the path, setting off little whispers, and Natasha began to whine; "Why are we going off the path? I don't want to. I'm going back."

"No!" I said it too loud, and she looked at me as though I was stupid as well as mad. "There's something in here I want to show you." And then, seeing she was about to turn away, I dealt my coup de grâce. "But you can't tell your mum. No one's meant to go there."

She shoved her hands in the pockets of her leather jacket and gave a weird sarcastic yip of a laugh. "Okay. If it shuts you up."

I spotted my landmark, the tree stump, but when I reached it, I didn't recognise the thick sawn welts across its top, and what fungus grew there had rotted down to ooze, and, the most important thing, there was no passageway behind. But I wasn't going to admit I'd made a mistake. "Up here," I said, avoiding Natasha's eyes, and as I began following the thorny wall in the other direction, I began to wonder how anyone had ever managed to cut their way through it, how I hadn't heard a chainsaw from the house. It was like a bank of coral, but as tough as rock, and the deepest parts couldn't have been touched by the sun for years. Behind me, twigs snapped angrily, and I heard a muttered "Moron", and I stopped, thinking with new clarity that the passageway must have been to the left of the tree stump, not the right, and we'd easily find it if we went back, and if we didn't, I'd tell Natasha it'd been a joke, that I was having fun with her, and that in itself would be a win. But when I turned, she was peering at the raw white of some newly cut twigs, and I couldn't quite take it in, how it was there, how I could have walked straight past.

"Are we meant to go in here?" she said. I nodded dumbly, and she disappeared before I could tell her anything else. She must have run, because I found her, when I emerged from the passageway—which seemed, if anything, slightly tighter—already standing in the centre of the grass between the chestnut trees, and when she turned her head, I was impressed by how suddenly her mood could change.

"Wow," she said. "Thanks for bringing me."

But it wasn't right. It was lovely, and above us, the heavy clouds had parted to clear, pure blue, and the overhanging branches, as they receded, trapped shivering, pearly light, like the air between them had a gleam, some strange and subtle shine. Natasha had paused beneath a tree that had no cruel twists in its bark, miraculously untouched by growths and knots. Its branches, young and pliable, lowered sprays of pinkish buds, like a dainty bridal veil.

I followed her, stunned by the difference the sky, the sun, simply not being alone, could make. They seemed so protective, those trees, their grotesqueness turned to sheltering solidity, and as we walked, their lowest branches brushed our heads with what felt like friendly reassurance. At the very end, we stared up at the stateliest amongst them; a straight strong giant whose cavities and growths were smooth and shallow, whose bark flowed peacefully around the junctures of its branches. Natasha turned a wondering face towards mine. "It's perfect, isn't it?" And as she spoke the sun struck the bark of the tree, lighting it with auburn warmth.

"Look!" She ran past, to the wall of thorn, and—too unlikely, too incredible—squatted down by a swathe of darkest green and spotless white; snowdrops, just coming into bloom. It was as though, I thought, it had all been prepared for us.

There was a rustle behind me, and I swung around to see the tail of a grey squirrel flicking down into the ivy that cloaked one of the trees. The leaves shook as the animal went deeper, and I was for a moment, mesmerised by their dark lustre, the vigour of their growth, and how they circled all the way to the forked, bare crown; how the life of the tree had been trapped and buried by another life's needs.

"Let's go, Tash," I said.

"Why?" Her eyes shone, impressionable, hurtable, young. I shouldn't have brought her. I'd preferred her as she was.

"Because we're not meant to be here."

"So what?"

"I'll leave you here then." And I turned back up the avenue. There were only trees, and flowers, and sunshine there, and I lacked the power to articulate my disappointment, or to understand that, in trying to create distance, to rationalise what had happened there before, I was really hoping I hadn't dreamt that apparitional form, and that it would appear again and prove itself not human.

Natasha came running when I reached the passageway, and when we were back to the woods, she said; "I don't know what the rush is. Those bitches wanted us out the house."

"Wanted *you* out the house, more like."

"Piss off, little girl."

We walked back to the path in angry silence, although I wondered why, if she liked the avenue so much, she didn't want to stay behind.

At the lawn, she went ahead of me, and she didn't see when I looked back and found no telltale trail of leaves. Nor did she notice, as she stomped off towards the rose beds, the figure at the far side of the lawn, just by the house, who, at first, I assumed must be Charlie, but who, as I crossed and gave one more glance, took on another form; grey, shawled, stooped over two walking sticks, hair frost-white, and her eyes, I felt even from that distance, fixed watchfully on me. Hadn't Belinda said that, in winter, the icy old woman never left the house? Maybe she'd experienced an early thaw this year.

Christmas Day felt awkward and forced in that place. Mum had hung a couple of paper chains, but they, and the tree, didn't really seem to belong to us. In the morning, when Mum and Dad were in the kitchen and I was still studying *The Big Book of Mysteries* they'd given me, I heard a clatter and the rise of politely enthusiastic voices, and I went over and closed the door so I wouldn't have to hear Belinda and Colin making the day even stranger; the day that had always been the same, just us three and no one else. They stayed for half an hour and I imagine sherry was drunk, and when the coast was clear, Mum called me into the kitchen to help with the Brussels sprouts, and the roast dinner smelled like it would in someone else's house.

In the afternoon we saw Charlie, out raking the lawn. "Unbelievable!" Dad said.

We went to the woods together on Boxing Day, and they didn't think of coming off the path, and I said nothing about the chestnut avenue, only pointing, when they asked, to where the walls of trees and bushes were.

I was taken to one of my friend's on the following Tuesday afternoon, and she and I roamed the waste ground near her house and set fire to some paper sacks in an abandoned shed and ran away when the flames started to spread out of control, watching at a distance as the wood slats burst apart and the roof caught and the whole thing became magnificent and wild, like the blazing heart of a star.

There was only one day left to go at the farm when it began to snow. The little tree and the few decorations we'd brought with us were taken down, and our bags were packed and I was more than anything looking forward to having my own bed back, and the flannelette sheets that Mum got out in winter, even if it was in a new house. When I opened the bedroom curtains and saw the first few wandering white dots, it felt like a celebration; the chance to see this place—the lawn, the woods, the long roof of the house—turned white and fantastical before we left for good.

When I went downstairs, the light in the sitting room had gathered a strange tinge of blue, and I didn't see Mum, at first, standing to the side of window, watching the snow, now much heavier, in its loose and sleepy fall.

"I expect you'll want to go out in this," she said, "as it's our last day." She spoke with her back to me and I had the oddest feeling, which I put down to that eerie light, that it wasn't quite her normal voice, and that it came from somewhere else.

"I'll just have some toast first," I said.

She turned, as though I'd startled her. "Okay, dear. Make sure you wear two scarves if you go out."

The snow had already feathered the margins of the roof tiles and filled in the crooks of the skinny rosebushes, and when I stepped onto the lawn, a gust sent flurries chasing sideways, skimming, and then the brief wind dropped, and I gazed up, dizzily, into spinning circles that seemed to centre themselves on me.

Only a few ragged black patches broke the clean white of the field, and as I entered the woods, the steady smothering of the snow brought a muffled quiet, sinking gently. I seemed so far away already, and as I went off the path, everything moved in and out of sight, blanking away and coming back, appearing in instants of monochrome, and it was as though I saw things in my memory only when I'd passed; the unburied sides of the dead leaves, the shadowed trees, and their terminal shoots, the coldest parts, gathering smooth white sheathes.

It was roughly where it had been before, the passageway—or do I mean roughly where I remembered it?—and the snow had collected thickly there, almost an inch deep, and had clumped in small irregular fins between the twigs, and when I came out into the avenue, I was overwhelmed for a moment by how remote, how distant from the real world it seemed, enclosed now from above as well as from the sides, the sky almost reachable, almost within touching distance.

I walked a little way. There was a tree like a black flame, all its branches gone, just the trunk tapering up, rising through the swarm of white that was like a million living things, seeking around, rising up a little, scouting. And then, a tree I'd noticed that first time, the illusion of movement even more convincing through the screen of the snow, even more like the two halves of it were trying to pull themselves apart.

The avenue was infinite, the trees, everything diffuse and dancing. A face, I thought, was up there, a young woman's face, and I immediately thought of Natasha, although, as I was about to call out, I knew it couldn't possibly be her, and yet she seemed familiar, that girl, someone I'd seen and of whom I had no fear. But I couldn't be sure of it. Was the face just something spun out of the snow, the strange remaking of it?

I advanced slightly, calling "Hello?" until, seeing a low branch not far ahead that was moving a little too much, I stopped. It lifted up, so it seemed to have two long, bowed legs. Could it be, though, only a branch that reared as if it had a spine and shoulders, whose semblance of arms, sharp-jointed, strung hard, flexured, swung into the air? Was it shadow, in tones of darkest blue, making it seem to have some kind of head, but with too many mouths, too many empty eyes? I could see the girl, leaning, gazing up. She wore a long and loose grey dress, and her hands fluttered in a mad, uncertain way, until they found whatever stooping thing it was, and finding it, clutched tight. Her hair touched her waist, white, as she gracefully, like a dancer, arched backwards, in a movement of complete surrender.

I turned, quite calmly, as I might if I'd come across two lovers doing something I wasn't ready to see. Some instinct, I suppose, told me to make no sudden moves—the preternatural detachment that takes over in disaster. They weren't quite voices, the sounds I tried not to hear, but rather insinuations, the thin leavings of hissed syllables, and if I screamed, I thought, it might hang, like shattered glass, in the air. For all my legs were moving, the passageway seemed to be further away, to not be coming any closer, and I hoped, for a desperate moment, that I was asleep, that I was dreaming, but then I saw, through the snow, the limbs, the crippled torsos, the black lightning of those trees, and I knew

I was really there and that I'd come there all too willingly, when I should have kept away.

Another shadow appeared, ahead of me, but straight-edged, grey, an opening, and I walked, still unhurriedly, towards it. It had grown in already, so I had to go through sideways, and as I turned my shoulders, I heard an unmistakable human sigh, and something flitted, dark and dipping, maybe only a bird, low over my head. In two pushes I was into the woods, and I made my way, letting my breath come back, through the trees and onto the path. The front of my coat was caked with white, except for one spot where it had fallen away, over my heart, and I felt cold inside, all the way through to my spine, but still I didn't run. I hunched forward, as though I were dragging a dead, invisible weight. I willed myself along, even though something inside was telling me to stop, lie down, and sleep.

The long low house had almost vanished in the snow. As I approached, as finally I was crossing the lawn and could at last see the windows and the light in our sitting room, I couldn't be sure if it was Mum, standing by the wall at our end of the house, or a bush I'd never noticed before. Only when I was a few feet away did I see the white hair, half-covered by a thick green shawl, the clouded blue of her stare, and the caved and wrinkled cheeks. She leaned on her two walking sticks, waiting.

"Did you see me?" she said. Her voice was phlegmy, rough.

"When do you mean?" I knew, though, it was no ordinary question.

She wobbled, steadied, coughed once, and took a shallow, shaking breath. "I let you see my ghost. Before they tried to dance with you. You understand it. I saw you."

It must have been slowing, the snow, because everything about her face—even the sparse white eyelashes—was very clear to me.

"Your ghost? You can't have a ghost when you're not dead," I said, and I turned away, wanting nothing more than to get inside and away from her. She spoke again, though, as I made to go.

"Maybe ghosts aren't what you think they are. Maybe there are many kinds."

I couldn't stop myself from looking round, ready to come up with some kind of answer, to tell her that she didn't know what she was talking about, but when I did, when I half-turned, with my eyes, at first, directed down, all my words, my defences, all the knowledge I'd gleaned from *The Big Book of Mysteries*, upped and left. There, wrapped around the old woman's bare feet, the lower part of the thin legs that showed beneath a fallen hem, clinging to her fragile skin as though attached by threads, were green sweet chestnut leaves, as flexible and fresh as the first new growth of spring.

It was the moment when something changed for me, the moment when my mind reformed, when it built itself a protective wall that stands to this day. What was there here that would be good to know or understand? Some knowledge leaves you with less. What losses may we suffer if we choose to cross the borders that should stay closed to us?

I raised my eyes to meet those of Great Aunt Lucy and, smiling sweetly before I walked away, I said: "I don't believe in ghosts."

Sam Hicks lives in south east London. Her fiction has appeared in various anthologies, including *Dark Lane, Nightscript, Vastarien, Supernatural Tales*, and *The Best Horror of The Year 11, 12 and 13*.

About the Editor

Rhonda Parrish lives in a place which is occasionally colder than Mars and is sometimes blessed by beautiful lights which dance across the sky. She is constantly creating shiny new poems and stories. She hoards them, like a magpie dragon, at https://www.patreon.com/RhondaParrish—the only place in the multiverse many of them can be found.

Acknowledgements

This book would not have been possible without the support of our Kickstarter backers. Thank you!

Krista D. Ball
Robert W. Easton
Zack Fissel
Skyla Cameron
summer-villain
Melissa Yuan-Innes
David Perlmutter
Jane G.
Robert Runté
Peter Halasz
Amanda Balter
Rebecca M. Senese
K. Bird Lincoln
Melanie Marttila
Charles Cousins
Alison Thurman
BD Wilson
Michelle Manus
Charlotte E. English
Applegate
Dead Fish Books
Steven Byrd
Joseph Halden
Derek Newman-Stille
Kristina Meschi
TinaFoo
Trysh L. Thompson

Ale C
Tonya Redpath
Chance
Colleen Feeney
K Hendrick
Cerise Cauthron
Andrew C
J. Peters
Jessica Arden Cline
Rebecca Brae
Diane Severson Mori
Sarena Ulibarri
Kordi Steck
Liz Crow
L Hutchings
Naticia
Rain Carling
Tracy H.
Crystal P
Mackenzie McDonald
Luke Danforth
Jessica Dennis
Gee Rothvus
James 'The Great Old One' Burke
Kristina Smith
Alexandra Corrsin
Ruth Ann Orlansky

Barbara Ann Paulson

Conor Neilson

Wendy Sparrow

Judy McClain

Jessica Enfante

Kerrie Koopman

Michèle Sharik

Kari Kilgore

Rueban Releeshahn

phoenix17

S. M. Davis

Frank Lewis

Kristopher Eklof

Lorena Skates

Dianthaa

Ron&Anne Mann

Will

Amarah Grove

J. M. Turner

Charlotte V Hooper

Jessica Richards

Nadz

E. Kim

Corinne Brucks

Chris Patrick Carolan

Eve Weaver

Chris Chastain

Adam Israel & Andrea Redman

Eron Wyngarde

The Selkie Delegation

Tanya Corbin

Aaron F. Huston

Mark Shaffer

Heather DeGrande

Sherry D. Ramsey

Kimberly J Kaiser

Jarrod Wade

In loving memory of Basil Martin